IN A FREE STATE

In a Free State is a sequence, beginning and ending with passages from the writer's journal, at the heart of which is the novel which gives its title to the whole. Two English people, Bobby and Linda, are driving back from the capital of an African country to their expatriates' compound in one of the regions, at a time of civil conflict. Neutral, white, protected, they have both in their different ways found liberation in Africa, and they too, like the country in which they are living, might be said to be "in a free state". But their neutrality will not last; there is danger on the open road. This novel, brilliant in every way (simply as an "adventure" it is masterly in its mounting menace), says more about colonialism and its consequences than has yet been said by anyone.

It is given a deeper meaning by two long studies of other men looking for liberation far from home, an Indian in Washington and two West Indian brothers in London; while the enclosing pieces of documentary admit us directly to the type of experience from which the fiction has grown.

V. S. NAIPAUL

In a Free State

ANDRE DEUTSCH

First published October 1971 by
André Deutsch Limited
105 Great Russell Street
London WC1

Second Impression November 1971
Third Impression January 1972

Printed in Great Britain
by Ebenezer Baylis & Son Ltd
The Trinity Press
Worcester and London

ISBN 0 233 95832 0

Contents

The Tramp at Piraeus

The Tramp at Piraeus

IT WAS ONLY a two-day crossing from Piraeus to Alexandria, but as soon as I saw the dingy little Greek steamer I felt I ought to have made other arrangements. Even from the quay it looked overcrowded, like a refugee ship; and when I went aboard I found there wasn't enough room for everybody.

There was no deck to speak of. The bar, open on two sides to the January wind, was the size of a cupboard. Three made a crowd there, and behind his little counter the little Greek barman, serving bad coffee, was in a bad mood. Many of the chairs in the small smoking-room, and a good deal of the floor space, had been seized by overnight passengers from Italy, among them a party of overgrown American schoolchildren in their mid-teens, white and subdued but watchful. The only other public room was the dining-room, and that was being got ready for the first of the lunch sittings by stewards who were as tired and bad-tempered as the barman. Greek civility was something we had left on shore; it belonged perhaps to idleness, unemployment and pastoral despair.

But we on the upper part of the ship were lucky. We had cabins and bunks. The people on the lower deck didn't. They were deck passengers; night and day they required only sleeping room. Below us now they sat or lay in the sun, sheltering from the wind, humped figures in Mediterranean black among the winches and orange-coloured bulkheads.

They were Egyptian Greeks. They were travelling to Egypt, but Egypt was no longer their home. They had been expelled; they were refugees. The invaders had left Egypt; after many humiliations Egypt was free; and these Greeks, the poor ones,

1*

who by simple skills had made themselves only just less poor than Egyptians, were the casualties of that freedom. Dingy Greek ships like ours had taken them out of Egypt. Now, briefly, they were going back, with tourists like ourselves, who were neutral, travelling only for the sights; with Lebanese businessmen; a troupe of Spanish night-club dancers; fat Egyptian students returning from Germany.

The tramp, when he appeared on the quay, looked very English; but that might only have been because we had no English people on board. From a distance he didn't look like a tramp. The hat and the rucksack, the lovat tweed jacket, the grey flannels and the boots might have belonged to a romantic wanderer of an earlier generation; in that rucksack there might have been a book of verse, a journal, the beginnings of a novel.

He was slender, of medium height, and he moved from the knees down, with short springy steps, each foot lifted high off the ground. It was a stylish walk, as stylish as his polka-dotted saffron neck-scarf. But when he came nearer we saw that all his clothes were in ruin, that the knot on his scarf was tight and grimy; that he was a tramp. When he came to the foot of the gangway he took off his hat, and we saw that he was an old man, with a tremulous worn face and wet blue eyes.

He looked up and saw us, his audience. He raced up the gangway, not using the hand-ropes. Vanity! He showed his ticket to the surly Greek; and then, not looking about him, asking no questions, he continued to move briskly, as though he knew his way around the ship. He turned into a passageway that led nowhere. With comical abruptness he swung right round on one heel and brought his other foot down hard.

"Purser," he said to the deck-boards, as though he had just remembered something. "I'll go and see the purser."

And so he picked his way to his cabin and bunk.

Our sailing was delayed. While their places in the smoking-room were being watched over, some of the American school-children had gone ashore to buy food; we were waiting for them to come back. As soon as they did – no giggles: the girls

were plain, pale and abashed – the Greeks became especially
furious and rushed. The Greek language grated like the anchor
chain. Water began to separate us from the quay and we could
see, not far from where we had been, the great black hulk of the
liner *Leonardo da Vinci*, just docked.

The tramp reappeared. He was without his hat and rucksack
and looked less nervous. Hands in trouser-pockets already stuffed
and bulging, legs apart, he stood on the narrow deck like an
experienced sea-traveller exposing himself to the first sea breeze
of a real cruise. He was also assessing the passengers; he was looking for company. He ignored people who stared at him; when
others, responding to his own stare, turned to look at him he
swivelled his head away.

In the end he went and stood beside a tall blond young man.
His instinct had guided him well. The man he had chosen was a
Yugoslav who, until the day before, had never been out of
Yugoslavia. The Yugoslav was willing to listen. He was baffled
by the tramp's accent but he smiled encouragingly; and the tramp
spoke on.

"I've been to Egypt six or seven times. Gone around the world
about a dozen times. Australia, Canada, all those countries.
Geologist, or used to be. First went to Canada in 1923. Been there
about eight times now. I've been travelling for thirty-eight years.
Youth-hostelling, that's how I do it. Not a thing to be despised.
New Zealand, have you been there? I went there in 1934. Between
you and me, they're a cut above the Australians. But what's
nationality these days? I myself, I think of myself as a citizen of
the world."

His speech was like this, full of dates, places and numbers, with
sometimes a simple opinion drawn from another life. But it was
mechanical, without conviction; even the vanity made no
impression; those quivering wet eyes remained distant.

The Yugoslav smiled and made interjections. The tramp neither
saw nor heard. He couldn't manage a conversation; he wasn't
looking for conversation; he didn't even require an audience. It
was as though, over the years, he had developed this way of

swiftly explaining himself to himself, reducing his life to names and numbers. When the names and numbers had been recited he had no more to say. Then he just stood beside the Yugoslav. Even before we had lost sight of Piraeus and the *Leonardo da Vinci* the tramp had exhausted that relationship. He hadn't wanted company; he wanted only the camouflage and protection of company. The tramp knew he was odd.

AT LUNCH I SAT with two Lebanese. They were both over-night passengers from Italy and were quick to explain that it was luggage, not money, that had prevented them travelling by air. They looked a good deal less unhappy with the ship than they said they were. They spoke in a mixture of French, English and Arabic and were exciting and impressing each other with talk of the money other people, mainly Lebanese, were making in this or that unlikely thing.

They were both under forty. One was pink, plump and casu-ally dressed, with a canary pullover; his business in Beirut was, literally, money. The other Lebanese was dark, well-built, with moustached Mediterranean good looks, and wore a three-piece check suit. He made reproduction furniture in Cairo and he said that business was bad since the Europeans had left. Commerce and culture had vanished from Egypt; there was no great demand among the natives for reproduction furniture; and there was growing prejudice against Lebanese like himself. But I couldn't believe in his gloom. While he was talking to us he was winking at one of the Spanish dancers.

At the other end of the room a fat Egyptian student with thick-lensed glasses was being raucous in German and Arabic. The German couple at his table were laughing. Now the Egyptian began to sing an Arabic song.

The man from Beirut said in his American accent, "You should go modern."

"Never," the furniture-maker said. "I will leave Egypt first. I will close my factory. It is a horror, the modern style. It is grotesque, totally grotesque. *Mais le style Louis Seize, ah, voilà l'âme* – " He broke off to applaud the Egyptian and to shout his congratulations in Arabic. Wearily then, but without malice, he said under his breath, "Ah, these natives." He pushed his plate from him, sank in his chair, beat his fingers on the dirty table-cloth. He winked at the dancer and the tips of his moustache flicked upwards.

The steward came to clear away. I was eating, but my plate went as well.

"You were dining, monsieur?" the furniture-maker said. "You must be *calme*. We must all be *calme*."

Then he raised his eyebrows and rolled his eyes. There was something he wanted us to look at.

It was the tramp, standing in the doorway, surveying the room. Such was the way he held himself that even now, at the first glance, his clothes seemed whole. He came to the cleared table next to ours, sat on a chair and shifted about in it until he was settled. Then he leaned right back, his arms on the rests, like the head of a household at the head of his table, like a cruise-passenger waiting to be served. He sighed and moved his jaws, testing his teeth. His jacket was in an appalling state. The pockets bulged; the flaps were fastened with safety pins.

The furniture-maker said something in Arabic and the man from Beirut laughed. The stewards shooed us away and we followed the Spanish girls to the windy little bar for coffee.

Later that afternoon, looking for privacy, I climbed some steep steps to the open railed area above the cabins. The tramp was standing there alone, stained trouser-legs swollen, turn-ups shredded, exposed to the cold wind and the smuts from the smokestack. He held what looked like a little prayer-book. He was moving his lips and closing and opening his eyes, like a man praying hard. How fragile that face was, worked over by distress; how frail that neck, below the tight knot of the polka-dotted scarf. The flesh around his eyes seemed especially soft; he looked close to tears. It was strange. He looked for company but needed solitude; he looked for attention, and at the same time wanted not to be noticed.

I didn't disturb him. I feared to be involved with him. Far below, the Greek refugees sat or lay in the sun.

IN THE SMOKING-ROOM after dinner the fat young Egyptian shouted himself hoarse, doing his cabaret act. People who understood what he was saying laughed all the time. Even the furniture-maker, forgetting his gloom about the natives, shouted and clapped with the rest. The American schoolchildren lay in their own promiscuous seasick heap and looked on, like people helplessly besieged; when they spoke among themselves it was in whispers.

The non-American part of the room was predominantly Arab and German and had its own cohesion. The Egyptian was our entertainer, and there was a tall German girl we could think of as our hostess. She offered us chocolate and had a word for each of us. To me she said: "You are reading a very good English book. These Penguin books are very good English books." She might have been travelling out to join an Arab husband; I wasn't sure.

I was sitting with my back to the door and didn't see when the tramp came in. But suddenly he was there before me, sitting on a chair that someone had just left. The chair was not far from the German girl's, but it stood in no intimate relationship to that chair or any other group of chairs. The tramp sat squarely on it, straight up against the back. He faced no one directly, so that in that small room he didn't become part of the crowd but appeared instead to occupy the centre of a small stage within it.

He sat with his old man's legs wide apart, his weighted jacket sagging over his bulging trouser-pockets. He had come with things to read, a magazine, the little book which I had thought was a prayer-book. I saw now that it was an old pocket diary with many loose leaves. He folded the magazine in four, hid it under his thigh, and began to read the pocket diary. He laughed, and looked up to see whether he was being noticed. He turned a page, read and laughed again, more loudly. He leaned towards the German girl and said to her over his shoulder, "I say, do you read Spanish?"

She said, carefully, "No."

"These Spanish jokes are awfully funny."

But though he read a few more, he didn't laugh again.

The Egyptian continued to clown; that racket went on. Soon the German girl was offering chocolate once more. "*Bitte?*" Her voice was soft.

The tramp was unfolding his magazine. He stopped and looked at the chocolate. But there was none for him. He unfolded his magazine. Then, unexpectedly, he began to destroy it. With nervous jigging hands he tore at a page, once, twice. He turned some pages, began to tear again; turned back, tore. Even with the raucousness around the Egyptian the sound of tearing paper couldn't be ignored. Was he tearing out pictures – sport, women, advertisements – that offended him? Was he hoarding toilet paper for Egypt?

The Egyptian fell silent and looked. The American schoolchildren looked. Now, too late after the frenzy, and in what was almost silence, the tramp made a show of reason. He opened the tattered magazine wide out, turned it around angrily, as though the right side up hadn't been easy to find, and at last pretended to read. He moved his lips; he frowned; he tore and tore. Strips and shreds of paper littered the floor around his chair. He folded the loose remains of the magazine, stuffed it into his jacket pocket, pinned the flaps down, and went out of the room, looking like a man who had been made very angry.

"I WILL KILL him," the furniture-maker said at breakfast the next morning.

He was in his three-piece suit but he was unshaved and the dark rings below his eyes were like bruises. The man from Beirut, too, looked tired and crumpled. They hadn't had a good night. The third bunk in their cabin was occupied by an Austrian boy, a passenger from Italy, with whom they were on good terms. They had seen the rucksack and the hat on the fourth bunk; but it wasn't until it was quite late, all three in their bunks, that they had discovered that the tramp was to be the fourth among them.

"It was pretty bad," the man from Beirut said. He felt for delicate words and added, "The old guy's like a child."

"Child! If the English pig comes in now" – the furniture-maker raised his arm and pointed at the door – "I will *kill* him. *Now*."

He was pleased with the gesture and the words; he repeated them, for the room. The Egyptian student, hoarse and hungover after the evening's performance, said something in Arabic. It was obviously witty, but the furniture-maker didn't smile. He beat his fingers on the table, stared at the door and breathed loudly through his nose.

No one was in a good mood. The drumming and the throbbing and bucking of the ship had played havoc with stomachs and nerves; the cold wind outside irritated as much as it refreshed; and in the dining-room the air was stale, with a smell as of hot rubber. There was no crowd, but the stewards, looking unslept and unwashed, even their hair not well combed, were as rushed as before.

The Egyptian shrieked.

The tramp had come in, benign and rested and ready for his coffee and rolls. He had no doubts about his welcome now. He came without hesitation or great speed to the table next to ours, settled himself in his chair and began to test his teeth. He was quickly served. He chewed and drank with complete relish.

The Egyptian shrieked again.

The furniture-maker said to him, "I will send him to your room tonight."

The tramp didn't see or hear. He was only eating and drinking. Below the tight knot of his scarf his Adam's apple was very busy. He drank noisily, sighing afterwards; he chewed with rabbit-like swiftness, anxious to be free for the next mouthful; and between mouthfuls he hugged himself, rubbing his arms and elbows against his sides, in pure pleasure at food.

The fascination of the furniture-maker turned to rage. Rising, but still looking at the tramp, he called, "Hans!"

The Austrian boy, who was at the table with the Egyptian, got up. He was about sixteen or seventeen, square and chunky, enormously well-developed, with a broad smiling face. The man from Beirut also got up, and all three went outside.

The tramp, oblivious of this, and of what was being prepared for him, continued to eat and drink until, with a sigh which was like a sigh of fatigue, he was finished.

IT WAS TO be like a tiger-hunt, where bait is laid out and the hunter and spectators watch from the security of a platform. The bait here was the tramp's own rucksack. They placed that on the deck outside the cabin door, and watched it. The furniture-maker still pretended to be too angry to talk. But Hans smiled and explained the rules of the game as often as he was asked.

The tramp, though, didn't immediately play. After breakfast he disappeared. It was cold on the deck, even in the sunshine, and sometimes the spray came right up. People who had come out to watch didn't stay, and even the furniture-maker and the man from Beirut went from time to time to rest in the smoking-room among the Germans and Arabs and the Spanish girls. They were given chairs; there was sympathy for their anger and exhaustion. Hans remained at his post. When the cold wind made him go inside the cabin he watched through the open door, sitting on one of the lower bunks and smiling up at people who passed.

Then the news came that the tramp had reappeared and had been caught according to the rules of the game. Some of the American schoolchildren were already on deck, studying the sea. So were the Spanish girls and the German girl. Hans blocked the cabin door. I could see the tramp holding the strap of his rucksack; I could hear him complaining in English through the French and Arabic shouts of the furniture-maker, who was raising his arms and pointing with his right hand, the skirts of his jacket dancing.

In the dining-room the furniture-maker's anger had seemed only theatrical, an aspect of his Mediterranean appearance, the moustache, the wavy hair. But now, in the open, with an expectant audience and a victim so nearly passive, he was working himself into a frenzy.

"Pig! Pig!"

"It's not true," the tramp said, appealing to people who had only come to watch.

"Pig!"

The grotesque moment came. The furniture-maker, so strongly built, so elegant in his square-shouldered jacket, lunged with his left hand at the old man's head. The tramp swivelled his head, the way he did when he refused to acknowledge a stare. And he began to cry. The furniture-maker's hand went wide and he stumbled forward against the rails into a spatter of spray. Putting his hands to his breast, feeling for pen and wallet and other things, he cried out, like a man aggrieved and desperate, "Hans! Hans!"

The tramp stooped; he stopped crying; his blue eyes popped. Hans had seized him by the polka-dotted scarf, twisting it, jerking it down. Kicking the rucksack hard, Hans at the same time flung the tramp forward by the knotted scarf. The tramp stumbled over Hans's kicking foot. The strain went out of Hans's smiling face and all that was left was the smile. The tramp could have recovered from his throw and stumble. But he preferred to fall and then to sit up. He was still holding the strap of his rucksack. He was crying again.

"It's not true. These remarks they've been making, it's not true."

The young Americans were looking over the rails.

"Hans!" the furniture-maker called.

The tramp stopped crying.

"Ha-ans!"

The tramp didn't look round. He got up with his rucksack and ran.

The story was that he had locked himself in one of the lavatories. But he reappeared among us, twice.

About an hour later he came into the smoking-room, without his rucksack, with no sign of distress on his face. He was already restored. He came in, in his abrupt way, not looking to right or left. Just a few steps brought him right into the small room and almost up against the legs of the furniture-maker, who was stretched out in an upholstered chair, exhausted, one hand over his half-closed eyes. After surprise, anger and contempt filled the tramp's eyes. He started to swivel his head away.

"Hans!" the furniture-maker called, recovering from his astonishment, drawing back his legs, leaning forward. "Ha-ans!"

Swivelling his head, the tramp saw Hans rising with some playing cards in his hand. Terror came to the tramp's eyes. The swivelling motion of his head spread to the rest of his body. He swung round on one heel, brought the other foot down hard, and bolted. Entry, advance, bandy-legged swivel and retreat had formed one unbroken movement.

"Hans!"

It wasn't a call to action. The furniture-maker was only under-lining the joke. Hans, understanding, laughed and went back to his cards.

The tramp missed his lunch. He should have gone down imme-diately, to the first sitting, which had begun. Instead, he went into hiding, no doubt in one of the lavatories, and came out again only in time for the last sitting. It was the sitting the Lebanese and Hans had chosen. The tramp saw from the doorway.

"Ha-ans!"

But the tramp was already swivelling.

Later he was to be seen with his rucksack, but without his hat, on the lower deck, among the refugees. Without him, and then without reference to him, the joke continued, in the bar, on the narrow deck, in the smoking-room. "Hans! Ha-ans!" Towards the end Hans didn't laugh or look up; when he heard his name he completed the joke by giving a whistle. The joke lived; but by nightfall the tramp was forgotten.

AT DINNER THE Lebanese spoke again in their disinterested

way about money. The man from Beirut said that, because of certain special circumstances in the Middle East that year, there was a fortune to be made from the well-judged exporting of Egyptian shoes; but not many people knew. The furniture-maker said the fact had been known to him for months. They postulated an investment, vied with each other in displaying knowledge of hidden, local costs, and calmly considered the staggering profits. But they weren't really exciting one another any longer. The game was a game; each had taken the measure of the other. And they were both tired.

Something of the lassitude of the American schoolchildren had come over the other passengers on this last evening. The Americans themselves were beginning to thaw out. In the smoking-room, where the lights seemed dimmer, their voices were raised in friendly boy-girl squabbles; they did a lot more coming and going; especially active was a tall girl in a type of ballet-dancer's costume, all black from neck to wrist to ankle. The German girl, our hostess of the previous evening, looked quite ill. The Spanish girls were flirting with nobody. The Egyptian, whose hangover had been compounded by seasickness, was playing bridge. Gamely from time to time he croaked out a witticism or a line of a song, but he got smiles rather than laughs. The furniture-maker and Hans were also playing cards. When a good card or a disappointing one was played the furniture-maker said in soft exclamation, expecting no response, "Hans, Hans." It was all that remained of the day's joke.

The man from Beirut came in and watched. He stood beside Hans. Then he stood beside the furniture-maker and whispered to him in English, their secret language, "The guy's locked himself in the cabin."

Hans understood. He looked at the furniture-maker. But the furniture-maker was weary. He played his hand, then went out with the man from Beirut.

When he came back he said to Hans, "He says that he will set fire to the cabin if we try to enter. He says that he has a quantity of paper and a quantity of matches. I believe that he will do it."

"What do we do?" the man from Beirut asked.

"We will sleep here. Or in the dining-room."

"But those Greek stewards sleep in the dining-room. I saw them this morning."

"That proves that it is possible," the furniture-maker said.

Later, the evening over, I stopped outside the tramp's cabin. At first I heard nothing. Then I heard paper being crumpled: the tramp's warning. I wonder how long he stayed awake that night, listening for footsteps, waiting for the assault on the door and the entry of Hans.

In the morning he was back on the lower deck, among the refugees. He had his hat again; he had recovered it from the cabin.

ALEXANDRIA WAS A long shining line on the horizon: sand and the silver of oil-storage tanks. The sky clouded over; the green sea grew choppier. We entered the breakwater in cold rain and stormlight.

Long before the immigration officials came on board we queued to meet them. Germans detached themselves from Arabs, Hans from the Lebanese, the Lebanese from the Spanish girls. Now, as throughout the journey since his meeting with the tramp, the tall blond Yugoslav was a solitary. From the lower deck the refugees came up with their boxes and bundles, so that at last they were more than their emblematic black wrappings. They had the slack bodies and bad skins of people who ate too many carbohydrates. Their blotched faces were immobile, distant, but full of a fierce, foolish cunning. They were watching. As soon as the officials came aboard the refugees began to push and fight their way towards them. It was a factitious frenzy, the deference of the persecuted to authority.

The tramp came up with his hat and rucksack. There was no nervousness in his movements but his eyes were quick with fear. He took his place in the queue and pretended to frown at its length. He moved his feet up and down, now like a man made impatient by officials, now like someone only keeping out the cold. But he was of less interest than he thought. Hans, mountainous with his own rucksack, saw him and then didn't see him. The Lebanese, shaved and rested after their night in the dining-room, didn't see him. That passion was over.

One out of Many

One out of Many

I AM NOW AN American citizen and I live in Washington, capital of the world. Many people, both here and in India, will feel that I have done well. But.

I was so happy in Bombay. I was respected, I had a certain position. I worked for an important man. The highest in the land came to our bachelor chambers and enjoyed my food and showered compliments on me. I also had my friends. We met in the evenings on the pavement below the gallery of our chambers. Some of us, like the tailor's bearer and myself, were domestics who lived in the street. The others were people who came to that bit of pavement to sleep. Respectable people; we didn't encourage riff-raff.

In the evenings it was cool. There were few passers-by and, apart from an occasional double-decker bus or taxi, little traffic. The pavement was swept and sprinkled, bedding brought out from daytime hiding-places, little oil-lamps lit. While the folk upstairs chattered and laughed, on the pavement we read newspapers, played cards, told stories and smoked. The clay pipe passed from friend to friend; we became drowsy. Except of course during the monsoon, I preferred to sleep on the pavement with my friends, although in our chambers a whole cupboard below the staircase was reserved for my personal use.

It was good after a healthy night in the open to rise before the sun and before the sweepers came. Sometimes I saw the street lights go off. Bedding was rolled up; no one spoke much; and soon my friends were hurrying in silent competition to secluded lanes and alleys and open lots to relieve themselves. I was spared this competition; in our chambers I had facilities.

Afterwards for half an hour or so I was free simply to stroll. I liked walking beside the Arabian Sea, waiting for the sun to come up. Then the city and the ocean gleamed like gold. Alas for those morning walks, that sudden ocean dazzle, the moist salt breeze on my face, the flap of my shirt, that first cup of hot sweet tea from a stall, the taste of the first leaf-cigarette.

Observe the workings of fate. The respect and security I enjoyed were due to the importance of my employer. It was this very importance which now all at once destroyed the pattern of my life.

My employer was seconded by his firm to Government service and was posted to Washington. I was happy for his sake but frightened for mine. He was to be away for some years and there was nobody in Bombay he could second me to. Soon, therefore, I was to be out of a job and out of the chambers. For many years I had considered my life as settled. I had served my apprenticeship, known my hard times. I didn't feel I could start again. I despaired. Was there a job for me in Bombay? I saw myself having to return to my village in the hills, to my wife and children there, not just for a holiday but for good. I saw myself again becoming a porter during the tourist season, racing after the buses as they arrived at the station and shouting with forty or fifty others for luggage. Indian luggage, not this lightweight American stuff! Heavy metal trunks!

I could have cried. It was no longer the sort of life for which I was fitted. I had grown soft in Bombay and I was no longer young. I had acquired possessions, I was used to the privacy of my cupboard. I had become a city man, used to certain comforts.

My employer said, "Washington is not Bombay, Santosh. Washington is expensive. Even if I was able to raise your fare, you wouldn't be able to live over there in anything like your present style.'

But to be barefoot in the hills, after Bombay! The shock, the disgrace! I couldn't face my friends. I stopped sleeping on the pavement and spent as much of my free time as possible in my cupboard among my possessions, as among things which were soon to be taken from me.

My employer said, "Santosh, my heart bleeds for you."

I said, "Sahib, if I look a little concerned it is only because I worry about you. You have always been fussy, and I don't see how you will manage in Washington."

"It won't be easy. But it's the principle. Does the representative of a poor country like ours travel about with his cook? Will that create a good impression?"

"You will always do what is right, sahib."

He went silent.

After some days he said, "There's not only the expense, Santosh. There's the question of foreign exchange. Our rupee isn't what it was."

"I understand, sahib. Duty is duty."

A fortnight later, when I had almost given up hope, he said, "Santosh, I have consulted Government. You will accompany me. Government has sanctioned, will arrange accommodation. But no expenses. You will get your passport and your P form. But I want you to think, Santosh. Washington is not Bombay."

I went down to the pavement that night with my bedding.

I said, blowing down my shirt, "Bombay gets hotter and hotter."

"Do you know what you are doing?" the tailor's bearer said. "Will the Americans smoke with you? Will they sit and talk with you in the evenings? Will they hold you by the hand and walk with you beside the ocean?"

It pleased me that he was jealous. My last days in Bombay were very happy.

I PACKED MY EMPLOYER'S two suitcases and bundled up my own belongings in lengths of old cotton. At the airport they made a fuss about my bundles. They said they couldn't accept them as luggage for the hold because they didn't like the responsibility. So when the time came I had to climb up to the aircraft with all my bundles. The girl at the top, who was smiling at everybody else, stopped smiling when she saw me. She made me go right to the back of the plane, far from my employer. Most of the seats there were empty, though, and I was able to spread my bundles around and, well, it was comfortable.

It was bright and hot outside, cool inside. The plane started, rose up in the air, and Bombay and the ocean tilted this way and that. It was very nice. When we settled down I looked around for people like myself, but I could see no one among the Indians or the foreigners who looked like a domestic. Worse, they were all dressed as though they were going to a wedding and, brother, I soon saw it wasn't they who were conspicuous. I was in my ordinary Bombay clothes, the loose long-tailed shirt, the wide-waisted pants held up with a piece of string. Perfectly respectable domestic's wear, neither dirty nor clean, and in Bombay no one would have looked. But now on the plane I felt heads turning whenever I stood up.

I was anxious. I slipped off my shoes, tight even without the laces, and drew my feet up. That made me feel better. I made myself a little betel-nut mixture and that made me feel better still. Half the pleasure of betel, though, is the spitting; and it was only when I had worked up a good mouthful that I saw I had a problem. The airline girl saw too. That girl didn't like me at all. She spoke roughly to me. My mouth was full, my cheeks were bursting, and I couldn't say anything. I could only look at her. She went and called a man in uniform and he came and stood over me. I put my shoes back on and swallowed the betel juice. It made me feel quite ill.

The girl and the man, the two of them, pushed a little trolley of drinks down the aisle. The girl didn't look at me but the man said, "You want a drink, chum?" He wasn't a bad fellow. I pointed at random to a bottle. It was a kind of soda drink, nice and sharp at first but then not so nice. I was worrying about it when the girl said, "Five shillings sterling or sixty cents U.S." That took me by surprise. I had no money, only a few rupees. The girl stamped, and I thought she was going to hit me with her pad when I stood up to show her who my employer was.

Presently my employer came down the aisle. He didn't look very well. He said, without stopping, "Champagne, Santosh? Already we are overdoing?" He went on to the lavatory. When he passed back he said, "Foreign exchange, Santosh! Foreign exchange!" That was all. Poor fellow, he was suffering too.

The journey became miserable for me. Soon, with the wine I had drunk, the betel juice, the movement and the noise of the aeroplane, I was vomiting all over my bundles, and I didn't care what the girl said or did. Later there were more urgent and terrible needs. I felt I would choke in the tiny, hissing room at the back. I had a shock when I saw my face in the mirror. In the fluorescent light it was the colour of a corpse. My eyes were strained, the sharp air hurt my nose and seemed to get into my brain. I climbed up on the lavatory seat and squatted. I lost control of myself. As quickly as I could I ran back out into the comparative openness of the cabin and hoped no one had noticed. The lights were dim now; some people had taken off their jackets and were sleeping. I hoped the plane would crash.

The girl woke me up. She was almost screaming. "It's you, isn't it? Isn't it?"

I thought she was going to tear the shirt off me. I pulled back and leaned hard on the window. She burst into tears and nearly tripped on her sari as she ran up the aisle to get the man in uniform.

Nightmare. And all I knew was that somewhere at the end, after the airports and the crowded lounges where everybody was dressed up, after all those take-offs and touchdowns, was the city of Washington. I wanted the journey to end but I couldn't say I wanted to arrive at Washington. I was already a little scared of that city, to tell the truth. I wanted only to be off the plane and to be in the open again, to stand on the ground and breathe and to try to understand what time of day it was.

At last we arrived. I was in a daze. The burden of those bundles! There were more closed rooms and electric lights. There were questions from officials.

"Is he diplomatic?"

"He's only a domestic," my employer said.

"Is that his luggage? What's in that pocket?"

I was ashamed.

"Santosh," my employer said.

I pulled out the little packets of pepper and salt, the sweets, the envelopes with scented napkins, the toy tubes of mustard. Airline trinkets. I had been collecting them throughout the journey, seizing a handful, whatever my condition, every time I passed the galley.

"He's a cook," my employer said.

"Does he always travel with his condiments?"

"Santosh, Santosh," my employer said in the car afterwards, "in Bombay it didn't matter what you did. Over here you represent your country. I must say I cannot understand why your behaviour has already gone so much out of character."

"I am sorry, sahib."

"Look at it like this, Santosh. Over here you don't only represent your country, you represent me."

For the people of Washington it was late afternoon or early evening, I couldn't say which. The time and the light didn't match, as they did in Bombay. Of that drive I remember green fields, wide roads, many motor cars travelling fast, making a steady hiss, hiss, which wasn't at all like our Bombay traffic noise. I remember big buildings and wide parks; many bazaar areas; then smaller houses without fences and with gardens like bush, with the *hubshi* standing about or sitting down, more usually sitting down, everywhere. Especially I remember the *hubshi*. I had heard about them in stories and had seen one or two in Bombay. But I had never dreamt that this wild race existed in such numbers in Washington and were permitted to roam the streets so freely. O father, what was this place I had come to?

I wanted, I say, to be in the open, to breathe, to come to myself, to reflect. But there was to be no openness for me that evening. From the aeroplane to the airport building to the motor car to the apartment block to the elevator to the corridor to the apartment itself, I was forever enclosed, forever in the hissing, hissing sound of air-conditioners.

I was too dazed to take stock of the apartment. I saw it as only another halting place. My employer went to bed at once, completely exhausted, poor fellow. I looked around for my room. I couldn't find it and gave up. Aching for the Bombay ways, I spread my bedding in the carpeted corridor just outside our apartment door. The corridor was long: doors, doors. The illuminated ceiling was decorated with stars of different sizes; the colours were grey and blue and gold. Below that imitation sky I felt like a prisoner.

WAKING, LOOKING UP at the ceiling, I thought just for a second that I had fallen asleep on the pavement below the gallery of our Bombay chambers. Then I realized my loss. I couldn't tell how much time had passed or whether it was night or day. The only clue was that newspapers now lay outside some doors. It disturbed me to think that while I had been sleeping, alone and defenceless, I had been observed by a stranger and perhaps by more than one stranger.

I tried the apartment door and found I had locked myself out. I didn't want to disturb my employer. I thought I would get out into the open, go for a walk. I remembered where the elevator was. I got in and pressed the button. The elevator dropped fast and silently and it was like being in the aeroplane again. When the elevator stopped and the blue metal door slid open I saw plain concrete corridors and blank walls. The noise of machinery was very loud. I knew I was in the basement and the main floor was not far above me. But I no longer wanted to try; I gave up ideas of the open air. I thought I would just go back up to the apartment. But I hadn't noted the number and didn't even know what floor we were on. My courage flowed out of me. I sat on the floor of the elevator and felt the tears come to my eyes. Almost without noise the elevator door closed, and I found I was being taken up silently at great speed.

The elevator stopped and the door opened. It was my

employer, his hair uncombed, yesterday's dirty shirt partly unbuttoned. He looked frightened.

"Santosh, where have you been at this hour of morning? Without your shoes."

I could have embraced him. He hurried me back past the newspapers to our apartment and I took the bedding inside. The wide window showed the early morning sky, the big city; we were high up, way above the trees.

I said, "I couldn't find my room."

"Government sanctioned," my employer said. "Are you sure you've looked?"

We looked together. One little corridor led past the bathroom to his bedroom; another, shorter corridor led to the big room and the kitchen. There was nothing else.

"Government sanctioned," my employer said, moving about the kitchen and opening cupboard doors. "Separate entrance, shelving. I have the correspondence." He opened another door and looked inside. "Santosh, do you think it is possible that this is what Government meant?"

The cupboard he had opened was as high as the rest of the apartment and as wide as the kitchen, about six feet. It was about three feet deep. It had two doors. One door opened into the kitchen; another door, directly opposite, opened into the corridor.

"Separate entrance," my employer said. "Shelving, electric light, power point, fitted carpet."

"This must be my room, sahib."

"Santosh, some enemy in Government has done this to me."

"Oh no, sahib. You mustn't say that. Besides, it is very big. I will be able to make myself very comfortable. It is much bigger than my little cubby-hole in the chambers. And it has a nice flat ceiling. I wouldn't hit my head."

"You don't understand, Santosh. Bombay is Bombay. Here if we start living in cupboards we give the wrong impression. They will think we all live in cupboards in Bombay."

"O sahib, but they can just look at me and see I am dirt."

"You are very good, Santosh. But these people are malicious. Still, if you are happy, then I am happy."

"I am very happy, sahib."

And after all the upset, I was. It was nice to crawl in that evening, spread my bedding and feel protected and hidden. I slept very well.

IN THE MORNING my employer said, "We must talk about money, Santosh. Your salary is one hundred rupees a month. But Washington isn't Bombay. Everything is a little bit more expensive here, and I am going to give you a Dearness Allowance. As from today you are getting one hundred and fifty rupees."

"Sahib."

"And I'm giving you a fortnight's pay in advance. In foreign exchange. Seventy-five rupees. Ten cents to the rupee, seven hundred and fifty cents. Seven fifty U.S. Here, Santosh. This afternoon you go out and have a little walk and enjoy. But be careful. We are not among friends, remember."

So at last, rested, with money in my pocket, I went out in the open. And of course the city wasn't a quarter as frightening as I had thought. The buildings weren't particularly big, not all the streets were busy, and there were many lovely trees. A lot of the *hubshi* were about, very wild-looking some of them, with dark glasses and their hair frizzed out, but it seemed that if you didn't trouble them they didn't attack you.

I was looking for a café or a tea-stall where perhaps domestics congregated. But I saw no domestics, and I was chased away from the place I did eventually go into. The girl said, after I had been waiting some time, "Can't you read? We don't serve hippies or bare feet here."

O father! I had come out without my shoes. But what a country, I thought, walking briskly away, where people are never allowed to dress normally but must forever wear their very best! Why must they wear out shoes and fine clothes for

2

no purpose? What occasion are they honouring? What waste, what presumption! Who do they think is noticing them all the time?

And even while these thoughts were in my head I found I had come to a roundabout with trees and a fountain where – and it was like a fulfilment in a dream, not easy to believe – there were many people who looked like my own people. I tightened the string around my loose pants, held down my flapping shirt and ran through the traffic to the green circle.

Some of the *hubshi* were there, playing musical instruments and looking quite happy in their way. There were some Americans sitting about on the grass and the fountain and the kerb. Many of them were in rough, friendly-looking clothes; some were without shoes; and I felt I had been over hasty in condemning the entire race. But it wasn't these people who had attracted me to the circle. It was the dancers. The men were bearded, barefooted and in saffron robes, and the girls were in saris and canvas shoes that looked like our own Bata shoes. They were shaking little cymbals and chanting and lifting their heads up and down and going round in a circle, making a lot of dust. It was a little bit like a Red Indian dance in a cowboy movie, but they were chanting Sanskrit words in praise of Lord Krishna.

I was very pleased. But then a disturbing thought came to me. It might have been because of the half-caste appearance of the dancers; it might have been their bad Sanskrit pronunciation and their accent. I thought that these people were now strangers, but that perhaps once upon a time they had been like me. Perhaps, as in some story, they had been brought here among the *hubshi* as captives a long time ago and had become a lost people, like our own wandering gipsy folk, and had forgotten who they were. When I thought that, I lost my pleasure in the dancing; and I felt for the dancers the sort of distaste we feel when we are faced with something that should be kin but turns out not to be, turns out to be degraded, like a deformed man, or like a leper, who from a distance looks whole.

I didn't stay. Not far from the circle I saw a café which

appeared to be serving bare feet. I went in, had a coffee and a
nice piece of cake and bought a pack of cigarettes; matches
they gave me free with the cigarettes. It was all right, but then
the bare feet began looking at me, and one bearded fellow came
and sniffed loudly at me and smiled and spoke some sort of
gibberish, and then some others of the bare feet came and
sniffed at me. They weren't unfriendly, but I didn't appreciate
the behaviour; and it was a little frightening to find, when I left
the place, that two or three of them appeared to be following
me. They weren't unfriendly, but I didn't want to take any
chances. I passed a cinema; I went in. It was something I wanted
to do anyway. In Bombay I used to go once a week.

And that was all right. The movie had already started. It was
in English, not too easy for me to follow, and it gave me time
to think. It was only there, in the darkness, that I thought about
the money I had been spending. The prices had seemed to me
very reasonable, like Bombay prices. Three for the movie ticket,
one fifty in the café, with tip. But I had been thinking in rupees
and paying in dollars. In less than an hour I had spent nine
days' pay.

I couldn't watch the movie after that. I went out and began
to make my way back to the apartment block. Many more of
the *hubshi* were about now and I saw that where they congregated the pavement was wet, and dangerous with broken
glass and bottles. I couldn't think of cooking when I got back
to the apartment. I couldn't bear to look at the view. I spread
my bedding in the cupboard, lay down in the darkness and waited
for my employer to return.

When he did I said, "Sahib, I want to go home."

"Santosh, I've paid five thousand rupees to bring you here.
If I send you back now, you will have to work for six or seven
years without salary to pay me back."

I burst into tears.

"My poor Santosh, something has happened. Tell me what
has happened."

"Sahib, I've spent more than half the advance you gave me

this morning. I went out and had a coffee and cake and then I went to a movie."

His eyes went small and twinkly behind his glasses. He bit the inside of his top lip, scraped at his moustache with his lower teeth, and he said, "You see, you see. I told you it was expensive."

I UNDERSTOOD I WAS a prisoner. I accepted this and adjusted. I learned to live within the apartment, and I was even calm.

My employer was a man of taste and he soon had the apartment looking like something in a magazine, with books and Indian paintings and Indian fabrics and pieces of sculpture and bronze statues of our gods. I was careful to take no delight in it. It was of course very pretty, especially with the view. But the view remained foreign and I never felt that the apartment was real, like the shabby old Bombay chambers with the cane chairs, or that it had anything to do with me.

When people came to dinner I did my duty. At the appropriate time I would bid the company goodnight, close off the kitchen behind its folding screen and pretend I was leaving the apartment. Then I would lie down quietly in my cupboard and smoke. I was free to go out; I had my separate entrance. But I didn't like being out of the apartment. I didn't even like going down to the laundry room in the basement.

Once or twice a week I went to the supermarket on our street. I always had to walk past groups of *hubshi* men and children. I tried not to look, but it was hard. They sat on the pavement, on steps and in the bush around their redbrick houses, some of which had boarded-up windows. They appeared to be very much a people of the open air, with little to do; even in the mornings some of the men were drunk.

Scattered among the *hubshi* houses were others just as old but with gas-lamps that burned night and day in the entrance. These were the houses of the Americans. I seldom saw these people; they didn't spend much time on the street. The lighted gas-lamp was the American way of saying that though a house looked

old outside it was nice and new inside. I also felt that it was
like a warning to the *hubshi* to keep off.

Outside the supermarket there was always a policeman with
a gun. Inside, there were always a couple of *hubshi* guards with
truncheons, and, behind the cashiers, some old *hubshi* beggar men
in rags. There were also many young *hubshi* boys, small but
muscular, waiting to carry parcels, as once in the hills I had
waited to carry Indian tourists' luggage.

These trips to the supermarket were my only outings, and I
was always glad to get back to the apartment. The work there was
light. I watched a lot of television and my English improved.
I grew to like certain commercials very much. It was in these
commercials I saw the Americans whom in real life I so seldom
saw and knew only by their gas-lamps. Up there in the apartment, with a view of the white domes and towers and greenery
of the famous city, I entered the homes of the Americans and
saw them cleaning those homes. I saw them cleaning floors and
dishes. I saw them buying clothes and cleaning clothes, buying
motor cars and cleaning motor cars. I saw them cleaning, cleaning.

The effect of all this television on me was curious. If by some
chance I saw an American on the street I tried to fit him or her
into the commercials; and I felt I had caught the person in an
interval between his television duties. So to some extent Americans have remained to me, as people not quite real, as people
temporarily absent from television.

Sometimes a *hubshi* came on the screen, not to talk of *hubshi*
things, but to do a little cleaning of his own. That wasn't the
same. He was too different from the *hubshi* I saw on the street
and I knew he was an actor. I knew that his television duties
were only make-believe and that he would soon have to return
to the street.

ONE DAY AT the supermarket, when the *hubshi* girl took my
money, she sniffed and said, "You always smell sweet, baby."

She was friendly, and I was at last able to clear up that mystery,
of my smell. It was the poor country weed I smoked. It was a

peasant taste of which I was slightly ashamed, to tell the truth;
but the cashier was encouraging. As it happened, I had brought
a quantity of the weed with me from Bombay in one of my
bundles, together with a hundred razor blades, believing both
weed and blades to be purely Indian things. I made an offering
to the girl. In return she taught me a few words of English.
"Me black and beautiful" was the first thing she taught me.
Then she pointed to the policeman with the gun outside and
taught me: "He pig."

My English lessons were taken a stage further by the *hubshi*
maid who worked for someone on our floor in the apartment
block. She too was attracted by my smell, but I soon began to
feel that she was also attracted by my smallness and strangeness.
She herself was a big woman, broad in the face, with high
cheeks and bold eyes and lips that were full but not pendulous.
Her largeness disturbed me; I found it better to concentrate on
her face. She misunderstood; there were times when she frolicked
with me in a violent way. I didn't like it, because I couldn't
fight her off as well as I would have liked and because in spite
of myself I was fascinated by her appearance. Her smell mixed
with the perfumes she used could have made me forget myself.

She was always coming into the apartment. She disturbed me
while I was watching the Americans on television. I feared the
smell she left behind. Sweat, perfume, my own weed: the smells
lay thick in the room, and I prayed to the bronze gods my employer had installed as living-room ornaments that I would not
be dishonoured. Dishonoured, I say; and I know that this might
seem strange to people over here, who have permitted the
hubshi to settle among them in such large numbers and must
therefore esteem them in certain ways. But in our country we
frankly do not care for the *hubshi*. It is written in our books,
both holy and not so holy, that it is indecent and wrong for a
man of our blood to embrace the *hubshi* woman. To be dishonoured in this life, to be born a cat or a monkey or a *hubshi*
in the next!

But I was falling. Was it idleness and solitude? I was found attractive: I wanted to know why. I began to go to the bathroom of the apartment simply to study my face in the mirror. I cannot easily believe it myself now, but in Bombay a week or a month could pass without my looking in the mirror; and then it wasn't to consider my looks but to check whether the barber had cut off too much hair or whether a pimple was about to burst. Slowly I made a discovery. My face was handsome. I had never thought of myself in this way. I had thought of myself as unnoticeable, with features that served as identification alone.

The discovery of my good looks brought its strains. I became obsessed with my appearance, with a wish to see myself. It was like an illness. I would be watching television, for instance, and I would be surprised by the thought: are you as handsome as that man? I would have to get up and go to the bathroom and look in the mirror.

I thought back to the time when these matters hadn't interested me, and I saw how ragged I must have looked, on the aeroplane, in the airport, in that café for bare feet, with the rough and dirty clothes I wore, without doubt or question, as clothes befitting a servant. I was choked with shame. I saw, too, how good people in Washington had been, to have seen me in rags and yet to have taken me for a man.

I was glad I had a place to hide. I had thought of myself as a prisoner. Now I was glad I had so little of Washington to cope with: the apartment, my cupboard, the television set, my employer, the walk to the supermarket, the *hubshi* woman. And one day I found I no longer knew whether I wanted to go back to Bombay. Up there, in the apartment, I no longer knew what I wanted to do.

I BECAME MORE CAREFUL of my appearance. There wasn't much I could do. I bought laces for my old black shoes, socks, a belt. Then some money came my way. I had understood that the weed I smoked was of value to the *hubshi* and the bare feet; I disposed of what I had, disadvantageously as I now know, through the *hubshi* girl at the supermarket. I got just under two hundred dollars. Then, as anxiously as I had got rid of my weed, I went out and bought some clothes.

I still have the things I bought that morning. A green hat, a green suit. The suit was always too big for me. Ignorance, inexperience; but I also remember the feeling of presumption. The salesman wanted to talk, to do his job. I didn't want to listen. I took the first suit he showed me and went into the cubicle and changed. I couldn't think about size and fit. When I considered all that cloth and all that tailoring I was proposing to adorn my simple body with, that body that needed so little, I felt I was asking to be destroyed. I changed back quickly, went out of the cubicle and said I would take the green suit. The salesman began to talk; I cut him short; I asked for a hat. When I got back to the apartment I felt quite weak and had to lie down for a while in my cupboard.

I never hung the suit up. Even in the shop, even while counting out the precious dollars, I had known it was a mistake. I kept the suit folded in the box with all its pieces of tissue paper. Three or four times I put it on and walked about the apartment and sat down on chairs and lit cigarettes and crossed my legs, practising. But I couldn't bring myself to wear the suit out of doors. Later I wore the pants, but never the jacket. I never bought another suit; I soon began wearing the sort of clothes I wear today, pants with some sort of zippered jacket.

Once I had had no secrets from my employer; it was so much simpler not to have secrets. But some instinct told me now it would be better not to let him know about the green suit or the few dollars I had, just as instinct had already told me I should keep my growing knowledge of English to myself.

Once my employer had been to me only a presence. I used to tell him then that beside him I was as dirt. It was only a way of talking, one of the courtesies of our language, but it had something of truth. I meant that he was the man who adventured in the world for me, that I experienced the world through him, that I was content to be a small part of his presence. I was content, sleeping on the Bombay pavement with my friends, to hear the talk of my employer and his guests upstairs. I was more than content, late at night, to be identified among the sleepers and greeted by some of those guests before they drove away.

Now I found that, without wishing it, I was ceasing to see myself as part of my employer's presence, and beginning at the same time to see him as an outsider might see him, as perhaps the people who came to dinner in the apartment saw him. I saw that he was a man of my own age, around thirty-five; it astonished me that I hadn't noticed this before. I saw that he was plump, in need of exercise, that he moved with short, fussy steps; a man with glasses, thinning hair, and that habit, during conversation, of scraping at his moustache with his teeth and nibbling at the inside of his top lip; a man who was frequently anxious, took pains over his work, was subjected at his own table to unkind remarks by his office colleagues; a man who looked as uneasy in Washington as I felt, who acted as cautiously as I had learned to act.

I remember an American who came to dinner. He looked at the pieces of sculpture in the apartment and said he had himself brought back a whole head from one of our ancient temples; he had got the guide to hack it off.

I could see that my employer was offended. He said, "But that's illegal."

"That's why I had to give the guide two dollars. If I had a bottle of whisky he would have pulled down the whole temple for me."

My employer's face went blank. He continued to do his duties as host but he was unhappy throughout the dinner. I grieved for him.

Afterwards he knocked on my cupboard. I knew he wanted to talk. I was in my underclothes but I didn't feel underdressed, with the American gone. I stood in the door of my cupboard; my employer paced up and down the small kitchen; the apartment felt sad.

"Did you hear that person, Santosh?"

I pretended I hadn't understood, and when he explained I
2*

tried to console him. I said, "Sahib, but we know these people
are Franks and barbarians."

"They are malicious people, Santosh. They think that because
we are a poor country we are all the same. They think an official
in Government is just the same as some poor guide scraping
together a few rupees to keep body and soul together, poor
fellow."

I saw that he had taken the insult only in a personal way, and
I was disappointed. I thought he had been thinking of the temple.

A FEW DAYS LATER I had my adventure. The *hubshi* woman
came in, moving among my employer's ornaments like a bull.
I was greatly provoked. The smell was too much; so was the
sight of her armpits. I fell. She dragged me down on the couch,
on the saffron spread which was one of my employer's nicest
pieces of Punjabi folk-weaving. I saw the moment, helplessly,
as one of dishonour. I saw her as Kali, goddess of death and
destruction, coal-black, with a red tongue and white eyeballs
and many powerful arms. I expected her to be wild and fierce;
but she added insult to injury by being very playful, as though,
because I was small and strange, the act was not real. She laughed
all the time. I would have liked to withdraw, but the act took
over and completed itself. And then I felt dreadful.

I wanted to be forgiven, I wanted to be cleansed, I wanted
her to go. Nothing frightened me more than the way she had
ceased to be a visitor in the apartment and behaved as though
she possessed it. I looked at the sculpture and the fabrics and
thought of my poor employer, suffering in his office somewhere.

I bathed and bathed afterwards. The smell would not leave
me. I fancied that the woman's oil was still on that poor part
of my poor body. It occurred to me to rub it down with half
a lemon. Penance and cleansing; but it didn't hurt as much as I
expected, and I extended the penance by rolling about naked
on the floor of the bathroom and the sitting-room and howling.
At last the tears came, real tears, and I was comforted.

It was cool in the apartment; the air-conditioning always

hummed; but I could see that it was hot outside, like one of our own summer days in the hills. The urge came upon me to dress as I might have done in my village on a religious occasion. In one of my bundles I had a dhoti-length of new cotton, a gift from the tailor's bearer that I had never used. I draped this around my waist and between my legs, lit incense sticks, sat down crosslegged on the floor and tried to meditate and become still. Soon I began to feel hungry. That made me happy; I decided to fast.

Unexpectedly my employer came in. I didn't mind being caught in the attitude and garb of prayer; it could have been so much worse. But I wasn't expecting him till late afternoon.

"Santosh, what has happened?"

Pride got the better of me. I said, "Sahib, it is what I do from time to time."

But I didn't find merit in his eyes. He was far too agitated to notice me properly. He took off his lightweight fawn jacket, dropped it on the saffron spread, went to the refrigerator and drank two tumblers of orange juice, one after the other. Then he looked out at the view, scraping at his moustache.

"Oh, my poor Santosh, what are we doing in this place? Why do we have to come here?"

I looked with him. I saw nothing unusual. The wide window showed the colours of the hot day: the pale-blue sky, the white, almost colourless, domes of famous buildings rising out of dead-green foliage; the untidy roofs of apartment blocks where on Saturday and Sunday mornings people sunbathed; and, below, the fronts and backs of houses on the tree-lined street down which I walked to the supermarket.

My employer turned off the air-conditioning and all noise was absent from the room. An instant later I began to hear the noises outside: sirens far and near. When my employer slid the window open the roar of the disturbed city rushed into the room. He closed the window and there was near-silence again. Not far from the supermarket I saw black smoke, uncurling, rising, swiftly turning colourless. This was not the smoke which some

of the apartment blocks gave off all day. This was the smoke of a
real fire.

"The *hubshi* have gone wild, Santosh. They are burning down
Washington."

I didn't mind at all. Indeed, in my mood of prayer and repen-
tance, the news was even welcome. And it was with a feeling of
release that I watched and heard the city burn that afternoon and
watched it burn that night. I watched it burn again and again on
television; and I watched it burn in the morning. It burned like
a famous city and I didn't want it to stop burning. I wanted the
fire to spread and spread and I wanted everything in the city,
even the apartment block, even the apartment, even myself, to
be destroyed and consumed. I wanted escape to be impossible;
I wanted the very idea of escape to become absurd. At every sign
that the burning was going to stop I felt disappointed and let
down.

For four days my employer and I stayed in the apartment
and watched the city burn. The television continued to show
us what we could see and what, whenever we slid the window
back, we could hear. Then it was over. The view from our
window hadn't changed. The famous buildings stood; the trees
remained. But for the first time since I had understood that I
was a prisoner I found that I wanted to be out of the apartment
and in the streets.

The destruction lay beyond the supermarket. I had never gone
into this part of the city before, and it was strange to walk in
those long wide streets for the first time, to see trees and houses
and shops and advertisements, everything like a real city, and
then to see that every signboard on every shop was burnt or
stained with smoke, that the shops themselves were black and
broken, that flames had burst through some of the upper windows
and scorched the red bricks. For mile after mile it was like that.
There were *hubshi* groups about, and at first when I passed them
I pretended to be busy, minding my own business, not at all
interested in the ruins. But they smiled at me and I found I was
smiling back. Happiness was on the faces of the *hubshi*. They were

like people amazed they could do so much, that so much lay in their power. They were like people on holiday. I shared their exhilaration.

THE IDEA OF escape was a simple one, but it hadn't occurred to me before. When I adjusted to my imprisonment I had wanted only to get away from Washington and to return to Bombay. But then I had become confused. I had looked in the mirror and seen myself, and I knew it wasn't possible for me to return to Bombay to the sort of job I had had and the life I had lived. I couldn't easily become part of someone else's presence again. Those evening chats on the pavement, those morning walks: happy times, but they were like the happy times of childhood: I didn't want them to return.

I had taken, after the fire, to going for long walks in the city. And one day, when I wasn't even thinking of escape, when I was just enjoying the sights and my new freedom of movement, I found myself in one of those leafy streets where private houses had been turned into business premises. I saw a fellow countryman superintending the raising of a signboard on his gallery. The signboard told me that the building was a restaurant, and I assumed that the man in charge was the owner. He looked worried and slightly ashamed, and he smiled at me. This was unusual, because the Indians I had seen on the streets of Washington pretended they hadn't seen me; they made me feel that they didn't like the competition of my presence or didn't want me to start asking them difficult questions.

I complimented the worried man on his signboard and wished him good luck in his business. He was a small man of about fifty and he was wearing a double-breasted suit with old-fashioned wide lapels. He had dark hollows below his eyes and he looked as though he had recently lost a little weight. I could see that in our country he had been a man of some standing, not quite the sort of person who would go into the restaurant business. I felt at one with him. He invited me in to look around, asked my name and gave his. It was Priya.

Just past the gallery was the loveliest and richest room I had ever seen. The wallpaper was like velvet; I wanted to pass my hand over it. The brass lamps that hung from the ceiling were in a lovely cut-out pattern and the bulbs were of many colours. Priya looked with me, and the hollows under his eyes grew darker, as though my admiration was increasing his worry at his extravagance. The restaurant hadn't yet opened for customers and on a shelf in one corner I saw Priya's collection of good-luck objects: a brass plate with a heap of uncooked rice, for prosperity; a little copybook and a little diary pencil, for good luck with the accounts; a little clay lamp, for general good luck.

"What do you think, Santosh? You think it will be all right?"

"It is bound to be all right, Priya."

"But I have enemies, you know, Santosh. The Indian restaurant people are not going to appreciate me. All mine, you know, Santosh. Cash paid. No mortgage or anything like that. I don't believe in mortgages. Cash or nothing."

I understood him to mean that he had tried to get a mortgage and failed, and was anxious about money.

"But what are you doing here, Santosh? You used to be in Government or something?"

"You could say that, Priya."

"Like me. They have a saying here. If you can't beat them, join them. I joined them. They are still beating me." He sighed and spread his arms on the top of the red wall-seat. "Ah, Santosh, why do we do it? Why don't we renounce and go and meditate on the riverbank?" He waved about the room. "The yemblems of the world, Santosh. Just yemblems."

I didn't know the English word he used, but I understood its meaning; and for a moment it was like being back in Bombay, exchanging stories and philosophies with the tailor's bearer and others in the evening.

"But I am forgetting, Santosh. You will have some tea or coffee or something?"

I shook my head from side to side to indicate that I was

agreeable, and he called out in a strange harsh language to someone behind the kitchen door.

"Yes, Santosh. Yem-*blems!*" And he sighed and slapped the red seat hard.

A man came out from the kitchen with a tray. At first he looked like a fellow countryman, but in a second I could tell he was a stranger.

"You are right," Priya said, when the stranger went back to the kitchen. "He is not of Bharat. He is a Mexican. But what can I do? You get fellow countrymen, you fix up their papers and everything, green card and everything. And then? Then they run away. Run-run-runaway. Crooks this side, crooks that side, I can't tell you. Listen, Santosh. I was in cloth business before. Buy for fifty rupees that side, sell for fifty dollars this side. Easy. But then. Caftan, everybody wants caftan. Caftan-aftan, I say, I will settle your caftan. I buy one thousand, Santosh. Delays India-side, of course. They come one year later. Nobody wants caftan then. We're not organized, Santosh. We don't do enough consumer research. That's what the fellows at the embassy tell me. But if I do consumer research, when will I do my business? The trouble, you know, Santosh, is that this shopkeeping is not in my blood. The damn thing goes *against* my blood. When I was in cloth business I used to hide sometimes for shame when a customer came in. Sometimes I used to pretend I was a shopper myself. Consumer research! These people make us dance, Santosh. You and I, we will renounce. We will go together and walk beside Potomac and meditate."

I loved his talk. I hadn't heard anything so sweet and philosophical since the Bombay days. I said, "Priya, I will cook for you, if you want a cook."

"I feel I've known you a long time, Santosh. I feel you are like a member of my own family. I will give you a place to sleep, a little food to eat and a little pocket money, as much as I can afford."

I said, "Show me the place to sleep."

He led me out of the pretty room and up a carpeted staircase.

I was expecting the carpet and the new paint to stop somewhere, but it was nice and new all the way. We entered a room that was like a smaller version of my employer's apartment.

"Built-in cupboards and everything, you see, Santosh."

I went to the cupboard. It had a folding door that opened outward. I said, "Priya, it is too small. There is room on the shelf for my belongings. But I don't see how I can spread my bedding inside here. It is far too narrow."

He giggled nervously. "Santosh, you are a joker. I feel that we are of the same family already."

Then it came to me that I was being offered the whole room. I was stunned.

Priya looked stunned too. He sat down on the edge of the soft bed. The dark hollows under his eyes were almost black and he looked very small in his double-breasted jacket. "This is how they make us dance over here, Santosh. You say staff quarters and they say staff quarters. This is what they mean."

For some seconds we sat silently, I fearful, he gloomy, meditating on the ways of this new world.

Someone called from downstairs, "Priya!"

His gloom gone, smiling in advance, winking at me, Priya called back in an accent of the country, "Hi, Bab!"

I followed him down.

"Priya," the American said, "I've brought over the menus."

He was a tall man in a leather jacket, with jeans that rode up above thick white socks and big rubber-soled shoes. He looked like someone about to run in a race. The menus were enormous; on the cover there was a drawing of a fat man with a moustache and a plumed turban, something like the man in the airline advertisements.

"They look great, Bab."

"I like them myself. But what's that, Priya? What's that shelf doing there?"

Moving like the front part of a horse, Bab walked to the shelf with the rice and the brass plate and the little clay lamp. It was only then that I saw that the shelf was very roughly made.

Priya looked penitent and it was clear he had put the shelf up himself. It was also clear he didn't intend to take it down.

"Well, it's yours," Bab said. "I suppose we had to have a touch of the East somewhere. Now, Priya – "

"Money-money-money, is it?" Priya said, racing the words together as though he was making a joke to amuse a child. "But, Bab, how can *you* ask *me* for money? Anybody hearing you would believe that this restaurant is mine. But this restaurant isn't mine, Bab. This restaurant is yours."

It was only one of our courtesies, but it puzzled Bab and he allowed himself to be led to other matters.

I saw that, for all his talk of renunciation and business failure, and for all his jumpiness, Priya was able to cope with Washington. I admired this strength in him as much as I admired the richness of his talk. I didn't know how much to believe of his stories, but I liked having to guess about him. I liked having to play with his words in my mind. I liked the mystery of the man. The mystery came from his solidity. I knew where I was with him. After the apartment and the green suit and the *hubshi* woman and the city burning for four days, to be with Priya was to feel safe. For the first time since I had come to Washington I felt safe.

I can't say that I moved in. I simply stayed. I didn't want to go back to the apartment even to collect my belongings. I was afraid that something might happen to keep me a prisoner there. My employer might turn up and demand his five thousand rupees. The *hubshi* woman might claim me for her own; I might be condemned to a life among the *hubshi*. And it wasn't as if I was leaving behind anything of value in the apartment. The green suit I was even happy to forget. But.

PRIYA PAID ME forty dollars a week. After what I was getting, three dollars and seventy-five cents, it seemed a lot; and it was more than enough for my needs. I didn't have much temptation to spend, to tell the truth. I knew that my old employer and the *hubshi* woman would be wondering about me in their respective ways and I thought I should keep off the streets for a while. That was no hardship; it was what I was used to in Washington. Besides, my days at the restaurant were pretty full; for the first time in my life I had little leisure.

The restaurant was a success from the start, and Priya was fussy. He was always bursting into the kitchen with one of those big menus in his hand, saying in English, "Prestige job, Santosh, prestige." I didn't mind. I liked to feel I had to do things perfectly; I felt I was earning my freedom. Though I was in hiding, and though I worked every day until midnight, I felt I was much more in charge of myself than I had ever been.

Many of our waiters were Mexicans, but when we put turbans on them they could pass. They came and went, like the Indian staff. I didn't get on with these people. They were frightened and jealous of one another and very treacherous. Their talk amid the biryanis and the pillaus was all of papers and green cards. They were always about to get green cards or they had been cheated out of green cards or they had just got green cards. At first I didn't know what they were talking about. When I understood I was more than depressed.

I understood that because I had escaped from my employer I had made myself illegal in America. At any moment I could be denounced, seized, jailed, deported, disgraced. It was a complication. I had no green card; I didn't know how to set about getting one; and there was no one I could talk to.

I felt burdened by my secrets. Once I had none; now I had so many. I couldn't tell Priya I had no green card. I couldn't tell him I had broken faith with my old employer and dishonoured myself with a *hubshi* woman and lived in fear of retribution. I couldn't tell him that I was afraid to leave the restaurant and that nowadays when I saw an Indian I hid from him as anxiously as the Indian hid from me. I would have felt foolish to confess. With Priya, right from the start, I had pretended to be strong; and I wanted it to remain like that. Instead, when we talked now, and he grew philosophical, I tried to find bigger causes for being sad. My mind fastened on to these causes, and the effect of this was that my sadness became like a sickness of the soul.

It was worse than being in the apartment, because now the responsibility was mine and mine alone. I had decided to be free, to act for myself. It pained me to think of the exhilaration I had felt during the days of the fire; and I felt mocked when I remembered that in the early days of my escape I had thought I was in charge of myself.

The year turned. The snow came and melted. I was more afraid than ever of going out. The sickness was bigger than all the causes. I saw the future as a hole into which I was dropping. Sometimes at night when I awakened my body would burn and I would feel the hot perspiration break all over.

I leaned on Priya. He was my only hope, my only link with what was real. He went out; he brought back stories. He went out especially to eat in the restaurants of our competitors.

He said, "Santosh, I never believed that running a restaurant was a way to God. But it is true. I eat like a scientist. Every day I eat like a scientist. I feel I have already renounced."

This was Priya. This was how his talk ensnared me and gave me the bigger causes that steadily weakened me. I became more and more detached from the men in the kitchen. When they spoke of their green cards and the jobs they were about to get I felt like asking them: Why? Why?

And every day the mirror told its own tale. Without exercise, with the sickening of my heart and my mind, I was losing my looks. My face had become pudgy and sallow and full of spots; it was becoming ugly. I could have cried for that, discovering my good looks only to lose them. It was like a punishment for my presumption, the punishment I had feared when I bought the green suit.

Priya said, "Santosh, you must get some exercise. You are not looking well. Your eyes are getting like mine. What are you pining for? Are you pining for Bombay or your family in the hills?"

But now, even in my mind, I was a stranger in those places.

Priya said one Sunday morning, "Santosh, I am going to take you to see a Hindi movie today. All the Indians of Washington will be there, domestics and everybody else."

I was very frightened. I didn't want to go and I couldn't tell him why. He insisted. My heart began to beat fast as soon as I got into the car. Soon there were no more houses with gas-lamps in the entrance, just those long wide burnt-out *hubshi* streets, now with fresh leaves on the trees, heaps of rubble on bulldozed, fenced-in lots, boarded-up shop windows, and old smoke-stained signboards announcing what was no longer true. Cars raced along the wide roads; there was life only on the roads. I thought I would vomit with fear.

I said, "Take me back, *sahib*."

I had used the wrong word. Once I had used the word a hundred times a day. But then I had considered myself a small part of my employer's presence, and the word was not servile; it was more like a name, like a reassuring sound, part of my employer's dignity and therefore part of mine. But Priya's dignity could never be mine; that was not our relationship. Priya I had always called Priya; it was his wish, the American way, man to man. With Priya the word was servile. And he responded to the word. He did as I asked; he drove me back to the restaurant. I never called him by his name again.

I was good-looking; I had lost my looks. I was a free man; I had lost my freedom.

ONE OF THE Mexican waiters came into the kitchen late one evening and said, "There is a man outside who wants to see the chef."

No one had made this request before, and Priya was at once agitated. "Is he an American? Some enemy has sent him here. Sanitary-anitary, health-ealth, they can inspect my kitchens at any time."

"He is an Indian," the Mexican said.

I was alarmed. I thought it was my old employer; that quiet

approach was like him. Priya thought it was a rival. Though Priya regularly ate in the restuarants of his rivals he thought it unfair when they came to eat in his. We both went to the door and peeked through the glass window into the dimly lit dining-room.

"Do you know that person, Santosh?"

"Yes, sahib."

It wasn't my old employer. It was one of his Bombay friends, a big man in Government, whom I had often served in the chambers. He was by himself and seemed to have just arrived in Washington. He had a new Bombay haircut, very close, and a stiff dark suit, Bombay tailoring. His shirt looked blue, but in the dim multi-coloured light of the dining-room everything white looked blue. He didn't look unhappy with what he had eaten. Both his elbows were on the curry-spotted tablecloth and he was picking his teeth, half closing his eyes and hiding his mouth with his cupped left hand.

"I don't like him," Priya said. "Still, big man in Government and so on. You must go to him, Santosh."

But I couldn't go.

"Put on your apron, Santosh. And that chef's cap. Prestige. You must go, Santosh."

Priya went out to the dining-room and I heard him say in English that I was coming.

I ran up to my room, put some oil on my hair, combed my hair, put on my best pants and shirt and my shining shoes. It was so, as a man about town rather than as a cook, I went to the dining-room.

The man from Bombay was as astonished as Priya. We exchanged the old courtesies, and I waited. But, to my relief, there seemed little more to say. No difficult questions were put to me; I was grateful to the man from Bombay for his tact. I avoided talk as much as possible. I smiled. The man from Bombay smiled back. Priya smiled uneasily at both of us. So for a while we were, smiling in the dim blue-red light and waiting.

The man from Bombay said to Priya, "Brother, I just have a few words to say to my old friend Santosh."

Priya didn't like it, but he left us.

I waited for those words. But they were not the words I feared. The man from Bombay didn't speak of my old employer. We continued to exchange courtesies. Yes, I was well and he was well and everybody else we knew was well; and I was doing well and he was doing well. That was all. Then, secretively, the man from Bombay gave me a dollar. A dollar, ten rupees, an enormous tip for Bombay. But, from him, much more than a tip: an act of graciousness, part of the sweetness of the old days. Once it would have meant so much to me. Now it meant so little. I was saddened and embarrassed. And I had been anticipating hostility!

Priya was waiting behind the kitchen door. His little face was tight and serious, and I knew he had seen the money pass. Now, quickly, he read my own face, and without saying anything to me he hurried out into the dining-room.

I heard him say in English to the man from Bombay, "Santosh is a good fellow. He's got his own room with bath and everything. I am giving him a hundred dollars a week from next week. A thousand rupees a week. This is a first-class establishment."

A thousand chips a week! I was staggered. It was much more than any man in Government got, and I was sure the man from Bombay was also staggered, and perhaps regretting his good gesture and that precious dollar of foreign exchange.

"Santosh," Priya said, when the restaurant closed that evening, "that man was an enemy. I knew it from the moment I saw him. And because he was an enemy I did something very bad, Santosh."

"Sahib."

"I lied, Santosh. To protect you. I told him, Santosh, that I was going to give you seventy-five dollars a week after Christmas."

"Sahib."

"And now I have to make that lie true. But, Santosh, you know that is money we can't afford. I don't have to tell you about overheads and things like that. Santosh, I will give you sixty."

I said, "Sahib, I couldn't stay on for less than a hundred and twenty-five."

Priya's eyes went shiny and the hollows below his eyes darkened. He giggled and pressed out his lips. At the end of that week I got a hundred dollars. And Priya, good man that he was, bore me no grudge.

Now here was a victory. It was only after it happened that I realized how badly I had needed such a victory, how far, gaining my freedom, I had begun to accept death not as the end but as the goal. I revived. Or rather, my senses revived. But in this city what was there to feed my senses? There were no walks to be taken, no idle conversations with understanding friends. I could buy new clothes. But then? Would I just look at myself in the mirror? Would I go walking, inviting passers-by to look at me and my clothes? No, the whole business of clothes and dressing up only threw me back into myself.

There was a Swiss or German woman in the cake-shop some doors away, and there was a Filipino woman in the kitchen. They were neither of them attractive, to tell the truth. The Swiss or German could have broken my back with a slap, and the Filipino, though young, was remarkably like one of our older hill women. Still, I felt I owed something to the senses, and I thought I might frolic with these women. But then I was frightened of the responsibility. Goodness, I had learned that a woman is not just a roll and a frolic but a big creature weighing a hundred-and-so-many pounds who is going to be around afterwards.

So the moment of victory passed, without celebration. And it was strange, I thought, that sorrow lasts and can make a man look forward to death, but the mood of victory fills a moment and then is over. When my moment of victory was over I discovered below it, as if waiting for me, all my old sickness and fears: fear of my illegality, my former employer, my presumption, the *hubshi* woman. I saw then that the victory I had had was not something I had worked for, but luck; and that luck was only fate's cheating, giving an illusion of power.

But that illusion lingered, and I became restless. I decided to act, to challenge fate. I decided I would no longer stay in my room and hide. I began to go out walking in the afternoons. I gained courage; every afternoon I walked a little farther. It became my ambition to walk to that green circle with the fountain where, on my first day out in Washington, I had come upon those people in Hindu costumes, like domestics abandoned a long time ago, singing their Sanskrit gibberish and doing their strange Red Indian dance. And one day I got there.

One day I crossed the road to the circle and sat down on a bench. The *hubshi* were there, and the bare feet, and the dancers in saris and the saffron robes. It was mid-afternoon, very hot, and no one was active. I remembered how magical and inexplicable that circle had seemed to me the first time I saw it. Now it seemed so ordinary and tired: the roads, the motor cars, the shops, the trees, the careful policemen: so much part of the waste and futility that was our world. There was no longer a mystery. I felt I knew where everybody had come from and where those cars were going. But I also felt that everybody there felt like me, and that was soothing. I took to going to the circle every day after the lunch rush and sitting until it was time to go back to Priya's for the dinners.

Late one afternoon, among the dancers and the musicians, the *hubshi* and the bare feet, the singers and the police, I saw her. The *hubshi* woman. And again I wondered at her size; my memory had not exaggerated. I decided to stay where I was. She saw me and smiled. Then, as if remembering anger, she gave me a look of great hatred; and again I saw her as Kali, many-armed, goddess of death and destruction. She looked hard at my face; she considered my clothes. I thought: is it for this I bought these clothes? She got up. She was very big and her tight pants made her much more appalling. She moved towards me. I got up and ran. I ran across the road and then, not looking back, hurried by devious ways to the restaurant.

Priya was doing his accounts. He always looked older when

he was doing his accounts, not worried, just older, like a man to whom life could bring no further surprises. I envied him.

"Santosh, some friend brought a parcel for you."

It was a big parcel wrapped in brown paper. He handed it to me, and I thought how calm he was, with his bills and pieces of paper, and the pen with which he made his neat figures, and the book in which he would write every day until that book was exhausted and he would begin a new one.

I took the parcel up to my room and opened it. Inside there was a cardboard box; and inside that, still in its tissue paper, was the green suit.

I FELT A HOLE in my stomach. I couldn't think. I was glad I had to go down almost immediately to the kitchen, glad to be busy until midnight. But then I had to go up to my room again, and I was alone. I hadn't escaped; I had never been free. I had been abandoned. I was like nothing; I had made myself nothing. And I couldn't turn back.

In the morning Priya said, "You don't look very well, Santosh."

His concern weakened me further. He was the only man I could talk to and I didn't know what I could say to him. I felt tears coming to my eyes. At that moment I would have liked the whole world to be reduced to tears. I said, "Sahib, I cannot stay with you any longer."

They were just words, part of my mood, part of my wish for tears and relief. But Priya didn't soften. He didn't even look surprised. "Where will you go, Santosh?"

How could I answer his serious question?

"Will it be different where you go?"

He had freed himself of me. I could no longer think of tears. I said, "Sahib, I have enemies."

He giggled. "You are a joker, Santosh. How can a man like yourself have enemies? There would be no profit in it. I have enemies. It is part of your happiness and part of the equity of the world that you cannot have enemies. That's why you can run-run-runaway." He smiled and made the running gesture with his extended palm.

So, at last, I told him my story. I told him about my old employer and my escape and the green suit. He made me feel I was telling him nothing he hadn't already known. I told him about the *hubshi* woman. I was hoping for some rebuke. A rebuke would have meant that he was concerned for my honour, that I could lean on him, that rescue was possible.

But he said, "Santosh, you have no problems. Marry the *hubshi*. That will automatically make you a citizen. Then you will be a free man."

It wasn't what I was expecting. He was asking me to be alone forever. I said, "Sahib, I have a wife and children in the hills at home."

"But this is your home, Santosh. Wife and children in the hills, that is very nice and that is always there. But that is over. You have to do what is best for you here. You are alone here. *Hubshi-ubshi*, nobody worries about that here, if that is your choice. This isn't Bombay. Nobody looks at you when you walk down the street. Nobody cares what you do."

He was right. I was a free man; I could do anything I wanted. I could, if it were possible for me to turn back, go to the apartment and beg my old employer for forgiveness. I could, if it were possible for me to become again what I once was, go to the police and say, "I am an illegal immigrant here. Please deport me to Bombay." I could run away, hang myself, surrender, confess, hide. It didn't matter what I did, because I was alone. And I didn't know what I wanted to do. It was like the time when I felt my senses revive and I wanted to go out and enjoy and I found there was nothing to enjoy.

To be empty is not to be sad. To be empty is to be calm. It is to renounce. Priya said no more to me; he was always busy in the mornings. I left him and went up to my room. It was still a bare room, still like a room that in half an hour could be someone else's. I had never thought of it as mine. I was frightened of its spotless painted walls and had been careful to keep them spotless. For just such a moment.

I tried to think of the particular moment in my life, the particular action, that had brought me to that room. Was it the moment with the *hubshi* woman, or was it when the American came to dinner and insulted my employer? Was it the moment of my escape, my sight of Priya in the gallery, or was it when I looked in the mirror and bought the green suit? Or was it much earlier, in that other life, in Bombay, in the hills? I could find no one moment; every moment seemed important. An endless chain of action had brought me to that room. It was frightening; it was burdensome. It was not a time for new decisions. It was time to call a halt.

I lay on the bed watching the ceiling, watching the sky. The door was pushed open. It was Priya.

"My goodness, Santosh! How long have you been here? You have been so quiet I forgot about you."

He looked about the room. He went into the bathroom and came out again.

"Are you all right, Santosh?"

He sat on the edge of the bed and the longer he stayed the more I realized how glad I was to see him. There was this: when I tried to think of him rushing into the room I couldn't place it in time; it seemed to have occurred only in my mind. He sat with me. Time became real again. I felt a great love for him. Soon I could have laughed at his agitation. And later, indeed, we laughed together.

I said, "Sahib, you must excuse me this morning. I want to go for a walk. I will come back about tea time."

He looked hard at me, and we both knew I had spoken truly.

"Yes, yes, Santosh. You go for a good long walk. Make yourself hungry with walking. You will feel much better."

Walking, through streets that were now so simple to me, I thought how nice it would be if the people in Hindu costumes in the circle were real. Then I might have joined them. We would have taken to the road; at midday we would have halted in the shade of big trees; in the late afternoon the sinking sun would have turned the dust clouds to gold; and every evening at some village there would have been welcome, water, food, a fire in the night. But that was a dream of another life. I had watched the people in the circle long enough to know that they were of their city; that their television life awaited them; that their renunciation was not like mine. No television life awaited me. It didn't matter. In this city I was alone and it didn't matter what I did.

As magical as the circle with the fountain the apartment block had once been to me. Now I saw that it was plain, not very tall, and faced with small white tiles. A glass door; four tiled steps down; the desk to the right, letters and keys in the pigeonholes; a carpet to the left, upholstered chairs, a low table with paper flowers in the vase; the blue door of the swift, silent elevator. I saw the simplicity of all these things. I knew the floor I wanted. In the corridor, with its illuminated star-decorated ceiling, an imitation sky, the colours were blue, grey and gold. I knew the door I wanted. I knocked.

The *hubshi* woman opened. I saw the apartment where she worked. I had never seen it before and was expecting something like my old employer's apartment, which was on the same floor. Instead, for the first time, I saw something arranged for a television life.

I thought she might have been angry. She looked only puzzled. I was grateful for that.

I said to her in English, "Will you marry me?"

And there, it was done.

"It is for the best, Santosh," Priya said, giving me tea when I got back to the restaurant. "You will be a free man. A citizen. You will have the whole world before you."

I was pleased that he was pleased.

So I am now a citizen, my presence is legal, and I live in Washington. I am still with Priya. We do not talk together as much as we did. The restaurant is one world, the parks and green streets of Washington are another, and every evening some of these streets take me to a third. Burnt-out brick houses, broken fences, overgrown gardens; in a levelled lot between the high brick walls of two houses, a sort of artistic children's playground which the *hubshi* children never use; and then the dark house in which I now live.

Its smells are strange, everything in it is strange. But my strength in this house is that I am a stranger. I have closed my mind and heart to the English language, to newspapers and radio and television, to the pictures of *hubshi* runners and boxers and musicians on the wall. I do not want to understand or learn any more.

I am a simple man who decided to act and see for himself, and it is as though I have had several lives. I do not wish to add to these. Some afternoons I walk to the circle with the fountain. I see the dancers but they are separated from me as by glass. Once, when there were rumours of new burnings, someone scrawled in white paint on the pavement outside my house: *Soul Brother*. I understand the words; but I feel, brother to what or to whom? I was once part of the flow, never thinking of myself as a presence. Then I looked in the mirror and decided to be free. All that my freedom has brought me is the knowledge that I have a face and have a body, that I must feed this body and clothe this body for a certain number of years. Then it will be over.

Tell Me Who to Kill

Tell Me Who to Kill

JUST LIKE MY brother. He choose a bad morning to get married. Cold and wet, the little country parts between towns white rather than green, mist falling like rain, fields soaking, sometimes a cow standing up just like that. The little streams have a dirty milky colour and some of them are full of empty tins and other rubbish. Water everywhere, just like back home after a heavy shower in the rainy season, only the sky is not showing in the places where the water collect, and the sun is not coming out to heat up everything and steam it dry fast.

The train hot inside, the windows running with water, people and their clothes smelling. My old suit is smelling too. It is too big for me now, but it is the only suit I have and it is from the time of money. Oh my God. Just little bits of country between the towns, and sometimes I see a house far away, by itself, and I think how nice it would be to be there, to be watching the rain and the train in the early morning. Then that pass, and it is town again, and town again, and then the whole place is like one big town, everything brown, everything of brick or iron or rusty galvanize, like a big wet rubbish dump. And my heart drop and my stomach feel small.

Frank is looking at me, watching my face. Frank in his nice tweed jacket and grey flannel trousers. Tall, thin, going a little bald. But happy. Happy to be with me, happy when people look at us and see that he is with me. He is a good man, he is my friend. But inside he is puffed up with pride. No one is nice to me like Frank, but he is so happy to make himself small, bringing his knees together as though he is carrying a little box of cakes on them. He don't smile, but that is because he is so wise and happy.

His old big shoes shining like a schoolteacher's shoes, and you could see that he shine them himself every evening, like a man saying his prayers and feeling good. He don't mean it, but he always make me feel sad and he always make me feel small, because I know I could never be as nice and neat as Frank and I could never be so wise and happy. But I know, oh God I know, I lose everybody else, and the only friend I have in the world is Frank.

A boy writing on the wet window with his finger and the letters melting down. The boy is with his mother and he is all right. He know where they are going when the train stop. It is a moment I don't like at all, when the train stop and everybody scatter, when the ship dock and everybody take away their luggage. Everybody have their own luggage, and everybody's luggage so different. Everybody is brisk then, and happy, no time for talk, because they can see where they are going. Since I come to this country that is something I can't do. I can't see where I am going. I can only wait to see what is going to turn up.

I am going to my brother's wedding now. But I don't know what bus we will take when we get to the station, or what other train, what street we will walk down, what gate we will go through, and what door we will open into what room.

MY BROTHER. I REMEMBER a day like this, but with heat. The sky set black night and day, the rain always coming, beating on the galvanize roof, the ground turn to mud below the house, in the yard the water frothing yellow with mud, the pará-grass in the field at the back bending down with wet, everything damp and sticky, bare skin itching.

The cart is under the house and the donkey is in the pen at the back. The pen is wet and dirty with mud and manure and fresh grass mixed up with old grass, and the donkey is standing up quiet with a sugarsack on his back to prevent him catching cold. In the kitchen shed my mother is cooking, and the smoke from the wet wood thick and smelling. Everything will taste of smoke, but on a day like this you can't think of food. The mud and the heat and the smell make you want to throw up instead. My father is upstairs, in merino and drawers, rocking in the gallery, rubbing his hands on his arms. The smoke is not keeping away the mosquitoes up there, but mosquitoes don't bite him. He is not thinking of anything too much; he is just looking out at the black sky and the sugarcane fields and rocking. And in one of the rooms inside, below the old galvanize roof, my brother is lying on the floor with the ague.

It is a bare room, and the bare cedar boards have nothing on them except nails and some clothes and a calendar. You build a house and you have nothing to put in it. And my pretty brother is trembling with the ague, lying on the floor on a floursack spread on a sugarsack, with another floursack for counterpane. You can see the sickness on his little face. The fever is on him but he is not sweating. He can't understand what you say, and what he is saying is not making sense. He is saying that everything around him and inside him is heavy and smooth, very smooth.

It is as if he is going to die, and you think it is not right that someone so small and pretty should suffer so much, while some-one like yourself should be so strong. He is so pretty. If he grow up he will be like a star-boy, like Errol Flim or Fairley Granger. The beauty in that room is like a wonder to me, and I can't bear the thought of losing it. I can't bear the thought of the bare room and the wet coming through the gaps in the boards and the black mud outside and the smell of the smoke and the mosquitoes and the night coming.

This is how I remember my brother, even afterwards, even when he grow up. Even after we sell the donkey-cart and start working the lorry and we pull down the old house and build a nice one, paint and everything. It is how I think of my brother, small and sick, suffering for me, and so pretty. I feel I could kill anyone who make him suffer. I don't care about myself. I have no life.

I know that it was in 1954 or 1955, some ordinary year, that my brother was sick, and from the weather I can tell you the month is January or December. But in my mind it happen so long ago I can't put a time to it. And just as I can't put a time to it, so in my mind I can't put a real place to it. I know where our house is and I know, oh my God, that if ever I go back I will get off the taxi at the junction and walk down the old Savannah Road. I know that road well; I know it in all sorts of weather. But what I see in my mind is in no place at all. Everything blot out except the rain and the night coming and the house and the mud and the field and the donkey and the smoke from the kitchen and my father in the gallery and my brother in the room on the floor.

And it is as though because you are frightened of something it is bound to come, as though because you are carrying danger with you danger is bound to come. And again it is like a dream. I see myself in this old English house, like something in *Rebecca* starring Laurence Oliver and Joan Fountain. It is an upstairs room with a lot of jalousies and fretwork. No weather. I am there with my brother, and we are strangers in the house. My brother is at college or school in England, pursuing his studies, and he is visiting this college friend and he is staying with the boy's family. And then in a corridor, just outside a door, something happen. A quarrel, a friendly argument, a scuffle. They are only playing, but the knife go in the boy, easy, and he drop without making a noise. I just see his face surprised, I don't see any blood, and I don't want to stoop to look. I see my brother opening his mouth to scream, but no scream coming. Nothing making noise. I feel his fright – the gallows for him, just like that, and it was only an accident, it isn't true – and I know at that moment that the love and the danger I carry all my life burst. My life finish. It spoil, it spoil.

The worst part is still to come. We have to eat with the boy's parents. They don't know what happen. And both of us, my brother and me, we have to sit down and eat with them. And the body is in the house, in a chest, like in *Rope* with Fairley Granger. It is there at the beginning, it is there forever, and everything else is only like a mockery. But we eat. My brother is trembling; he is not a good actor. The people we are eating with, I can't see their faces, I don't know what they look like.

They could be like any of the white people on this train. Like that woman with the boy writing on the wet window.

I CAN'T HELP ANYBODY now. My life spoil. I would like the train never to stop. But look, the buildings are getting higher and closer together and now they are right beside the tracks, and you can see rooms and washing and other things hanging up in kitchens behind the wet windows. London. I am glad Frank is with me. He will look after me when the train stop. He will take me to the wedding house, wherever it is. My brother is getting married. And inside me is like lead.

When the train stop we let the others rush, and I calm down. No rain when we go outside, and it even look as if the sun is going to break through. Frank say we have a lot of time and we decide to walk a little. The streets dirty after the rain, the buildings black, old newspapers in the gutters. I follow Frank and he lead me to streets I know well. I wonder whether it is an accident or whether he know. He know everything.

And then I see the shop. Like a dirty box with a glass front. Now it is a jokes-shop, with little cards in the dusty window. Amuse your friends, frighten your friends. Card tricks, false false-teeth, solid glasses of Guinness, rubber spiders, itching powder, plastic dog-mess. It isn't much, but you wouldn't believe that once upon a time for a few months the place was mine.

"This is the place," I tell Frank. "The mistake of my life. This is where all my money went. Two thousand pounds. It take me five years to save that. In five months it went there."

Two thousand pounds. Pounds don't sound like real money if you spend most of your life dealing in dollars and cents. But in ten years my father couldn't make two thousand pounds. How a man could revive after that? You can say: I will do it again, I will work again and save again. You can say that, but you know that when your courage break, it break.

Frank put his arm around my shoulders to take me away from

the shop window. The owner, the new owner, the man with the lease, look at us. A yellow little bald fellow with a soft little paunch, and everything in his window already look as if it is collecting dust. Frank stiffen a little, the old pride puffing him up, and he is acting for the bald fellow and anybody else who is watching us.

I say, "You white bitch."

It is as though Frank love the obscene language. He get very tender and gentle, and because he is tender I start saying things I don't really feel.

"I am going to make a lot more money, Frank. I am going to make more money than you will ever make in your whole life, you white bitch. I will buy the tallest building here. I will buy the whole street."

But even as I talk I know it is foolishness. I know that my life spoil and even I myself feel like laughing.

I don't want to be out in the street now. It isn't that I don't want people to see me; I don't want to see people. Frank tell me it is because they are white. I don't know, when Frank talk like that I feel he is challenging me to kill one of them.

I want to get off the street, to calm down. Frank take me to a café and we sit right at the back, facing the wall. He sit beside me. And he is talking to me. He talk about his own childhood, and I feel he is trying to show me that he too as a child had ague in a bare room. But he win through in life, he is in his city, he is now wise and strong. He don't know how jealous he is making me of him. I don't want to listen. I look at the flowers on the paper napkins and I lose myself in the lines. He can't see what is locked up in my mind. He will never in a hundred years understand how ordinary the world was for me, with nothing good in it, nothing to see except sugarcane and the pitch road, and how from small I know I had no life.

ORDINARY FOR ME, but for my brother it wasn't going to be like that. He was going to break away; he was going to be a professional man; I was going to see to that. For the rich and the professional the world is not ordinary. I know, I see them. Where you build a hut, they build a mansion; where you have mud and a pará-grass field, they have a garden; when you kill time on a Sunday, they have parties. We all come out of the same pot, but some people move ahead and some people get left behind. Some people get left behind so far they don't know and they stop caring.

Like my father. He couldn't read and write and he didn't care. He even joke about his illiteracy, slapping his fat arms and laughing. He say he is happy to leave that side of life to his younger brother, who is a law clerk in the city. And whenever he meet this brother, my father is always turning his own life into a story and a joke, and he turn us his children into a joke too. But for all the jokes he make, you could see that my father feel that he is very wise, that it is he who pick up the bargain. My two older sisters and my older brother are like that too. They learn just so much in school; then – it was the way of the old days – they get married, and my older brother start beating his wife and so on, doing everything in the way people before him do, getting drunk on a Friday and Saturday, wasting his money, without shame.

I was the fourth child and the second son. The world change around me when I was growing up. I see people going away to further their studies and coming back as big men. I know that I miss out. I know how much I lose when I have to stop school, and I decide that it wasn't going to be like that for my younger brother. I feel I see things so much better than the rest of my family; they always tell me I am very touchy. But I feel I become like the head of the family. I get the ambition and the shame for all of them. The ambition is like shame, and the shame is like a secret, and it is always hurting. Even now, when it is all over, it can start hurting again. Frank can never see what I see in my mind.

A MAN USED TO live near us in a big two-storey house. The house was of concrete, with decorated concrete blocks, and it was in a lovely ochre colour with chocolate wood facings, everything so neat and nice it look like something to eat. I study this house every day and I think of it as the rich man's house, because the man was rich. He was rich, but once upon a time he was poor, like us, and the story was that he had a few acres of oil land in the south. A simple man, like my father, without too much education. But in my eyes the oil land and the luck and the money and the house make this man great.

I worship this man. Nothing extravagant about him; sometimes you could see him standing up on the road waiting for a bus or a taxi to go to town, and if you didn't know who he was you wouldn't notice him. I study everything about him, seeing luck and money in everything, in the hair he comb, in the shirt his hands button, in the shoes his hands lace up. He live alone in the house. His children married, and the story is that he don't get on with his family, that he is a man with a lot of worries. But to me even that is part of the greatness.

One time there was a wedding in the village, the old-fashioned all-night wedding, and the rich man lend his house. And on the wedding night I went in the house for the first time. The house that look so big from the outside is really very small inside. Downstairs is just concrete pillars, walls around open space. Upstairs is five small rooms, not counting galleries back and front. The lights dim, dim. It is what I remember most. That and the dead-rat smell. You feel dust everywhere, dust falling on you even while you walk. It isn't dust, it is the droppings from woodlice, hard smooth tiny eggs of wood that roll below your hand if you put your hand down anywhere.

The drawing-room choke up with furniture, Morris suite and centre tables and everything else; but you feel that if you press too hard on anything it will crush. Just the furniture, nothing else in the drawing-room, no pictures or calendars even, nothing except for a pile of Christian magazines, Jehovah's Witness or something like that, things that the rest of us throw away but he the rich man keep, and he is not even a Christian. The place is like a tomb. It is as though nobody live there, as though the rich man don't know why he build the house.

And then one day somebody shoot the man. For money, for

some family bad blood, nobody know. It is another country mystery. The black police nail up Five Hundred Dollars Reward posters everywhere, as though the village is suddenly like Dodge City or like something in *Jesse James*, with Henry Fonda and Tyrum Powers just around the corner.

Everybody wait for the drama. But no drama happen. The posters fade and tear, the police forget, the house remain. The ochre paint discolour, the galvanize roof rust and the rust run down the walls, and the damp run up fast from the ground like a bright green bush. The bright green get dark, it get black, real bush grow up in front of it. Mildew stain the house, the roof is all rust. The paint wash off the woodwork, the grain of the wood begin to show, the wood begin to get hollow, the soft parts melting away, until only the hard grain remain, like a skeleton. And all the time I live there the house just standing there like that.

I see now that the man I thought was a rich man wasn't rich at all. And from here, from this city which is like a country, I feel I could look down and see that whole village in the damp flat lands, the lumpy little pitch road, black between the green sugarcane, the ditches with the tall grass, the thatched huts, water in the yellow yards after rain, and the rusty roof of that one concrete house rotting.

YOU WONDER HOW people get to a village like that, how that place become their home. But it is home, and on a sunny Sunday morning, nobody working, see everybody relaxing in their front yards, a few zinnias growing here and there, a few marigolds and old maid and coxcomb and lady's slipper and the usual hibiscus. The barber making his round, people sitting down below mango trees and getting their hair cut. And in my mind it is on a morning like this that I can see my father's younger brother coming up the pitch road on his bicycle.

My father's brother is living in the city. How he get there, how he get education when my father get none, how he get this job with the lawyer, all of this happen a long time ago, before I was born, and is now like a mystery. He is a Christian, or he take a Christian name, Stephen, as a mark of his progressiveness. My father does mock him behind his back for that name, but all of us are proud of Stephen and we well enjoy the little fame and respect he give us in the village.

It is a big thing when he come to visit us. The neighbours spreading the news in advance, my mother chasing and killing a chicken right away, my father getting out the rum bottle and glasses and water. Fête! And at the end, just before he leave, Stephen sharing out coppers to the children for the Sunday 4.30 matinée double.

Or so it used to be. I adore Stephen when I was small. And adoring him like this, I used to think that he live alone in the city, that we was his only family. But then I get let down. I realize that Stephen have his own family, that he have a whole heap of girl children, going to the Convent, and that he have his own son, a bright boy, a great student, and he worship this son. The boy is my own age too, or just a little older. Once or twice he come to see us. He is nice and quiet, not pulling any style on us, and you could see that in a special way my father is prouder of him than he is of me or my younger brother, that Stephen's son is what he expect, different, a bright boy and a future professional. My father don't give him coppers for a matinée. He send him a Shirley Temple fountain pen, a Mickey Mouse wristwatch.

Stephen never tell us when he is coming, and you wonder why a man like that would decide to leave his family on a Sunday morning to come and have a country fête with us. My father say that Stephen is glad to get away from that modern life sometimes, that Stephen is not happy with his Christian wife, and that Stephen, because of his progressiveness, is full of worries. I don't know what worries a man like Stephen could have. And if he have worries, they don't always show.

Stephen is a joker and a mocker. Even before he put his bicycle in the shade, even before he take off his hat and bicycle clips, even before he take the first shot of rum, Stephen start mocking. I don't know why he find our donkey so funny; it is as though he never see one before. He mock us because of the donkey; he mock us when the donkey die. Then when we buy the lorry and it get laid up for a few weeks below the house, blocks of wood below the axle, he mock us because of that. Everything we do is only like a mockery to Stephen, and my father encourage him by laughing.

Stephen mock me a lot too, in the beginning. "When you marrying off this one?" he used to ask my father, even when I was small. My father always laugh and say, "Next season. I got a nice girl for him." But as I grow older I show I don't appreciate the humour, and Stephen stop mocking me.

He is not a bad or cruel man, Stephen. He is just a natural joker, with all his so-called worries. Sometimes he mock himself. One time, when he bring his son to see us, he say, "My son never yet tell a lie." I ask the boy, "It is true?" He say, "No." Stephen burst out laughing and say, "My God, the influence of you people! The boy just tell his first lie." This is Stephen, a little seriousness always below the mockery, and you feel that one reason he mock us is because he would like us to be a little more progressive.

Stephen is always asking my father what we are doing to educate my younger brother. "The others are lost," Stephen say. "But you could still give this one a little education. Dayo, boy, you would like to take some studies?" And Dayo would rub his foot against his ankle and say, "Yes, I would like to take some studies." It was the beauty of the boy that attract Stephen, I feel. He used to say, "I will take away Dayo with me." – "Yes," my father would say, "you take him away and give him some studies. In this school here he learning nothing at all. I don't know what teachers teaching these days."

I always think it would be nice if Stephen could take an interest in Dayo and use his contacts to get Dayo in a good school in the city. But I know that Stephen is just talking, or rather, it is the rum and curry chicken talking, and I don't see how I can talk to him seriously about Dayo. If Stephen was a stranger it would have been different. But Stephen is family, and family is funny. I don't want to give Stephen or his son the idea that I am running them competition. Stephen would more than mock, if he feel that; he might even get vexed.

So I let Stephen talk. I know that he will drink and mock, that his eyes will get redder and redder until his worries begin to show on his face in truth, and that when the fête is over he will jump on his bicycle and ride off back to the city and his family.

I know that Stephen can't really take an interest in Dayo, because Stephen's whole mind and heart is full of his own son. For years Stephen talk of his son's further studies, and for years he save for these further studies; he don't keep it secret. Even when the time for these studies get close, when everything is fixed up with the university in Canada, Stephen don't relax. You begin to feel then that Stephen is more than ambitious for his son, that he is a little frightened too. He is like a man carrying something that could break and cut him. Even my father notice the difference, and he begin to say behind Stephen's back, "My brother Stephen is going to get throw down by his son." Like a happy man, my father. He educate none of his own children to throw him down.

Then one Sunday afternoon, some months before the boy leave, Stephen come. Without warning, as usual. This time he is not on a bicycle and he is not alone. He is in a motor car and he is with his whole family. From the pará-grass field at the back of the house I see the car stop and I see all Stephen's girl children get out, and I remember the condition of our house. I race up in a foolish kind of way trying to sweep and straighten up. But my heart is failing me, because I can see the house as the girls will see it. And in the end, hearing the voices coming up the steps at the side, I pretend to be like my father, not caring, ready to make a joke of everything, letting people know that we have what we have, and that is that.

So they all come upstairs. And you could see the scorn in the face of Stephen's Christian wife and his Christian daughters. It would be much more bearable if they was ugly. But they are not ugly, and I feel that their scorn is right. I try to stay in the background. But then my mother, rubbing her dirty foot against her ankle, grin and pull up her veil over the top of her head, as though it is the only thing she have to do to make herself present-able, and she say, "But, Stephen, you didn't give us warning. You had this boy" – and she point to me – "running about trying to clean up the place." And she laugh, as though she make a good joke.

The foolish woman didn't know what she was saying. I run out of the house to the pará-grass field at the back and then through the sugarcane, trying to fight down the shame and the vexation.

I walk and walk, and I feel I would never like to go back to the house. But the day finish, I have to go back. The frogs croak-ing and singing in the canals and the ditches, the dim lights on in the house. Nobody miss me. Nobody care what they did say to me. Nobody ask where I went or what I do. Everybody in the house is just full of this piece of news. Dayo is going to live in the city with Stephen and his family. Stephen is going to send him to school or college and look after his studies. Stephen is going to make him a doctor, lawyer, anything. Everything settled.

It was like a dream. But it come at the wrong moment. I should be happy, but I feel that everything is now poisoned for me. Now that Dayo is about to go away, I begin to feel that I am carrying him inside me the way Stephen is carrying his own son, like something that might break and cut. And at the same time, forgive me, a new feeling is in my heart. I am just waiting for my father and mother, for Stephen and all Stephen's family, for all of them who was there that day, I am just waiting for all of them to die, to bury my shame with them. I hate them.

Even today I can hate them, when I should have more cause to hate white people, to hate this café and this street and these people who cripple me and spoil my life. But now the dead man is me.

I USED TO HAVE a vision of a big city. It wasn't like this, not streets like this. I used to see a pretty park with high black iron railings like spears, old thick trees growing out of the wide pave-ment, rain falling the way it fall over Robert Taylor in *Waterloo*

Bridge, and the pavement covered with flat leaves of a perfect shape in pretty colours, gold and red and crimson.

Maple leaves. Stephen's son send us one, not long after he went to Montreal to pursue his higher studies. The envelope is long, the stamp strange, and inside the envelope and his letter is this pretty maple leaf, one leaf from the thousands on that pavement. I handle the envelope and the leaf a lot, I study the stamp, and I see Stephen's son walking on the pavement beside the black railing. It is very cold, and I see him stopping to blow his nose, looking down at the leaves and then thinking of us his cousins. He is wearing an overcoat to keep out the cold and he have a brief-case under his arm. That is how I think of him in Montreal, furthering his studies, and happy among the maple leaves. And that is how I want to see Dayo.

IT WAS AFTER Stephen's son went to Montreal that the jealousy really did break out in Stephen's family against Dayo. They did always scorn the boy. They used to make him sleep in the draw-ing-room, and he had to make up a bed on the floor after every-body else went to sleep. He didn't have a room to pursue his studies in, like Stephen's son. He used to read his books in the tiny front gallery of Stephen's tiny house. The gallery was almost on the pavement, so that he could see everybody that pass and they could see him. See him? They could reach out a hand and turn the page of the book he was reading. Still, this regular read-ing and studying he do in the gallery win him a little fame and respect in the area, and I feel it was this little respect that the poor boy start to pick up that make Stephen's family vexed. They feel they are the only ones who should pursue studies.

Stephen's daughters especially take against the boy, when you would think they ought to have been proud of their handsome cousin. But no, like all poor people, they want to be the only ones to rise. It is the poor who always want to keep down the poor. So they feel that Dayo is lowering them. It wouldn't have sur-prised me to get a message one day from Stephen that Dayo was interfering and tampering with his daughters.

You can imagine how glad they all was when Dayo sit his various exams and fail. You can imagine how much that make their heart rejoice. The reason was the bad school Dayo was going to. He couldn't get into any of the good ones. Those schools always talk about a lack of background and grounding, and Dayo had to go to a private school where the teachers themselves was a set of dunces without any qualifications. But Stephen's daughters don't look at that.

You would think that Stephen, after all his grand charge about progressiveness, would stand up for Dayo and do something to give the boy a little help and courage. But Stephen himself, when his son went away, get very funny. He is not interested in anything at all; he is like a man in mourning. He is like a man expecting bad news, the thing that would break in his hands and cut him. His face get puffy, his hair get grey and coarse.

But the first bad news was mine. I come home one weekday, tired after my lorry work, and I find Dayo. He is well dressed, he is like a man on a visit. But he say he leave Stephen's house for good, he is not going back. He say, "They try to make me a yard-boy. They try to get me to run messages for them." I could see how much he was suffering, and I could see that he was frightened we wouldn't believe him and would force him to go back.

It is what my father would like to do. He scratch his arms and rub his hand over the stiff grey hair on his chin, making that sound he does like, and he say, as though he know everything and is very wise, "It is what you have to put up with."

So poor Dayo could only turn to me. And when I look at his face, so sad and frightened, I feel my body get weak and trembling. The blood run up and down my veins, and my arms start hurting inside, as though inside them there is wire and the wire is being pulled.

Dayo say, "I got to go away. I got to leave. I feel that if I stay here those people are going to cripple me with their jealousy."

I don't know what to say. I don't know the ropes, I don't have any contacts. Stephen is the man with the contacts, but now I can't ask Stephen anything.

"There is nothing for me to do here," Dayo say.

"What about the oilfields?" I ask him.

"Oilfields, oilfields. The white people keep the best jobs for themselves. All you could do there is to become a bench-chemist."

Bench-chemist, I never hear this word before, and it impress me to hear it. Stephen's family don't give Dayo any credit for learning, but I can see how much the boy improve in the two years and how he develop a new way of talking. He don't talk fast now, his voice is not going up and down, he use his hands a lot, and he is getting a nice little accent, so that sometimes he sound like a woman, the way educated people sound. I like his new way of talking, though it embarrass me to look at him and think that he my brother is now a master of language. So now he start talking, and I let him talk, and as he talk he lose his sadness and fright.

Then I ask him, "What you would study when you go away? Medicine, chartered accountancy, law?"

My mother jump in and say, "I don't know, ever since Dayo small, I always feel I would like him to do dentistry."

That is her intelligence, and you well know that she never think of dentistry or anything else for Dayo until that moment. We let her say what she have to say, and she go down to the kitchen, and Dayo begin to talk in his way. He don't give me a straight answer, he is working up to something, and at last it come. He say: "Aeronautical engineering."

This is a word, like bench-chemist, that I never hear before. It frighten me a little bit, but Dayo say they have a college in England where you just go and pay the fees. Anyway, so we agree. He was going to go away to further his studies in aeronautical engineering.

And as soon as we agree on that Dayo start behaving as though he is a prisoner on the run, as though he have a ship to catch, as though he couldn't stay another month on the island. It turn out in truth that he had a ship to catch. It turn out that he had some friends he did want to go to England with. So I run about here and there, raising money from this one and that one, signing my name on this paper and that paper, until the money side was settled.

Everything happen very fast, and I remember thinking, watching Dayo go aboard the ship with a smile, that it was one of those moments you can only properly think about afterwards. When the ship pull away and I see the oily water between the ship and the dock, my heart sink. I feel sick, I feel the whole thing was too easy, that something so easy cannot end well. And on top of all this is my grief for the boy, that slender boy in the new suit.

The grief work on me. In my mind I blame Stephen and his family for their jealousy. And, I couldn't help it, two or three days after Dayo leave I went to the city and went to Stephen's house.

It was a poky little old-fashioned wood house in a bad part of the city, and it shame me to think that once upon a time I used to look on Stephen as a big man. Now I see that in the city Stephen is not much, that all his hope and all his daughters' hope is in that son who is studying in Montreal. He is like the Prince to them. And in that little house, with no front yard and next to no backyard, they are living like Snow White and the seven dwarfs, with their little foreign pictures in their little drawing-room, and their little pieces of polished furniture. You feel you have to stoop, that if you take a normal step you will break something.

It was late afternoon when I went. Everybody home, Stephen rocking in the gallery. It surprise me to see him looking so old. The hair on his head really grey now, standing up short and stiff. Everybody is looking at me as though they feel I come to make trouble. I disappoint them. I kiss Stephen on his cheek and I kiss his wife. The girls pretend they don't see me, and that is all right by me.

They give me tea. Not in our crude country fashion, condensed milk and brown sugar and tea mixed up in one. No, man. Tea, milk, white sugar, everything separate. I pretend I am one of the seven dwarfs and I do everything they want me to do. Then, as I was expecting, they ask about Dayo.

I stir my tea with their little teaspoon and take a sip and I put the cup down and say, "Oh, Dayo. He gone away. On the *Colombie*."

Stephen is so surprised he stop rocking. Then he begin to smile. He look just like my father.

Stephen's wife, Miss Shameless Christian Short-Dress herself, she ask, "And what he gone away for? To look for a work?"

I lift up the teacup and say, "To pursue his higher studies."

Stephen is vexed now. "Higher studies? But he didn't even begin his lower studies."

"That is an opinion," I say, using some words I pick up from Dayo.

One of the girls, a real pretty and malicious little one, come out and ask, "What he is going to study?"

"Aeronautical engineering."

The shock show on Stephen's face, and I feel I could laugh. All of them are mad with jealousy now. All the girls come out and stand up around me in that little drawing-room as though I am the brown girl in the ring. I just drinking my tea out of their little teacup. On the walls they have all those pictures and photographs of foreign scenes, as though because they are Christian and so on, they alone must know about these things.

"Aeronautical engineering," Stephen say. "He would be better off piloting a taxi between the airport and the city."

The girls giggle and Stephen's wife smile. Stephen is the mocker and joker again, the man in control, and it is all right again for his family. They get a little happier. I see that if I stay any longer I would have to start insulting them, so I get up and leave. As I leave I hear one of the girls laugh. I can't tell you how full my heart get with hate.

Next morning I wake up at four o'clock, and the hate is still with me. The hate eat me and eat me until the day break and

I get up, and all that day the hate eating me while I am working, driving the lorry to and from the gravel pits.

In the afternoon, work over, the lorry parked below the house, I take a taxi and went back to the city, to Stephen's house. I didn't know what I was going to do. Half the time I was thinking that I would go and make friends with them again, that I would go and take Stephen's jokes and show that I could laugh at the jokes.

But that is the way of weakness and it would be foolish and wrong, because you cannot really joke with your enemy. When you find out who your enemy is, you must kill him before he kill you. And so with the other half of my mind I was thinking I would go there and break everything in the house, swinging one of those drawing-room bentwood chairs from wall to wall, from jalousie to jalousie, in all those tiny rooms, through all that damn fretwork.

Then a strange thing happen. Perhaps it was because I did wake up so early that morning. The constipation that was with me all day suddenly stop, and by the time I reach Stephen's house all I want is a toilet.

So I rush in the house. Stephen rocking in the little gallery. But I didn't tell him anything. I didn't say good afternoon or anything to his wife and his daughters. I went straight through to their toilet and I stay there a long time, and I pull the chain and I wait until the cistern full again and I pull the chain again. Then I walk out and I walk through the house and I didn't tell anybody anything, and I walk out on the street, and the feeling come back to my arms, no more stretched wires inside them, and I walk and walk until my head cool down, and then I take a taxi home, to the junction.

And next morning again I wake up in the darkness at four o'clock, but this time I am frightened. I only feel like crying and praying for forgiveness, and I begin to know something gone wrong with me, that my life and my mind not right. Even the hate break inside me. I can't feel the hate. I begin to feel lost. I think of Dayo lying sick on the floor in the old house and I think of him leaving on the white *Colombie*. And even when I get up in the morning I feel lost.

I expect punishment. I don't know how it is coming, but every day I wait for it. Every day I wait to hear from Dayo, but he don't write. I feel I would like to go back to Stephen's house, just go back and sit down and do nothing, not even talk. But I never go.

And then Stephen get news of his son. And the news is that Stephen's son gone foolish in Montreal. The further studies and his father too much for him, and in Montreal he is foolish, like those police dogs that get foolish, like pets, if you kill their handlers. Stephen get his bad news now! The Prince is not coming, and in that little house in the city the whole family mash up, in truth.

My father say, "I always say that Stephen was going to get throw down by that boy."

He feel he win. He do nothing; he just wait and win. But I remember my own hate, the hate that make me sick, and I feel I kill all of them.

I THINK NOW OF the maple leaf the boy send us in the airmail envelope with the strange stamp. Walking on the street with his overcoat and briefcase, when he was pursuing his studies. The street is still there, the rain fall on it a thousand times, the leaves still on the pavement beside the black railings. Now I feel I walk on that pavement myself, among the strange leaves. Strange leaves, strange flowers that sometimes I pick. I have paper; the paper have lines like a schoolchild's copybook, and a number; and Frank write my name in his own handwriting at the top on the dotted line. But I have nobody to write and send a leaf or a flower to.

THE WATER BLACK, the ship white, the lights blazing. And inside the ship, far below, everybody like prisoners already. The lights dim, everyone in their bunk. In the morning the water is blue, but you can't see land. You are just going where the ship is going, you will never be a free man again. The ship smelling, like vomit, like the back door of a restaurant. Night and day the ship is moving. The sea and sky lose colour, everything is grey.

I don't want the ship to stop, I don't want to touch land again. On the bunk below me is a jeweller fellow called Khan or Mohammed. He is wearing a hat all the time, all the time, and you would think he is wearing it for the joke. But he is not laughing, his face is small, and he is talking already of going back. I can't go back, I will have to stay. I don't know how I trap myself.

The land come nearer, and one morning through the rain you see it, more white than green, no colours there. The ship stop suddenly and it is very quiet, and there in the water below is a boat and some men in oilskins. You see them move but you can't hear them. And after all the days at sea everything in and around that little boat is very bright, as though a black-and-white picture suddenly turn Technicolor. The rocking water is deep and green, the oilskins very yellow, the faces of the people very pink.

The mystery land is theirs, the stranger is you. None of those houses in the rain there belong to you. You can't see yourself walking down those streets set down so flat on that cliff. But that is where you have to go, and as soon as everybody get down in the launch with their luggage the ship hoot. It is white and big and safe, it is saying goodbye, it is in a hurry to get away and to leave you behind. The Technicolor is over, the picture change. Now is only noise and rush and luggage, train and traffic. This is it, and already you are like a man in blinkers.

I TELL MYSELF I come to England to be with Dayo and to look after him, to keep him well while he is pursuing his studies. But I didn't see Dayo at the dock and I didn't see him at the railway station. He leave me alone. I do what I see other people do, and I manage. I find a job, I get some rooms in Paddington. I learn bus numbers and place names; I watch the season change from cold to warm. I manage, I am all right, but only because I feel it is not my life. I feel as I feel on the ship, that I lose that, that I throw that away.

Then, after all those weeks when he leave me guessing, Dayo write. He try to blame me; he say he had to write home to get my address. He is in another town. He write nothing about his aeronautical engineering, but he say he just finish one particular course of studies and he get a diploma, and now he want some help to move down to London to do some more studies.

I take the day off from the cigarette factory and draw out a few pounds from the post office and went up by train to the town where he was staying. It is always like this now. You are always taking trains and buses to strange places. You never know what sort of street you are going to find yourself in, what sort of house you will be knocking at.

The street is solid with little grey brick houses. Only a few steps from the gate of the house to the door, and the man who open the door get mad as soon as he hear my name. He is a small old man, his neck very loose in his collar, and I can't understand his accent too well. But I understand him to say that Dayo is owing him twelve pounds in rent, that Dayo run away without paying, and that he is not giving up Dayo's suitcase until he get his money. I begin to hate the little fellow and his mildewed house. Dirt shining on the walls, and when I see the little cubicle he is charging three pounds a week for, I had to control myself. You always have to control yourself now, I don't know for what reward.

In the cubicle I see Dayo's suitcase, still with the *Colombie* sticker. I pay and take it straightaway. I don't know where in this town Dayo can be, where he is hiding these last four weeks, but like a fool with this heavy suitcase, as though I just get off the ship myself, I walk up and down the streets, looking.

Even when I went back to the railway station I couldn't make up my mind to leave. The waiting-room empty, the seats cut up with long knife slashes that set your teeth on edge just to see them. I try to think of all the days that Dayo spend alone in this town, all the times he too see the day turn to evening, and he don't know who to turn to. And as the train take me back to London, I hate everything I see, houses, shops, traffic, all those settled people, those children playing games in fields.

At the station I wait again and take a bus and then another bus. Then there, outside my house, when I turn the corner with that heavy suitcase, I see Dayo, in the suit he went aboard the *Colombie* with.

He look as if he was waiting a long time, as if he nearly forget what he was waiting for. He is not thin; if anything, he is a little stouter. As soon as he see me he get sad, and the tears run to my eyes. When we go down to the basement we embrace and we sit down together on the sofa-bed. I am ashamed to notice it, but he is smelling, his clothes are dirty.

He put his head on my lap and I pat him like a baby, thinking of all those days he spend alone, without me. He knock his head on my knee and say, "I don't have confidence, brother. I lose my confidence." I look at his long hair that no barber cut for weeks, I see the inside of his dirty collar, I see his dirty shoes. Again and again he say, "I don't have confidence, I don't have confidence."

All the bad things I did want to say to him drop away. I rock him on my lap until I come to myself and see that it is dark, the street lamp on outside. I don't want him to do anything foolish because of false pride. I want to give him a way out. So I ask, "You don't want to go through with your studies?" He don't answer. He only sob. I ask him again, "You don't want to take any more studies?" He lift his head up and blow his nose and say, "It is all right, brother. I like studies." And I can tell he is happier, that he was only a little worried and lonely and down-couraged; and that it is going to be all right in truth.

In the kitchen, as soon as I turn on the light, cockroaches scatter everywhere, over dirty old stove and mash-up pot and pan. I bring out bread and milk and a tin of New Brunswick sardines.

It is full-moon night, and the old white woman upstairs start getting on the way she does always get on when the moon is full, shouting and fighting with her husband, screaming and cursing until one of them shut the other one outside.

I light a little fire, more firelighter and newspaper than coal, and Dayo and I sit and eat. I just regret the basement have no bath. But Dayo will go next day to the public baths, sixpence with the smooth old towel. Right now the little fire make the room more than warm, the damp dry out a little. The rat smell the food right away: I hear him scratching at the box I put over his hole. It is like living in a camp, in this basement. Not long after I move in I make a joke by putting a tiny lady's hand mirror right in the centre of the wall over the fireplace. Now Dayo is here to appreciate that joke.

We pull out the bed part of the sofa-bed and make it up. I even forget the smell, of dead rat and old dirt and gas and rust. Upstairs, the old woman shut her husband out. When I wake up in the night it is because the husband is either shouting from the pavement or banging on the door. In the morning all is calm. The monthly madness is over.

SO, SUDDENLY, THE sadness and the fright pass, and the happy time come. The happy time come and it don't go away, and I start forgetting. Stephen and his family, my father and mother, the sugarcane and the mud and the rich man's rotting house, the ship at night and the mystery land in the morning, all of that I forget. It is far away, like another life; none of that can touch me again. And in that basement, with the old mad woman upstairs, I feel as the London months pass that I get back my life, living with Dayo alone, knowing nobody else.

I fix up the little back bedroom for Dayo, with a reading-light and everything, and he start taking some regular studies. He get back his confidence and it look as though what he say is true, that he really like studies, because as fast as he finish one diploma he start another. In the new clothes I buy for him he is looking nice, even sharp. He develop his way of talking and he is looking good to me, like any professional. I know my own ignorance and I don't interfere with his studies. I let him go his own way and take his own time. I don't want anything to happen to him again. It is enough for me that he is there.

And you could say that I begin to like big-city life. At home, where people treat you rough and generally get on as though work is a crime and a punishment, I did always prefer to be my own boss. But here I get to like the factory. Nobody watching you; you lower nobody; nobody mock you. I like the nice sharp tobacco smell, and I get to like the machine I mind, with the cigarettes coming out in one long piece, so long and strong you could skip with it. I never think work would be like this, that it would make me feel good to think that the factory is always there and I could always go to it on a morning.

Every Friday they give you a hundred free cigarettes. These cigarettes have a special watermark, but those fellows from Pakistan don't always appreciate this and some of them get catch. A white fellow start walking out one day like a cowboy on high heels. When they stop him they find his shoes stuff up with tobacco. Things like this always happen. The factory is like a school that you don't like at first but then you like more and more.

No hustling with the lorry, nobody beating you down all the time, and you get your money in a little brown envelope, as though you are some kind of civil servant or professional. Regular work, regular money. After some months I finish paying off the moneylender at home, and then I even start saving a little for myself. I am not keeping this money at home, as my father used to do with his few cents. It is going straight in the post office; I have my own little book. One day I find I have a hundred pounds. Mine, not money I borrow. A hundred pounds. I feel safe. I can't tell you how safe I feel. Whenever I think of it I close my eyes and put my hand to my heart.

BUT IT IS so when you get too happy. You forget too much. That hundred pounds make me forget myself. It give me ideas. It make me forget why I am in London. I want to feel more than safe now. I want to see that money grow, I want to see the clerks writing in my book in their different handwriting every week. That become like a craze with me. I know it is foolishness, and I don't tell Dayo about it; but at the same time I enjoy the secret. And it is because I want to see this money grow week after week that I take a second job. I look around and I get a night work in a restaurant kitchen.

So I start stunning myself with work, and my life become one long work. I get up about six. By seven, Dayo still sleeping, I leave for the cigarette factory. I come back about six to the basement, sometimes Dayo there, sometimes he is not there. By eight I leave for the restaurant, and I come back about midnight or later. London for me is the bus rides, morning, evening, night, the factory, the restaurant kitchen, the basement. I know it is too much, but for me even that is part of the pleasure. Like when you are sick and thin, you want to get thinner and thinner, just to see how thin you could get. Or like some fat people who don't like being fat but still they just want to see how fat they could get: they are always looking at their shadow, and that is like their secret hobby. So now I am always tired when I go to sleep and tired in the morning, but I like and enjoy the tiredness. That is like the secret too, like the money adding up, fifty, sixty pounds a month. And the tiredness does always go in the middle of the morning.

I feel Dayo would mock me if he get to find out what possess my mind. He don't say anything, but I know that he, as a student in London, can't really appreciate having his brother working in a restaurant kitchen. But as the months pass, as one year pass, and two years, as the life hold out and the money add up, I find the money making me strong. And because the money make me strong I can put up with anything. I don't mind what people say or how they watch me. When I didn't have money I used to hate the basement, and I used to daydream about buying nice clothes not only for Dayo but for me too. But now my clothes don't matter to me, and I even get a thrill to think that nobody seeing me in my working clothes, on that street, coming out of that basement, would believe that I have a thousand pounds in the post office, that I have twelve hundred, that I have fifteen.

I scarcely believe it myself. Life in London! This was what people say at home, to mean everything nice. I didn't look for it; it wasn't what I come for. But I feel that that life come now, and if I was frightened of anything it was that my strength wouldn't hold out, that Dayo would finish his studies and leave me alone in the basement, and that the life would end.

It is true. This was the happy time, when Dayo live in my basement and I work like a man in blinkers, when I have the factory to go to every morning and the restaurant every evening, when I can enjoy a Sunday the way I never enjoy a Sunday before. Sometimes I think of the first day, and those men in yellow oilskins in the deep green water in the morning. But that to me is now like a memory from somewhere else, like something I make up.

CRANINESS. HOW A man could fool himself like that? Look at these streets now. Look at these things and people I never did see. They have their life too; the city is theirs. I don't know where I thought I was, behaving as though the city was a ghost city, working by itself, and that it is something I discover by myself. Frank will never understand. He will never see the city I see; he will never understand how I work like that.

He is only querying and probing me about foremen who insult me at the factory, about people who fight with me at the restaurant. He is forever worrying me with his discrimination inquiries. He is my friend, the only friend I have. I alone know how much he help me, from how far he bring me back. But he is digging me all the time because he prefer to see me weak. He like opening up manholes for me to fall in; he is anxious to push me down in the darkness.

His attitude, in the café and then at the bus stop and then in the bus, is: keep off, this man is weak, this man is under my protection. When he is like this he have the power to draw all

the strength from me, he with his shining shoes and his nice
tweed jacket. As though one time I couldn't go in a shop and
buy twelve tweed jackets and pay in cash.

But now the money gone and everything gone and I only
have this suit, and it is smelling. But everything does smell
here. At home, at home, windows are always open and everything get clean in the open air. Here everything is locked up.
Even on a bus no breeze does blow.

Somewhere in the city Dayo is getting married today. I don't
know where he think he is.

I WORK AND WORK and save and save and the money grow
and grow, and when it reach two thousand pounds, I get stunned.
I don't feel I can go on. I know the life have to stop sometime,
that I can't go on with two jobs, that something have to happen.
And now the thought of working and saving another thousand
is too much for me. So I stop work altogether. I leave the cigarette factory, I leave the restaurant. I take out my two thousand
from the post office and I decide to use it.

It is ignorance, it is madness. It is the madness the money
itself bring on. The money make me feel strong. The money
make me feel that money is easy. The money make me forget
how hard money is to make, that it take me more than four
years to save what I have. The money in my hand, two thousand
pounds, make me forget that my father never get more than
ten pounds a month for his donkey-cart work, that he bring
all of us up on that ten pounds a month, and that ten by twelve
is one hundred and twenty, that the money I have in my hand
is the pay of my father for fifteen or sixteen years. The money
make me feel that London is mine.

I take my money out and I do with it what I see people do
at home. I buy a business. It is the madness working on me,
the money madness. I don't know London and I know nothing
about business, but I buy a business. In my mind I am only
calculating like those people at home who buy one lorry and
work that and buy a second lorry and buy another and another.

The business I had in mind was a little roti-and-curry shop. Not a restaurant, something more like a stall you get at a race-course, two or three little basins of curry on the counter on this side, a little pile of rotis or chapattis or dalpuris on that side. A lot of women at home do very well that way. The idea come to me just like that one day when I was still at the cigarette factory, and it never leave me. And because the idea come just like that, as though somebody give it to me, I feel it is right. Dayo wasn't too interested. He talk a lot in that way he have, talking and talking and leaving you guessing about what he mean. I don't know whether he is ashamed or whether he find the idea of a roti-shop in London too funny, a reminder of home and simple things. I let him talk.

The first shock I get was the price of properties. But I didn't get frightened and stop. No, the madness is on me, I can't pull back. I am behaving as though I have a train to catch and must spend my money first. And the strange thing is that as soon as that first piece of money go, for the lease for a few years of a rundown little place in that scruffy street, as soon as that piece of money actually leave my hand, I know it is foolishness and I feel that all the money gone, that I have nothing. I feel the business bust already. I feel I start to bleed, and I am like a man only looking to down-courage himself.

So in just four or five weeks the whole world change for me again. I am no longer strong and rich, not caring what people say or think. Now, suddenly, I am a pauper, and my shabbiness worry me, and I begin to pine for the little things I didn't give myself, like twelve-pound tweed jackets, which now, after I pay decorators, electricians and the catering company, I can't afford.

Then I run into prejudice and regulations. At home you can put up a table outside your house any time and start selling what you want. Here they have regulations. Those suspicious men in tweeds and flannels, some of them young, young fellows, are coming round with their forms and pressing me on every side. They are not leaving me any peace of mind at all. They are full of remarks, they don't smile, they like nothing I do.

And I have to shop and cook and clean, and the area is not good and business is bad, and no amount of hard work and early rising will help.

I see I kill myself. The little courage that still remain with me wash away, and the secret vision I had of buying up London, the foolishness I always really know was foolishness, burst. Without my two thousand pounds in the post office, without my real cash, I was without my strength, like Samson without his hair.

When the men in flannels go, the young English louts come. I don't know what attract them to the place, why they pick on me. Half the time I can't understand what they say, but they are not people you can get on with at all. They only dress up and come to make trouble. Sometimes they eat and don't pay; sometimes they mash up plates and glasses and bend the cutlery. That become like their hobby, a lot of them against me alone. That is their bravery and education. And nobody on my side.

Before, in the days of the hard work, of the two jobs, in the days of money, this was the sort of thing that didn't bother me at all. But now everything is hurting. I can't bear the way those louts talk or laugh or dress, and I feel my heart getting full of hate again, as it used to be for Stephen and his family, that hate that make me sick.

DAYO SHOULD HAVE helped me. He was my brother. He was the man I make the money for. He was the man I went aboard the ship for. But now he leave me alone. He is there with me in the basement; sometimes we still eat together on a Sunday; but his attitude is that what I do is my business alone, he have his own things to do. He is going his own way, pursuing his studies or doing whatever he is doing. Sometimes the light is on in his room when I come in; sometimes he come tiptoeing in afterwards; in the morning I always leave him sleeping. He is there. You can't forget him. And then my heart begin to set against him too.

I begin to hate the way he talk. I begin to look at him. Once he was the pretty boy, using Vaseline Hair Tonic and combing his hair like Fairley Granger. Now you could see the face becoming just a labourer's face, without even the hardness that my father's face get from work and sun. And when he start talking in that way he have – and he can start talking about anything: all you have to say is "Dayo, give me a match" – he make me feel that something is wrong with him, that someone who is using words in this way is not right. He still have his accent, but he is like a man who have no control over his speech, as though it is the first time he talk that day, as though he have nobody in London to talk to.

So in these days I start worrying about Dayo. The roti-shop is always there to worry about, but that to me is in the past now. I do my hard work, I waste my money and my reward. I can't start again. I can't go back to the cigarette factory and those insulting illiterate girls and that long ride in the cold morning to the factory. That finish. Now I concentrate on Dayo, my brother. I watch his face, I watch the way he walk, the way he shave. He don't understand; he is just talking in his womanish way. I don't tell him anything. I don't even know what I think. I just look at him and study him.

I WAKE UP EARLY one morning with a wet-dream. It was the second wet-dream I had; the first happen when I was a boy. It leave me exhausted and dirty and ashamed. I want to go to Dayo and beg him to forgive me, because this, the thing that just happen to me, is something I never did think about for him. I feel I let him down, that I betray him in my heart, and I feel I would like to go to him and make up and talk as in the old days. I feel I must show him that I always love him.

I go in his little room at the back, the early backyard light showing through the thin curtains, and I look at the boy with the labourer's face sleeping on the narrow iron bed. On the table, that I cover with red oilcloth for him, is the reading-lamp I fix up for him for his studies, and his big books, and the paperbacks he read for relaxation sometimes, and the little transistor radio he get me to buy for him so that he could listen to his pop music.

A labourer's face. But the sadness of the sleeping face hit me, and the smallness of the room, and the concrete wall outside the window, and that yard where no sun fall. And I wonder what it is leading to, what will happen to him and me, whether he will ever take that ship back and get off one bright morning and take a taxi to the junction and drive through places he know.

I notice the saucer he is using as an ashtray, and the expensive cigarettes. I notice the dirtiness of his finger-nails and hands, the fatness at the top of his arms. Once those arms was so strong. Once he used to walk so nice, I used to think like Fonda.

I stand and watch him in the cold room. He twist and turn, he open his eyes, he recognize me. He get frightened. He jump up. And how dirty the sheets he is sleeping in. How dirty.

He say, "What happen?"

He talk without his accent. He look at me as though I come in the room to kill him. He say nothing else; he suddenly lose his way of talking. The labourer's face.

Sadness, but my sadness. It flow through my body like a fluid.

I say, "What course of studies you are now pursuing, Dayo?"

The fright leave his face. He try to get vexed. Try. He say, "Somebody make you a policeman or what?" He is not talking with his accent now, he is not going on and on. He is like a child again, back home.

I say, "I just want to talk with you. You know I am busy with the shop. It is a long time since we talk seriously."

He say, and as he talk he get back his accent, "Well, since you ask, and you have every right to ask, I will tell you. It isn't easy to take studies in this place as you and other people believe. A lot of people come here with their own ideas and they think they will start taking studies – "

I had to stop him. "What you are taking?"

"I am preparing myself for the modern world. I am taking a course in computer programming, if you want to know. Compu-ter pro-gram-ming. I hope this meet with your approval and satisfaction."

I lift up the pack of cigarettes from the table. I say, "Expensive."

He say, in his accent, "I smoke good cigarettes."

The labourer's face. The labourer's backchat. I feel that if I stay in that room I would hit him.

And yet I went to his room with love and shame.

The shame stay with me all day. In the evening, after a bad time in the shop, more trouble with those white louts, my arms getting the feeling that there is stretched wire inside them, I travel back by the night bus. When I get off, a black dog with a collar round its neck start following me. The street lamps shining on the trees, those trees with the peeling bark that is a little bit like the bark of our guava trees. The pavements damp, footmarks in the thin black mud. The big dog is friendly. I know it is making a mistake and I try to chase it away. But it only look at me, wagging its tail, and as soon as I walk on it follow me again, really close, as though it want to feel me all the time.

It follow me and follow me, right down past the rubbish bins to the basement. You would think that it would know now that it make a mistake. But no, it slip inside as soon as I open the door and it run up and down the hall, happy, wagging its tail, leaving footmarks everywhere.

I look for Dayo in his room, and the dog look too. I just see the dirty bed when I switch on the light, the sheet gathered up in the centre, the sheet and the pillow brown with dirt, the saucer full of cigarette ends. Oh my God.

I am hungry, but I can't stand the thought of food. I make a little Ovaltine. When I start to drink, the dog come right up to me again, wagging its tail. And wagging its tail, it follow me to the hall. I open the door. The dog know now it make a mistake. It race up the steps, not looking back at me, and run away in the night. It leave me feeling lonely.

4

Later, lying down, I hear Dayo tiptoeing in and switching on his light.

And it was the next morning, leaving Dayo sleeping in his room, and taking the Underground to the market, it was then that I see the advertisement in the carriage: PREPARE YOURSELF FOR TOMORROW'S WORLD WITH A COURSE IN COMPUTER PROGRAMMING.

I understand. I am not surprised. But the hate fill my heart. I want to see his face get frightened again. I get off the train after a couple of stops. I walk about the platform, I don't know what I want to do. I smoke a couple of cigarettes, I let the trains pass. I feel people start looking at me. I cross over to the other platform, not many people waiting that side, and take the train back.

The smart labourer boy. He only smoke good cigarettes. Oh God. I see myself going down to the basement to that room with the dirty sheets and the saucer with the expensive good cigarettes. I see myself lifting him out of that bed and hitting him on that lying labourer's mouth.

But I can't bring myself to go down the basement steps. I stand up for a long time looking down at the dustbins and the breakdown fence with two or three hedge plants that grow too big, like little trees, nobody trimming them, the basement window dull with dirt, scraps of wet-and-dried paper and other rubbish scattered about the little garden where somehow a type of grass is still growing.

The moon-mad white woman open the front door. Her face wrinkled and yellow, and you get a glimpse of the blackness behind her. The woman is dazed; the monthly madness tire her out; you can see that every night she is fighting in her sleep. As she bend down to take the milk, I see her yellow hair thin like a baby's. She look at me and I can see that she recognize me but she isn't sure. I nearly say good morning. It is the only thing we say to one another after five years. But then I change my mind and walk away fast to the corner. And I think: Oh my God, I am glad I change my mind.

But I can't leave and go to the market. I can't face that now, I feel I have to settle this thing first. I wait and wait at the corner, I don't know what for. I don't know what I want to do. Until I see Dayo stepping out, in his suit, with his books.

I know the bus stop he is going to. I turn left and walk to the stop before. The bus come; I get on and find a seat on the right-hand side. At the next stop Dayo is waiting. It is funny, studying him like this, as though he is a stranger, and he not knowing that you are studying him. You could see that he just throw some cold water over his face this morning, that his shirt is dirty, that he is not taking care of himself. He get on; he go upstairs; he does smoke good cigarettes.

He get off at Oxford Circus, and at the traffic lights I get off and follow him down Oxford Street through the crowds. At the end of Oxford Street he buy a paper and go inside a Lyons. I wait a good time. It is getting late now, the morning half gone. I follow him down Great Russell Street, and now I can see that he is idling in truth, looking at the window of the Indian food-shop, the noticeboards outside the newsagent selling foreign papers, crossing the road to look at the dusty books outside the bookshop. A lot of Africans knocking around here, with jacket and tie and briefcase; I don't know what good the studies they are taking will ever do them.

No more shops, only tall black iron railings beside the pavement, and then Dayo turn in the big open yard of the British Museum. A lot of foreign tourists here, in light tourist clothes. It is like a different city, and he is like a man among the tourists: watch him going up the wide steps with his suit and his books. But these people come for the day; they are happy, they have buses to take them back to their hotels; they have countries to go back to, they have houses. The sadness I feel make my heart seize.

He go inside. I know I have no more to see, but I decide to wait. I look at the tourists and walk about. I walk about the portico, the yard, and out in the street below the trees. One time I walk back nearly to Tottenham Court Road. The Indian restaurant is hot and smelling. It make me think of my own shop, the way I trap myself and throw away my life there. Lunchtime, I nearly forget. I run back to the Museum and I run straight up the steps through the tourists coming and going and I nearly run through the door. But then I see him outside, in the portico, sitting on a wood bench and smoking.

He still have the books with him, and he is sitting very sprawled. The hate rush in my heart, I want to punish him in public, I want a big thing right there in the open, in front of everybody. But then I catch sight of his face, and I stay behind the pillar and study him.

It isn't only the sadness of the face. It isn't only the way he is smoking, letting the cigarette hand drop from his mouth like a man who don't care. He is not sprawling to show off. He is like a man who break his back in truth. It is the face of a tired, foolish boy. It is the face of someone lost. It is the same face of the boy who wake up in the room and look at me with terror. And I feel that if anything happen now to frighten him that mouth will open in a scream.

The sun shining bright now. The grass green and level and pretty. You can see the edges of the lawn black and rich, like the first time you clear a piece of bush and you know anything will grow: you can feel the damp with your foot when you walk, you can see the seeds coming up, splitting and tiny, growing day after day. The schoolgirls sitting young and indecent on the concrete kerb in their very short blue skirts, laughing and talking loud to get people to look at them. The buses come and go. The taxis come and turn, and men and women get out and get in. The whole world going on. And I feel outside it, seeing only my brother and myself in this place, among the pillars, me in my working clothes, he in his suit that is so cheap it can't hold a crease or a shape, smoking his cigarette. I would like him to smoke the best cigarettes in the world.

I don't want him to turn foolish like Stephen's son. I don't want that to happen. I want to go to him and embrace him and put my hand on his head and smell his body. I want to tell him that it is all right, that I will protect him, that he must take no more studies, that he is a free man. I would like him then to smile at me. But he wouldn't smile at me. If I go to him now I will frighten him and he will open his mouth to scream. This is what I do, this is what I bring on myself. I can't go to him. I can only stand behind the pillar and watch him.

He put out his cigarette. Then with his books he walk out through the gate between the big black railings. Lunchtime now, pub, sandwich, people coming out of offices, walking below the trees. He mingle with them. But he have nowhere to go. And after I watch him leave I feel that I too have nowhere to go, and that the life in London is over.

I HAVE NOWHERE to go and I walk now, like Dayo, where the tourists walk. The roti-shop: that noose I put my neck in. I think how nice it would be if I could just leave it, leave it just like that. Let the curry from yesterday go stale and rotten and turn red like poison, let the dust fall from the ceiling and settle. Take Dayo home before he get foolish. If a man could do that, if a man could just leave a life that spoil.

To leave the basement with the moon-mad woman upstairs, to leave the windows that look out on nothing back and front. Night after night in the basement the rat scratch. One time, when I did take away the box to stop up the hole with Polyfilla, I see where the claws scratch and scratch in the dark. Something like white fur cover that part of the box. Let the rat come out. The life is over. I am like a man who is giving up. I come with nothing, I have nothing, I will leave with nothing.

All afternoon as I walk I feel like a free man. I scorn everything I see, and when I tire myself out with walking, and the afternoon gone, I still scorn. I scorn the bus, the conductor, the street.

I scorn the white boys who come in the shop in the evening. They come to make trouble. But it is different tonight. I am fighting for nothing here. They are provoking me. But they give me strength. Samson get back his hair, he is strong. Nothing can touch him. He is going back on the ship, and no matter how black the water is at night, in the morning it will be blue. Just for a little bit more he must be strong, and he will leave. He will go away and let the dust fall and the rats come.

The glasses and the plates are breaking. The words and that laugh are everywhere. Let everything break. I will take Dayo on that ship with me, and his face will not be sad, his mouth will not open to scream. I am walking out, I will go now, the knife is in my hand. But then at the door I feel I want to bawl. I see Dayo's face again, I feel the strength run right out of me, my bones turning to wire in my arms. These people take my money, these people spoil my life. I close the door and turn the key, and I know then I turn around and I hear myself say, "I am taking one of you today. Two of us going today." I hear nothing else.

Then, always, in the quiet, I see the boy's face surprised. And it is strange, because he and Dayo are college friends and Dayo is staying with him in this old-fashioned wood house in England. It is an accident; they was only playing. But how easy the knife go in him, how easy he drop. I can't look down. Dayo look at me and open his mouth to bawl, but no scream coming. He want me to help him, his eyes jumping with fright, but I can't help him now. It is the gallows for him. I can't take that for him. I only know that inside me mash up, and that the love and danger I carry all this time break and cut, and my life finish. Nothing making noise now. The body is in the chest, like in *Rope*, but in this English house. Then the worst part always come: the quiet dark ride, and the sitting down at the dining-table with the boy's parents. Dayo is trembling; he is not a good actor; he will give himself away. It is like his body in that chest, it is like mine. I can't see what the house is like. I can't see the boy's parents. It is like a dream, when you can't move, and you want to wake up quick.

Then noise come back, and I know that something bad happen to my right eye. But I can't even move my hand to feel it.

FRANK IS SITTING beside me on the bus now. I am on the inside, looking down on the road. He is on the outside, pressing against me. We will go to another railway station and take a train; then we will take a bus again. And at the end, in some building, in some church, I will see my brother and the white girl he is going to marry. In these three years Dayo make his own way. He give up studies, he get a work.

I used to think of him going back to the basement that day and finding nobody there, and nobody coming home; and I used to think of that as the end of the world. But he do better without me; he don't need me. I lose him. I can't see the sort of life he get into, I can't see the people he is going to mix with now. Sometimes I think of him as a stranger, different from the man I did know. Sometimes I see him as he was, and feel that he is alone, like me.

The rain stop, the sun come out. In the train we go past the backs of tall houses. The brick grey; no paint here, except for the window frames, bright red and bright green. People living one on top of the other. All kinds of rubbish on top of the flat roofs over projecting back rooms, and sometimes a little plant in a pot inside, behind windows running with wet and steam. Everybody on his shelf, in his little place. But a man can leave everything, a man can just disappear. Somebody will come after him to clean up and clear away, and that new person will settle down there until his own time come.

When we come to the station it is as though we are out of London again. The station building small and low, the houses small and neat in red brick, the little chimneys smoking. The big advertisements in the station yard make you feel that everybody here is very happy, laughing below an umbrella in the shape of a house-roof, eating sausages and making funny faces, the whole family sitting down to eat together.

As we wait for the bus, for this last lap, my nervousness return. The street is wide, everything is clean, and I feel exposed. But Frank know me well. He edge up close, as though he want to protect me from the little cold wind that is blowing. The wind make Frank's face white and it lift a little of his thin hair, so that he look a little bit like a boy.

I see him playing as a boy in streets like this one. I don't know why, I see him with a dirty face and dirty clothes, like those children asking for a penny for the guy. And as I am thinking this, looking down at Frank's big shining shoes, a very little girl in very small jeans come right up to Frank and embrace his knees and ask for a penny. He say no, and she hit him on his leg and say, "You *have* a penny." She is a very young child; she don't know what she is doing, rubbing up against strangers; she don't even know what money is. But Frank's white face get very hard, and even after the girl go away Frank is nervous still. He is glad to get on the bus when it come.

Now on this last lap to the church I feel I am entering enemy territory. I can't see my brother living in this sort of place. I can't see him getting mixed up with these people. The streets wide, the trees without leaves, and everything is looking new. Even the church is looking new. It is of red brick; it don't have a fence or anything; it is just there, on the main road.

We stand up on the pavement and wait. The wind cold now, and I am nervous. But I feel Frank is even more nervous. A woman in a tweed suit come out of the church. She is about fifty and she have a nice face. She smile at us. And now Frank is shyer than me. I don't know whether the woman is my brother's mother-in-law or whether she is just someone who is helping out. You think of a wedding, you think of people waiting outside the church or hall or whatever it is. You don't think of it like this.

Some more people come, not many, with one or two children. And they looking hard at me, like an enemy, these people who spoil my life.

Frank touch me on the arm. I am glad he touch me, but I shrug his hand away. I know it isn't true, but I tell myself he is on the other side, with those others, looking at me without looking at me. I know it isn't true about Frank because, look, he too is nervous. He want to be alone with me; he don't like being with his own people. It isn't like being on a bus or in a café, where he can be like a man saying: I protect this man with me. It is different here outside the church, with the two of us standing on the pavement on one side, and the other sad people standing on another side, the sun red like an orange, the trees hardly throwing a shadow, the grass wild all around the brick church.

A taxi stop. It is my brother. He have a thin white boy with him, and the two of them in suits. Taxi today, wedding day. No turban, no procession, no drums, no ceremony of welcome, no green arches, no lights in the wedding tent, no wedding songs. Just the taxi, the thin white boy with sharp shoes and short hair, smoking, and my brother with a white rose in his jacket. He is just the same. The ugly labourer's face, and he is talking to his friend, showing everybody he is very cool. I don't know why I did think he would get different in three years.

When he and his friend come to me I look at my brother's eyes and his big cheeks and the laughing mouth. It is a soft face and a frightened face. I hope nobody take it into their head one day to break that face up. The friend looking at me, smoking, squinting with the smoke, sly eyes in a rough thin face.

I can feel Frank stiffening and getting more nervous. But then the nice woman in the tweed suit come and start talking in her very brisk way. She is making a noise, breaking up the silence rather than talking, and she take my brother and his friend away and she start moving about among the people on the other side, always making this noise. She is a nice woman; she have this nice face; at this bad moment she is being very nice.

We go in the church and the nice lady make us sit on the right side. Nobody else there but Frank and me, and then the other people come in and sit on the left side, and the ugly church is so big it is as though nobody is there at all. It is the first time I am in a church and I don't like it. It is as though they are making me eat beef and pork. The flowers and the brass and the old smell and the body on the cross make me think of the dead.

4*

The funny taste is in my mouth, my old nausea, and I feel I would vomit if I swallow.

I look down, I do what Frank do, and all the time the taste is in my mouth. I don't look at my brother and the girl until it is all over. Then I see this girl in white, with her veil and flowers, like somebody dead, and her face is blank and broad and very white, the little make-up shining on cheeks and temples like wax. She is a stranger. I don't know how my brother allow himself to do this thing. It is not right. He is a lost man here. You can see it on everybody's face except the girl's.

Outside, the air is fresh. They take a lot of pictures, and still it is more like a funeral than a wedding. Then the nice lady make Frank and me get in the photographer's car. He is a business-man with worries, this photographer. With his gold-rimmed glasses and his little moustache, business is all he is talking about, and he is driving very fast, like one of our mad taxi-drivers. He is talking about the jobs he have to do, about how he start in the photography business, his contacts with newspapers and so on, and even as he is driving he is digging in his breast pocket and turning round to smile and give us his card.

He drive us to a sort of restaurant and straightaway he is busy with his camera and he forget us. It is an old-fashioned building and you go inside a courtyard in the middle, galleries all around. A lot of crooked brown beams everywhere, like in some old British picture, and they take us into a crooked little room with some very crooked beams. In that room everybody gather again and get photographed. Everybody can fit in that small room, everybody at the wedding.

Some of the women crying, my brother looking tired and stunned, the girl looking tired. His wife. How quick a big thing like that settle, how quick a man spoil his life. Frank stick close to me, and when the time come for us to sit down he sit next to me. Nobody talking too much. You get more talk at a wake. Only the pretty waitress, so nice and neat in her white apron and black dress, is happy. She is outside it, and only she is behaving as though it is a wedding party.

No meat for me, and Frank say no meat for him either. He want to do everything like me now. The nice waitress bring us trout. The skin burn black and crispy at the top, and when I eat a piece of the fish it is raw and rotten, so that the church taste come back in my mouth, and I think of the dead again, and brass and flowers.

The waitress come in, her armpits smelling now, and ask if anybody want wine. She say she forget to ask the first time. Nobody hear, nobody answer. She ask again; she say some people drink wine at wedding parties. Still nobody answer. And then an old man who never say anything before, he looking so sad, he lift his face up, he laugh and say, "*There's* your answer, miss." And I feel he must be like Stephen, the wise and funny man of the family, and that people expect to laugh at what he say. And people laugh, and I feel I like that man.

I love them. They take my money, they spoil my life, they separate us. But you can't kill them. O God, show me the enemy. Once you find out who the enemy is, you can kill him. But these people here they confuse me. Who hurt me? Who spoil my life? Tell me who to beat back. I work four years to save my money, I work like a donkey night and day. My brother was to be the educated one, the nice one. And this is how it is ending, in this room, eating with these people. Tell me who to kill.

And now my brother come to me. He is going away with his wife, for good. He hold me by the hand, he look at me, tears come in his eyes, and he say, "I love you." It is true, it is like the time he cry and say he didn't have confidence. I know that he love me, that now it is true, but that it will not be true as soon as he go out of this room, that he will have to forget me. Because it was my idea after my trouble that nobody should know, that the message should go back home that I was dead. And for all this time I am the dead man.

I have my own place to go back to. Frank will take me there when this is over. And now that my brother leave me for good I forget his face already, and I only seeing the rain and the house and the mud, the field at the back with the pará-grass bending down with the rain, the donkey and the smoke from the kitchen, my father in the gallery and my brother in the room on the floor, and that boy opening his mouth to scream, like in *Rope*.

In a Free State

In a Free State

IN THIS COUNTRY in Africa there was a president and there
was also a king. They belonged to different tribes. The enmity
of the tribes was old, and with independence their anxieties about
one another became acute. The king and the president intrigued
with the local representatives of white governments. The white
men who were appealed to liked the king personally. But the
president was stronger; the new army was wholly his, of his
tribe; and the white men decided that the president was to be
supported. So that at last, this weekend, the president was able
to send his army against the king's people.

The territory of the king's people lay to the south and was
still known by its colonial name of the Southern Collectorate.
It was there that Bobby worked, as an administrative officer
in one of the departments of the central government. But during
this week of crisis he had been in the capital, four hundred miles
away, attending a seminar on community development; and in
the capital there was no sign of war or crisis. The seminar had
more English participants than African; the Africans were well-
dressed and dignified, with little to say; and the seminar ended on
Sunday with a buffet lunch in a half-acre garden in what was
still an English suburb.

It was like another Sunday in the capital, which, in spite of the
white exodus to South Africa and in spite of deportations,
remained an English-Indian creation in the African wilderness.
It owed nothing to African skill; it required none. Not far from
the capital were bush villages, half-day excursions for tourists.
But in the capital Africa showed only in the semi-tropical suburban gardens, in the tourist-shop displays of carvings and leather

goods and souvenir drums and spears, and in the awkward liveried boys in the new tourist hotels, where the white or Israeli supervisors were never far away. Africa here was décor. Glamour for the white visitor and expatriate; glamour too for the African, the man flushed out from the bush, to whom, in the city, with independence, civilization appeared to have been granted complete. It was still a colonial city, with a colonial glamour. Everyone in it was far from home.

IN THE BAR of the New Shropshire, once white, now the capital's interracial pick-up spot, with a reputation for racial "incidents", the white men wore open shirts and drank beer. The Africans drank shorter, prettier drinks with cocktail sticks and wore English-made Daks suits. Their hair was parted low on the left and piled up on the right, in the style known to city Africans as the English style.

The Africans were young, in their twenties, and plump. They could read and write, and were high civil servants, politicians or the relations of politicians, non-executive directors and managing directors of recently opened branches of big international corporations. They were the new men of the country and they saw themselves as men of power. They hadn't paid for the suits they wore; in some cases they had had the drapers deported. They came to the New Shropshire to be seen and noted by white people, however transient; to be courted; to make trouble. There were no Asiatics in the bar: the liberations it offered were only for black and white.

Bobby was wearing a saffron cotton shirt of a type that had begun to be known as a "native shirt". It was like a smock, with short, wide sleeves and a low open neck; the fabric, with its bold "native" pattern in black and red, was designed and woven in Holland.

The small young African at Bobby's table was not a native. He was, as he had quickly let Bobby know, a Zulu, a refugee from South Africa. He was in light-blue trousers and a plain white shirt, and he was further distinguished from the other

Africans in the bar by his cloth cap, of a plaid pattern, with which, as he slumped low in his chair, he continually played, now putting it on and pulling it over his eyes, now using it as a fan, now holding it against his chest and kneading it with his small hands, as though performing an isometric exercise.

Conversation with the Zulu wasn't easy. There too he was fidgety. The king and the president, sabotage in South Africa, seminars, tourists, the natives: he hopped from subject to subject, never committing himself, never relating one thing to another. And the cloth cap was like part of his elusiveness. The cap made the Zulu appear now as a dandy, now as an exploited labourer from the South African mines, now as an American minstrel, and sometimes even as the revolutionary he had told Bobby he was.

They had been together for more than an hour. It was nearly half-past ten; it was getting late for Bobby. Then, after a silence, during which they had both been looking at the rest of the bar, the Zulu said, "In this town there are even white whores now."

Bobby, looking at his beer, sipping his beer, not hurrying himself, refusing to meet the Zulu's eyes, was glad that the talk had at last touched sex.

"It isn't nice," the Zulu said.

"What isn't nice?"

"Look." The Zulu sat up, his cap on his head, and put his hand to his hip pocket, thrusting forward his small but well-developed chest as he did so, tight within the white shirt. He took out a wallet and flipped his thumb through many new banknotes. "I could go now to places where this would make me welcome. I don't think it is nice."

Bobby thought: this boy is a whore. Bobby was nervous of African whores in hotel bars. But he prepared to bargain. He said, "You are a brave man. Going about with all that cash. I never carry more than sixty or eighty shillings on me."

"You need two hundred to do anything in this town."

"A hundred at the outside is enough for me."

"Enjoy it."

Bobby looked up and held the Zulu's gaze. The Zulu didn't flinch. It was Bobby who looked away.

Bobby said, "You South Africans are all arrogant."

"We are not like your natives here. These people are the most ignorant people in the world. Look at them."

Bobby looked at the Zulu. So small for a Zulu. "You must be careful what you say. They might deport you."

The Zulu fanned himself with his cap and turned away. "Why do these white women want to be with the natives? A couple of years ago the natives couldn't even come in here. Now look. It isn't nice. I don't think it is nice."

"It must be different in South Africa," Bobby said.

"What do you want to hear, mister? Listen, I'll tell you. I did pretty well in South Africa. I bought my whisky. I had my women. You'd be surprised."

"I can see that many people would find you attractive."

"I'll tell you." The Zulu's voice dropped. His tone became conspiratorial as he began to give the names of South African politicians with whose wives and daughters he had slept.

Bobby, looking at the Zulu's tense little face, the eyes that held such hurt, felt compassion and excitement. It was the African thrill: Bobby forgot his nervousness.

"South Africans," the Zulu said, raising his voice again. "Over here they never leave you alone. They always look for you. 'You from South Africa?' I'm tired of being accosted by them."

"I don't blame them."

"I thought you were South African when you came in."

"Me!"

"They always sit with me. They always want to start a conversation."

"What a nice cap."

Bobby leaned to touch the plaid cap, and for a while they held the cap together, Bobby fingering the material, the Zulu allowing the cap to be fingered.

Bobby said, "Do you like my new shirt?"

"I wouldn't be seen dead in one of those native shirts."

"It's the colour. We can't wear the lovely colours you can wear."

The Zulu's eyes hardened. Bobby's fingers edged along the cap until they were next to the Zulu's. Then he looked down at the fingers, pink beside black.

"When I born again – " Bobby stopped. He had begun to talk pidgin; that wouldn't do with the Zulu. He looked up. "If I come into the world again I want to come with your colour." His voice was low. On the plaid cap his fingers moved until they were over one of the Zulu's.

The Zulu didn't stir. His face, when he lifted it to Bobby's, was without expression. Bobby's blue eyes went moist and seemed to stare; his thin lips trembled and seemed set in a half-smile. There was silence between the two men. Then, without moving his hand or changing his expression, the Zulu spat in Bobby's face.

For a second or so Bobby's fingers remained on the Zulu's. Then he took his hand away, found his handkerchief, dabbed at his face; and when he put away the handkerchief his eyes were still staring at the Zulu, his lips still seemed set in their half-smile. The Zulu never moved.

The bar had seen. Blacks stared, whites looked away. Conversation faltered, then recovered.

Bobby got up. The Zulu continued to stare, into space now, never changing the level of his gaze. Deliberately, Bobby moved his chair back. Then, plump and sacrificial-looking in his loose, dancing native shirt, not looking down, left arm at his side, right arm jerking from the elbow, he walked with a fixed smile towards the door.

The Zulu sank lower in his armchair. He put on his cap and took it off; he pressed his chin into his neck, opened his mouth, closed his mouth. His face had been taut and expressionless; now it had the calm of a child. This was what remained of his revolution: these visits to the New Shropshire, this fishing for white men. In the capital the Zulu was a solitary, without employment, living on a small dole from an American foundation. In this part of Africa the Americans – or simply Americans – supported everything.

The liveried barboy, remembering his duties, ran after Bobby with the bill. He stopped Bobby in the doorway, beside the large native drum, part of the new decorations of the New Shropshire. Bobby, at first not hearing, then relieved that it was only the boy, overacted confusion. Feeling below the yellow native shirt for his wallet, in the hip pocket of his soft light-grey flannel trousers, he smiled, as at a private joke, without looking at the boy's face. He gave the boy a twenty-shilling note. Then, absurd chivalry overcoming him, he gave the boy another note, to pay for the Zulu's drinks as well; and he didn't wait for change.

IN THE LOBBY there was the new official photograph of the president. It had appeared in the city only that weekend. In the old photographs the president wore a headdress of the king's tribe, a gift of the king at the time of independence, a symbol of the unity of the tribes. The new photograph showed the president without the headdress, in jacket, shirt and tie, with his hair done in the English style. The bloated cheeks shone in the studio lights; the hard opaque eyes looked directly at the camera. Africans were said to attribute a magical power to the president's eyes; and the eyes seemed to know their reputation.

From the floodlit forecourt of the New Shropshire – the rock garden, the white flagpole with the limp national flag – Bobby drove down the sloping drive to the dark highway. At night in every suburb the bush began there, on the highway. Every week men of the forest came to settle in the usurped city. They brought only the skills of the forest; they found no room; and at night they prowled the city's unenclosed spaces. There were many frightening stories. Normally Bobby scoffed, rejecting, as much as the stories, the expatriates who told them. But now he drove very fast, down the bush-lined highways, past the wide roundabouts, through the bumpy lanes of the Indian bazaar –

houses, shops and warehouses – to the city centre, with its complex one-way system, its half a dozen skyscrapers dark above the bright square and the wide dusty car-park.

In the cramped lobby of his hotel there was again the new photograph of the president, between English foxhunting prints. The hotel, built in colonial days, was where up-country government officers like Bobby were lodged when they came to the capital on government business. It looked older than it was. Rough timber merged into mock-Tudor: the hotel was partly "pioneer", partly suburban, still English, home from home. Bobby didn't like it. His room, which had an open fireplace, was white and furry, with white walls, white sheepskin rugs, a white candlewick bedspread and a zebra-skin pouffe.

The evening was over, the week was over. This was his last night in the capital; early in the morning he was driving back to the Collectorate. His packing had already been done. He left a tip for the roomboy in an envelope. Soon he was in bed. He was quite calm.

AFRICA WAS FOR Bobby the empty spaces, the safe adventure of long fatiguing drives on open roads, the other Africans, boys built like men. "You want lift? You big boy, you no go school? No, no, you no frighten. Look, I give you shilling. You hold my hand. Look, my colour, your colour. I give you shilling buy schoolbooks. Buy books, learn read, get big job. When I born again I want your colour. You no frighten. You want five shillings?" Sweet infantilism, almost without language: in language lay mockery and self-disgust.

All week, while being the government officer at the seminar, he had rehearsed that drive back to the Collectorate. But then, at the buffet lunch, he had been asked to give Linda a lift back; and he couldn't refuse. Linda was one of the "compound wives" from the Collectorate, one of those who lived in the government compound. She had flown up to the capital with her husband, who was taking part in the seminar; but she wasn't flying back with him. Bobby knew Linda and her husband and had even been once to dinner at their house; but after three years they were still no more than acquaintances. It was one of those difficult half-relationships, with uncertainty rather than suspicion on both sides. So the prospect of adventure had vanished; and the drive, which had promised so much, seemed likely to be full of strain.

Disappointment rather than need, then, had sent Bobby to the New Shropshire. And even while he was making his preparations to go out he had known that the evening wouldn't end well. He didn't like places like the New Shropshire. He didn't have the bar-room skills, the bar-room toughness. Instinct had told him, from the first exchange of glances, that the Zulu was only a tease. But he had gone to the table and committed himself. He didn't like African whores. A whore in Africa was a boy who wanted more than five shillings; any boy who wanted more than five was dealing only in money, and was wrong. Bobby had decided that long ago; but he had started to bargain with the Zulu.

That evening he had broken all his rules; the evening had shown how right his rules were. He felt no bitterness, no hurt. He didn't blame the Zulu, he didn't blame Linda. Before Africa, the incident of the evening might have driven him out adventuring for hours more in dangerous places; and then in his room might have driven him to a further act of excess and self-mortification. But now he knew that the mood would pass, the morning would come. Even with Linda as his passenger, the drive remained.

He was awakened by a sound as of crowing cocks. It came from the lane at the side of the hotel. It was one of the sounds of the African night: a prowler had been disturbed, the African hue and cry was being raised. Later, he saw himself again in a place like the New Shropshire. He was on his back and the liveried boy was standing above him; but he couldn't raise his head to see the boy's face, to see whether the face laughed. His head was aching; the pain began to shoot and then it was as if his head were exploding. Even when he awakened, the pain remained, the sense of the drained head. It was some time before he fell asleep again. And when next he was awakened, by the helicopter circling near, then far, then so close it seemed to be directly over the hotel, it was well past five, light in the white room, and time to get up.

2

YAK-YAK-YAK-YAK. The helicopter, flying low, as if examining the hotel car-park, drowned the braying of the burglar alarm on Bobby's car as Bobby unlocked the door. Bobby, feeling himself examined, didn't look up. The helicopter hovered, then rose again at an angle.

In the bazaar area, through which Bobby had driven so recklessly the previous evening, the shops and warehouses of concrete and corrugated iron were closed; the long Indian names on plain signboards looked as cramped as the buildings. When the road left the bazaar it ran beside a wide dry gully, cool now, but promising dust and glare later; and then, the gully disappearing, the road became a dual-carriageway with flowers and shrubs on the central reservation.

The Union Club had been founded by some Indians in colonial days as a multi-racial club; it was the only club in the capital that admitted Africans. After independence the Indian founders had been deported, the club seized and turned into a hotel for tourists. The garden was a wild dry tangle around a bare yard. And in the main doorway, level to the dusty ground, below a cantilevered concrete slab, Linda stood beside her ivory-coloured suitcase and waved.

She was cheerful, with no early-morning strain on her thin face. No need to ask what had kept her overnight in the capital. Her cream shirt hung out of her blue trousers, which were a little loose around her narrow, low hips; her hair was in a pale brown scarf. In those clothes, and below that concrete slab, she looked small, boyish, half-made. She was hardly good-looking, and she showed her age; but in the Collectorate compound she had a reputation as a man-eater. Bobby had heard appalling stories about Linda. As appalling, he thought, getting out of the car, as the stories she must have heard about him.

With loud words in the empty yard, they fell on one another, conducting this meeting, their first without witnesses, as though they had witnesses; so that all at once, after silence and tension, they were like actors in a play, neither really listening to the other, Linda tinkling, apologetic, grateful, explaining, Bobby simultaneously rejecting explanations and gratitude and fussing tremendously with the ivory-coloured suitcase, as with a stage property.

Yak-yak-yak-yak.

Silenced, they both looked up. The men in the helicopter were white.

"They are looking for the king," Linda said, when the helicopter moved away. "They say he's in the capital. He got away from the Collectorate in one of those African taxis. In some sort of disguise."

Last night's expatriate gossip: Bobby began to be depressed about his passenger. Over rocks and broken pavement they bumped out of the yard.

"I hope they haven't done anything too awful to the poor wives," Linda said. Her manner was still affected. "Were you *persona* very *grata* in that quarter?"

"Not very. I'm not a great one for high society."

She giggled, out of her own cheerfulness.

Bobby set his face. He decided to be sombre, to give nothing away. He had shown goodwill and that was enough for the time being.

Sombrely, then, he drove along the dual-carriageway; and sombrely many minutes later he took the gentle curves of the suburban road, with its wide grass verges, hedges, big houses, big gardens, with here and there now a barefoot yard-boy in khaki.

"You wouldn't believe you were in Africa," Linda said. "It's so much like England here."

"It's a little grander than the England I know."

She didn't answer. And for some time she said nothing.

He felt he had been too aggressive. He said, "Of course, they didn't allow Africans to live here."

"They had their servants, Bobby."

"Servants, yes." She caught him unprepared. He hadn't expected her to be so provocative so early. He said, with the calm grim satisfaction of a man prophesying the racial holocaust, "I suppose that is why someone like John Mubende-Mbarara has refused to move out of the *native* quarter."

"How well you pronounce those names."

Bobby's sombreness turned to gloom. "Well, he won't come to you. If you want to see his work you have to go to him. In the native quarter."

Linda said, "When Johnny M. began, he was a good primitive painter and we all loved his paintings of his family's lovely ribby cattle. But he churned out so many of those he got to be a little better than primitive. Now he's only bad. So I don't suppose it matters if he does continue to paint his cattle in the native quarter."

"That's been said before."

"About him living in the native quarter?"

"About his painting." Bobby hated himself for answering.

"He's got awfully fat," Linda said.

Bobby decided to say no more. He decided again to be sombre and this time not to be drawn.

SUBURBAN GARDENS GAVE way to African urban allotments with fewer trees, and at the edge of the town the land felt open and the light was like the light that announces the nearness of the ocean. Here, serving both town and wilderness, weathered painted hoardings on tall poles showed laughing Africans smoking cigarettes, drinking soft drinks and using sewing machines.

Allotments turned to smallholdings and secondary bush. A few Africans were about, most on foot, one or two on old bicycles. Their clothes were patched with large oblongs of red, blue, yellow, green; it was a local style. Bobby was on the point of saying something about the African colour-sense. But he held back; it was too close to the subject of the painter.

The land began to slope; the view became more extensive. The Indian-English town felt far away alraedy. To one side of the road the land was hummocked, as with grassed-over ant-hills. Each hump marked the site of a tree that had been felled. Wasteland now, emptiness; but here, until just seventy years before, Africans like those on the road had lived, hidden from the world, in the shelter of their forests.

Yak-yak. At first only a distant drone, the helicopter was quickly overhead; and for a while it stayed, touched now with the morning light, killing the noise of the car and the feel of its engine. The road curved downhill, now in yellow light, now in damp shadow. The helicopter receded, the sound of wind and motor-car tyres returned.

From beside mounds of fruit and vegetables heavy-limbed African boys ran out into the road, holding up cauliflowers and cabbages. There had been accidents here; offending motorists had been manhandled by enraged crowds, gathering swiftly from the roadside bush. Bobby slowed down. He hunched over the wheel and gave a slow, low wave to the first boy. The boy didn't respond, but Bobby continued to smile and wave until he had passed all the boys. Then, remembering Linda, he went sombre again.

She was serene, full of her own cheerfulness. And when she said, "Did you notice the size of those cauliflowers?" it was as though she didn't know they were quarrelling.

He said, grimly, "Yes, I noticed the size of the cauli-flowers."

"It's something that surprised me."

"Oh?"

"It's foolish really, but I never thought they would have fields. I somehow imagined they would all be living in the jungle. When Martin said we were being posted to the Southern Collectorate I imagined the compound would be in a little clearing in the forest. I never thought there would be roads and houses and shops – "

"And radios."

"It was ridiculous. I knew it was ridiculous, but I sort of saw them leaning on their spears under a tree and standing around one of those big old-fashioned sets. His Master's Voice."

Bobby said, "Do you remember that American from the foundation who came out to encourage us to keep statistics or something? I took him out for a drive one day, and as soon as we were out of the town he was terrified. He kept on asking, 'Where's the Congo? Is that the Congo?' He was absolutely terrified all the time."

The road was now cut into a hill and the curves were sharp. A sign said: *Beware of Fallen Rocks*.

"That's one of my favourite road-signs," Bobby said. "I always look for it."

"So precise."

"Isn't it?"

His sombreness had gone; it would be hard now for him to reassume it. Already he and Linda had become travellers together, sensitive to the sights, finding conversation in everything.

"I love being out this early," Linda said. "It reminds me of summer mornings in England. Though in England I never liked the summer, I must say."

"Oh?"

"I always felt I should be enjoying myself, but I never seemed to. The day would go on and on, and I could never find much to do. The summer always made me feel I was missing a lot. I preferred the autumn. I was much more in control then. To me autumn is the great season of renewal. All very girlish, I'm sure."

"I wouldn't say girlish. I would say unusual. I once had a psychiatrist who thought we were all reminded of death in October. He said that as soon as he realized this he stopped being rheumatic in the winter. Of course at the same time he'd put in central heating."

"I somehow thought, Bobby, that you would have a psychiatrist." She was being bright again. "Tell me exactly what was wrong."

He said, calmly, "I had a breakdown at Oxford."

He had spoken too calmly. Linda remained bright. "I've long wanted to ask someone who had one. Exactly what is a breakdown?"

It was something he had defined more than once. But he pretended to fumble for the words. "A breakdown. It's like watching yourself die. Well, not die. It's like watching yourself become a ghost."

She matched his tone. "Did it last long?"

"Eighteen months."

She was impressed. He could tell.

With a chuckle, as though speaking to a child, he said, "Look at that lovely tree." She obeyed. And when the tree had been looked at, he said, solemnly again, "Africa saved my life." As though it was a complete statement, explaining everything; as though he was at once punishing and forgiving all who misunderstood him.

She was stilled. She could find nothing to say.

THIS WAS THE famous view. This was the openness the sky had been promising. The land dropped and dropped. The continent here was gigantically flawed. The eye lost itself in the colourless distances of the wide valley, dissolving in every direction in cloud and haze.

Linda said, "Africa, Africa."

"Shall we stop and have a look?"

He pulled in where the verge widened. They got out of the car.

"So cool," Linda said.

"You wouldn't believe you were almost on the Equator."

They had both seen the view many times and neither of them wanted to say anything that the other might have heard before or anything that was too fanciful.

"It's the clouds that do it," Linda said at last. "When we first came out Martin took photographs of clouds all the time."

"I never knew Martin was a photographer."

"He wasn't. He'd just got himself a camera. He used to use my name when he sent the film off to be processed, so that no one at Kodak would think he'd taken the pictures. I suppose they must get an awful lot of junk. After he got tired of clouds he began crawling about on his hands and knees snapping toadstools and the tiniest wildflowers he could find. The camera wasn't built for that. All he got were greeny-brown blurs. The people at Kodak dutifully sent every blur back, addressed to me."

They were in danger of forgetting the view.

"So cool here," Bobby said.

A white Volkswagen went past, travelling out of the town. A white man was at the wheel. He blew his horn long and hard when he saw Bobby and Linda, and accelerated down the hill.

"I wonder who he's showing off to," Bobby said.

Linda found this very funny.

"It's absurd," Bobby said, when they were sitting in the car again, "but I feel all this" – he indicated the great valley – "belongs to me."

She had been close to laughter. Now she leaned forward and laughed. "It *is* absurd, Bobby. When you say it like that."

"But you know what I mean. I couldn't bear looking at this if I didn't know that I was going to look at it again. You know," he said, sitting up, as stiff as a driving pupil, looking left and right, driving off, "I never knew a place like Africa existed. I wasn't interested. I suppose, like you, I thought of tribesmen and spears. And of course I knew about South Africa."

"I've just thought. We haven't heard the helicopter for some time."

"Helicopters don't have much of a range. It's almost the only thing I learned in the Air Force."

"Bobby!"

"Just National Service."

"Do you think they've got the king?"

"It must be awful for him," Bobby said, "having to run from the wogs. I am in a minority on this, I know, but I always found him embarrassing. He was far too English for me. We'll see what his smart London friends do for him now. Such a foolish man. I feel sure some of them put him up to all this talk of secession and so on."

" 'I say, awfully stuffy here, with all these wogs, what?' "

"And they found it very charming and funny. I never did, I must say. You know, there's going to be an awful lot of ill-informed criticism. And we won't be exempt. Serving dictatorial African regimes and so on."

"It's something that worries Martin," Linda said.

"Oh?"

"The criticism."

"I am here to serve," Bobby said. "I'm not here to tell them how to run their country. There's been too much of that. What sort of government the Africans choose to have is none of my business. It doesn't alter the fact that they need food and schools and hospitals. People who don't want to serve have no business here. That sounds brutal, but that's how I see it."

She didn't respond.

"It isn't a popular attitude, I know," he said. "What is it our Duchess says?"

"Duchess?"

"That's how I call her."

"You mean Doris Marshall?"

"I bend over 'black-wards'. Isn't that what she says?"

Linda smiled.

"Very original," Bobby said. "But I don't know why we think the African don't have eyes. You think the Africans don't know that the Marshalls are on the old South African railroad?"

"She's South African."

"As she tells everybody," Bobby said.

" 'And proud of it, my dear.' "

" 'When I was steddying ittykit in Suffafrica – ' "

"That's it," Linda said. "You've got it exactly. And there's this thing about 'glove-box'. Do you know about that?"

"You mean you don't say glove-compartment."

"You always say glove-box."

" 'Because it's ittykit in Suffafrica, my dear.' "

"That's it, that's it," Linda said.

"I think the sooner they finish putting the screws on Denis Marshall and send the two of them packing to South Africa, the better for everybody."

She rearranged the scarf around her hair and rolled down the window a little.

"It's almost cold," she said, and took a deep breath. "That's the nice thing about the capital. The open fires."

After the way they had just been talking, this expatriate commonplace disappointed him. He said, "The nicest thing about the capital is this. This drive back. I don't think I'll ever get tired of it."

"Stop it. You'll make me sad."

"There's a splendid thing I read by Somerset Maugham somewhere. He's not much admired now, I know. But he said that if you wanted only the best and held out for it, really held out, you usually got it. I must say I've begun to feel like that. I feel we can always do what we really want to do."

"It's easy for you now, Bobby. But you were saying there was a time when you didn't even know a place like Africa existed."

"I know now."

"I know it too. But it doesn't help. I may want to stay, but I know I can't."

She closed the window and took a deep breath again. She gazed at the wide valley.

She said, "If I weren't English I think I would like to be a Masai. So tall, those women. So elegant."

It was a compliment to Africa: he took it as a sign of her new attitude to him. But he said, "How very Kenya-settler. The romantic blacks are the backward ones."

"Are they backward? I was thinking of the *manyattas* or whatever they are. Like the drawings in a geography book. You know, your little hut, your tall fence, and bringing home your cattle for the night to protect them against marauders."

"That's what I meant. Peter Pan in Africa."

"But doesn't the pre-man side of Africa have this effect on you sometimes?"

He didn't reply. They both became embarrassed.

He said, "I can't see you in a *manyatta*, I must say."

She accepted that.

A little later she said, "Marauders. I love that word."

The emptiness of the road couldn't now be taken for granted. Traffic to the capital was light but steady: old lorries, tankers driven by turbanned Sikhs, a few European and Asian cars, African-driven Peugeot estate-cars, often looking brand-new, always speeding, packed with rocking Africans.

These Peugeot cars were the country's long-distance taxi-buses. One, horn blaring, surprised and overtook Bobby on a steep slope. The Africans in the back turned round to smile. Linda looked away. The horn continued. Almost immediately the road curved and the Peugeot's brake-lights came on.

"I can't understand why some people like to drive with their brakes," Bobby said.

Linda said, "For the same reason that they sell their spare tyres."

Bend by bend, brake-lights intermittently flashing, the Peugeot pulled away.

"It was one of the things I noticed when I first came out," Linda said. "Nearly everybody you met had been in an accident or knew someone who had been in an accident. There were so many people in splints in the compound it looked like a ski resort."

It was an old joke, but Bobby acknowledged it. "There was an accident right here not long ago. One of our Singer-Singer Sikh friends turned off his ignition, to coast down. But somehow that locked his steering."

"What happened?"

"He ran off the road and was killed."

"Martin says they are the worst drivers."

"Whenever you see a Mercedes in the middle of the road you can be sure it's an Asian at the wheel. I can't stand those shops. They don't sell the Africans a pack of cigarettes. They sell them just one or two cigarettes at a time. They make a fortune out of the Africans."

"A good way of getting something out of them is to say, 'Hello, isn't this made in South Africa?' They get so terrified they virtually give you the shop free."

She stopped then, feeling she had gone too far.

AT LAST THEY were at the foot of the cliff and on the floor of the valley. The sun was getting high; the land was scrub and open; it became warm in the car. Linda rolled down her window a crack. At the other side of the valley the escarpment was blurred; colour there was insubstantial, like an illusion of light and distance. They were headed for that escarpment, for the high plateau; and the road before them was straight.

Sixty, seventy, eighty miles an hour: without effort or thought Bobby was accelerating, drawn on by the road. Here, after the hillside windings, the adventure of the drive as speed, distance and tension always began. As he concentrated on the car and the black road, Bobby's sense of time became acute. Without looking at his watch he could measure off quarter-hours.

A derelict wooden building; a warning to slow down, on a washed-out red-and-white roadside board and then in elongated white letters on the road itself. A right-angled turn over the narrow-gauge, desolate-looking railroad track; and the highway became the worn main road of a straggling settlement: tin and old timber, twisted hoardings, a long wire fence with danger signs stencilled in red, dirt branch-roads, trees rising out of dusty yards, crooked shops raised off the earth. And then, making the road narrow, an African crowd.

They wore felt hats with conical crowns and brims pulled

5

down low. Many were in long drooping jackets, brown or dark-grey, which looked like cast-off European clothes. Quite a few, men and women, were brilliantly patched. Two or three men with pencils and pads were marshalling the Africans into open lorries with high canopy-frames. Policemen in black uniforms watched.

"They are restless today," Linda said.

Bobby, driving very slowly, let the old joke pass. Africans stared from the road and down from the lorries, their black faces featureless below their felt hats. Bobby began a low wave but didn't complete it. Linda, encountering stares, adjusted her scarf and looked straight ahead. Even when they had passed the crowd Bobby continued to drive slowly, anxious not to appear to be running away. In the rear-view mirror the blank-faced Africans with their patches and hats grew small. Out of the settlement, past a curve, Bobby checked again: the road behind showed clear.

The light hurt. Linda put on her dark glasses. The scrub stretched in every direction and seemed to end only with the hazy mountains. In the high sky clouds grew swiftly from the merest white wisps, became silver and black with storm, then disintegrated and reshaped. Bobby and Linda didn't talk. It was some time before Bobby took the car up to speed again.

Linda said, "You know what they're up to, don't you?"

Bobby didn't reply.

"They are going to swear their oaths of hate. You know what that means, don't you? You know the filthy things they are going to do? The filth they are going to eat? The blood, the excrement, the dirt."

Bobby leaned over the wheel. "I don't know how much of those stories one can believe."

"I believe you know. It's been going on all weekend in the capital."

"There's an awful lot of gossip in the capital. Some people will insist on their thrills."

"Hate against the king and the king's people. And against you and me. I can do without that sort of thrill."

"I know, I know. You think oaths, you think terrorists and *pangas*. But that's not the issue today, thank goodness. And you know, all I believe they do is to eat a piece of meat. I don't think they even eat it. They just bite on it."

"Well, I suppose going up to Government House to eat dirt and hold hands and dance naked in the dark is no better and no worse than going up to sign the visitors' book."

She laughed. It broke the mood.

"I must say I didn't like the looks we got there," Bobby said. "For a minute it made me feel we were back in the old days. I would've hated to be here then, wouldn't you?"

"Oh, I don't know. I suppose I would have adjusted. I adjust very easily."

"I wonder whether we aren't a little jealous of the president and his people. At a time like this we feel excluded, and naturally we resent it. I'm sure we would like them a lot more if they were more easygoing. Like the Masai. Speaking personally, I haven't found any . . . 'prejudice'."

Above her dark glasses her narrow forehead twitched. "Oh, it's easy for you, Bobby."

"What do you mean?"

"I think it's going to rain this afternoon. Just when we leave the tar. I'm looking at those clouds piling up there. If you travel a lot with Martin you get this eye for clouds. That untarred bit of road is my private nightmare. Just half an hour of rain and it's all mud. I can't stand skids. It's like being in an earthquake. It's the one thing that really makes me hysterical. That and earthquakes."

"I wouldn't say the clouds are 'piling up'."

"Still, wouldn't it be romantic if we had to spend the night at the colonel's, watching the rain come sweeping in across the lake?"

"He's very much the sort of character I prefer to keep away from. Everything I hear about him leads me to believe he's a total bore."

"He's a very settler settler, I must say. He doesn't care for anyone."

"I suppose you mean Africans."

"Bobby. Pay attention. The first time the Marshalls went there she asked for a port and lemon."

" 'My dear!' "

"My dear. He just lifted up his scrawny arm and pointed to the door and shouted, 'Get out!' Even the barboy jumped."

"Ittykit in Suffafrica. I forgive him that. I might almost say it's a point in his favour. But why do you say it's easier for me?"

"Oh, Bobby, I've gone over this so often with Martin. We appear to talk of nothing else. When I was a girl lapping up my Somerset Maugham and learning about the great world I never dreamt that so much of my married life would have been spent anguishing about things like 'terms of service'."

"Ogguna Wanga-Butere is my superior," Bobby said. "He is my – 'boss'. I show him respect. And I believe he respects me."

"I'm sorry, but when those names trip off your tongue like that, you make them sound very funny."

"I very much feel that Europeans have themselves to blame if there's any prejudice against them. Every day the president travels up and down, telling his people that we are needed. But he's no fool. He knows the old colonial hands are out to get every penny they can before they scuttle South. It makes me laugh. We lecture the Africans about corruption. But there's a lot of anguish and talk about prejudice when they rumble our little rackets. And not so little either. We were spending thousands on overseas baggage allowances for baggage that never went anywhere."

"It was nice to have," Linda said.

She was abstracted; her good humour had gone. Her bony forehead, curving sharply from the flat, thinning hair below her scarf, had begun to shine; above her dark glasses the worry-lines were beginning to show.

"Busoga-Kesoro brought me the papers. He said, 'Bobby,

this claim by Denis Marshall has been passed and paid. But we know he didn't take any baggage anywhere this last leave. What do we do?' What could I say? I knew very well there would be talk over the coffee-cups about my 'disloyalty'. But who are my loyalties to? I told B-K, 'I think this should go up to the minister.' "

He was exaggerating his role; he was talking too much. He saw that; he saw he was losing Linda's interest. He leaned over the wheel, smiled at the road, shifted about on his seat and said, "Where shall we stop for coffee?"

"The Hunting Lodge?"

He didn't approve. But he said, "What a good idea. I hear it's under new management."

She said in her new abstracted manner, "After the property scare."

"The Asians did very well out of that."

She didn't reply. He fell silent. He would have liked to abolish the impression of talkativeness, to be again, as at the beginning, the man with personality in reserve. But now the sombre person was she.

The road ran black and straight between the flat scrub.

"I believe you are right," he said after a time. "The clouds are piling up. At times like this one doesn't know whether to press on or to hang back."

His manner was conciliating. She made no effort to match it. She said firmly, "I want coffee."

They looked at the road.

"I'd heard," he said, "that Sammy Kisenyi wasn't the easiest of men. But I didn't know that Martin was so unhappy."

She sighed. Bobby was stilled; he leaned back against his seat. Then, stilling him further, keeping up the tension, Linda with great weary self-possession rearranged her hair and scarf.

Far away on the road something shimmered. It was more than a mirage. They concentrated on it. A mangled dog.

"I'm glad I've seen it," Linda said. "I was waiting for it." Her tone was mystical. "You always have to see one."

"So you'll be leaving?"

"Oh, Bobby, it's so different for you. In your department the work goes on and there's always something to show. But radio is radio. You have to put out programmes. And if you're an old radio man, as Martin is, you know when you are putting out rubbish. And surely the point of coming out here and giving up the BBC was to do something a little better than that. I suppose it's Martin's fault in a way. He was never one of the pushing P.R.O. types."

"I see that. About the radio. I do feel they overdo the politics and the speeches. There could be a little more editing."

"When I think that Martin was offered the job of Regional Director. But he said, 'No. This is an African country. This is a job for someone like Sammy.'"

"They say that Sammy had a rough time in England."

"Of course it hasn't been a disaster. There are still people in the BBC who remember Martin. When we were there on leave last year someone at the Club said to Martin, 'Oh, but you're pretty high-powered over there, aren't you?'"

"But of course. No one spoils his career by coming out here. So you think you'll be going back to England?"

"One has to think of the future. But England: I don't know. Martin has put out feelers here and there. I have no doubt that something will happen."

"I'm sure it will." But his question hadn't been answered. He asked, "Where do you think it'll be?"

He waited.

She said, "South."

He said, "My life is here."

3

THE SCRUB, WHEN it ruled, had appeared to stretch all the way to the escarpment across a flat valley. But for some time the land had been getting broken and greener. The escarpment still bounded the view, but less and less abruptly. There were now low, spreading, isolated hills; dark trees in the distance hinted at water and streams; here and there hummocked fields spoke of recent forests. Dirt roads began to meet the highway; simple road-signs gave the names of places twenty, thirty, sixty miles away. There were a few small hoardings. Traffic was still light.

Linda said, in her even mystical voice, "That's my favourite hill on this drive. It looks as though some giant hand had clawed down the side."

The description was accurate. It was what Bobby himself felt about the hill.

He said, "Yes."

Ahead of them, a tall covered van entered the highway from a side road. Beagles pushed their heads above the tailboard of the van. Hanging on at the back, badly jolted, were two Africans in jodhpurs and riding boots, red caps and jackets.

"Such a strange part of Africa," Linda said.

She sat up, took her bag from the floor and brought out her vanity case. She began to make her face up. Her mystical manner had disappeared. Bobby was now the gloomy one.

"When we were in West Africa for those few months," she said, patting powder, squinting at the hand mirror, "you would never have said that the Africans there were remotely English. But as soon as you crossed the border into the French place there you saw black men just like ours sitting on the roadside and eating French bread and drinking red wine and wearing little French berets. Now you come here and see these black English grooms."

The road had begun to curve; the way ahead was no longer clear. They stayed behind the van with the yelping, interested beagles. The grooms eyed the car without friendliness. A sign announced the Hunting Lodge, one mile on.

"We'll have to be quick," Bobby said. "I don't like the way those clouds are piling up there."

"I told you I was the expert."

The road they turned off into dipped sharply from the embankment of the highway. It ran dark-red and narrow, with deep wheeltracks about a central ridge, between humped fields. Rain had fallen the previous day or early that morning. The car slithered in the wheeltracks; the steering-wheel jumped in Bobby's hands.

"Still hasn't dried out," Bobby said. "It must have rained pretty hard."

"It will rain again soon," Linda said. But she didn't sound anxious.

The red road curved, following a shallow depression between gentle slopes. Bobby and Linda were enclosed by green; the highway was hidden. Not far ahead of them a line of trees, some white and leafless, marked the course of a stream. Beyond that the land sloped up again, parkland.

"Like England," Linda said.

"Or Africa."

Past a turning the land on the left was shaved of humps and was as flat as a swamp, with scattered tussocks of grass and reeds breaking the surface, as in a swamp. At one end of the levelled area was a derelict timber pavilion, the roof partly collapsed.

"Polo," Linda said.

"Does Martin play?"

As they drove past they saw the ruin in elevation. Light showed through the missing boards in the exposed back wall at the top and between the broken planking of the steps below, so that the pavilion looked like a dark-grey cut-out against the green. The pavilion had not been built to last. It was a structure such as an army might put up and leave behind.

"Do you think those beagles will go back home when the time comes?" Linda said. "Or will they grow wild?"

The red road ran beside the line of trees, some of which, on the bank of the stream, had died, their roots drowned. Water roared over stones and could be heard above the beat of the car engine. Sometimes the stream itself could be seen, brimming and muddy.

"Goodness," Bobby said. "It must have rained heavily."

The road turned off, twisted and climbed. Broken rocks had been beaten into the road here and they showed jagged where the surrounding earth had been washed away. The car rocked but did not skid; the hill flattened, became open; and they were at the Hunting Lodge: a separate little creosoted office-shed, marked with a board, a mock-pioneer, mock-Tudor hall, and two rows of cottages flat to the ground, with tiled roofs and chimneys and rough casement windows above a profusion of seed-packet flowers drooping from the recent rain.

A white Volkswagen was parked in the yard, the manœuvres of its wheels showing fresh on the wet sand. Bobby recognized it as the Volkswagen that had passed them when they had stopped to look at the view. The driver, the man who had sounded the horn, a short, sturdy man of about forty, with dark glasses, khaki slacks and a conventional sports shirt, was waiting.

Bobby, sensing Linda fresh and alert beside him, wondered how he had allowed himself to forget. More, he wondered how he had allowed himself to be brought so directly to the Hunting Lodge. He decided to be grim.

FROWNING, HE PARKED.

"Too late for coffee," the man from the Volkswagen said. He was American, of moderate accent.

"But perhaps in time for lunch," Linda said.

Bobby, concentrating on his frown and his parking and his general silent grimness, missed his chance to object.

"Bobby," Linda said, "do you know Carter?"

Bobby, locking the car door, barely looked up. "I don't think I do."

"Well. Bobby, Carter."

"That's a nice shirt you're wearing, Bobby," Carter said, taking off his dark glasses, extending a hand.

And Bobby knew he had already been described to Carter by Linda.

"They start serving lunch at twelve," Carter said. "But we'll

5*

have to order it now if we want it. As you can see, the place isn't exactly packed out. All right, lunch? I'll go and tell her."

"I'll go," Bobby said.

He moved off towards the hall.

"In the office, Bobby," Carter said. "She's in the office."

Bobby turned and smiled, as though he knew but had forgotten. Then he thought that it was foolish to smile; and sternly, left arm rigid, soft mouth set, eyes blank, native shirt jumping, he crossed the yard and went up the steps into the little office-shack.

Below the new photograph of the president, with the hair done in the English style, a middle-aged white woman stood writing at a little counter with her left hand. Her right arm was in plaster, in a sling. She looked up as Bobby entered, then went on writing. In another country this would not have been notice-able; here it was unusual. In the corner of the office, out of the light that came through the door, Bobby saw an African. The African was smiling.

The African was dressed like those labourers they had seen that morning being marshalled into the lorries. But his clothes looked more personal and less like cast-offs. His striped brown jacket was stained in many places and the bloated tips of the wide lapels curled; but the jacket fitted. The pullover, rough with little burrs of dirt, fitted; and the shirt, oily black around the collar, with two or three old tidemarks of sweat, was like a second skin. Seen from the car, the labourers on the road were expressionless and blank, their black faces in shadow below hats pulled down to the crown. But the African in the office carried his round-topped hat in his hand, and his face was exposed. It was a face as plain as the president's in the photograph, showing age alone rather than a quality of experience. Liveliness and emotion lay only in the eyes.

The eyes now smiled, turning from the middle-aged woman writing at the counter to Bobby. When Bobby smiled back the African did not respond. His smile was fixed.

The woman looked up.

"Can we have lunch for three?"

"We start at twelve."

And then, as though not wishing to show too much interest in Bobby while the smiling African looked on, she returned to her writing.

Bobby didn't see Linda and Carter when he came out of the office. He walked down the gravelled path between the cottages and the drooping flowers. Outside each door there was a little pile of split eucalyptus logs, wet from the rain. An old grey-and-black spaniel was worrying one pile, sniffing loudly. From the cottages the hummocked open land, so recently forest, sloped down to what was still woodland. The stream roared there, its course marked by the bare white branches of those trees whose roots it had drowned.

A forest stream, it turned out, with the forest debris of collapsed trees. But from the high bank on which he stood Bobby saw flat stones and boulders below the raging red water: stepping stones: the small thrills, perhaps, of an ordered garden in a gentler season. A little way up there was a remnant of a retaining brick wall. The stream had long ago breached that and now in flood was making another channel through what had once been a garden, swamping the arum lilies that had grown wild. Sunlight, coming through the trees, lit up some of the white lilies and showed them as patches of pure colour against the tangled weeds pulled flat by the flow of water, silent here, and already in places gathered into stagnant pools.

All at once the lilies lost their brightness; it grew dark below the trees; the swamped garden was silent. The stream raged on. On the other bank tree trunks were black in the gloom; leaves and branches hung low. The wood of a fairy-tale, far from home: what was so recently man-made, after the forests had been cut down and the forest-dwellers flushed out and dismissed, what had perhaps been intended only as an effect of art in a landscape made secure, had become natural. It spoke of an absence of men, danger. Bobby thought of the king, hunted from the sky. He looked up.

The rainclouds had massed; the road ahead was untarred for a hundred miles.

He went out of the wood into the open and walked back up the hill. The spaniel was still worrying the pile of split logs and had partly pulled it down. The African with the smile was now outside the office, his hat still in his hand. Bobby acknowledged the African's gaze, turned into the hall and went into the room marked *Lounge*.

It was a long wide room. Small-paned windows with chintz curtains gave clear views of the woodland, the hills beyond with irregular blocks of pine forest, the play of rain-clouds. The furniture looked used but not recently used. The new photograph of the president, the man of the forest with his hair now in the English style, stood between coloured prints of English scenes. There were old magazines: photographs of parties, dances, country houses, furniture: an England, as it were, for export, carefully photographed, with what was offending left out. The English countryside Bobby knew best was a spreading semi-industrial confusion of housing developments like tent-cities, old houses lost on busy main roads, railroad tracks, factory buildings; where what remained of Nature – a brook, it might be, with pollarded willows – looked only like semi-urban wasteland. But the room he was in echoed the photographs in the magazines. The scale was too large, for him, for the injured woman in the tiny office; and perhaps it had always been too large.

Someone shrieked: "Three lunches, was it?"

The shriek, really a hoarse, piercing whisper, came from a middle-aged white man in a state of great ruin. He was bandaged and plastered all the way up one leg and all the way up one arm. He barely supported himself on metal crutches and at every step he seemed about to fall on his face.

"Motor accident," the man hissed, with some pride. "They say lightning never strikes twice. . . ." He shook his head. "You saw my wife?"

"In the office?"

"Got her too." He leaned forward at a steep angle like a

comedian. "Oh yes. But all right now. Just the itching. Funny thing about plaster. You know, when they take it out at the end, they will still find that little bit at the centre wet. You heading south? Work there? Short-contract man?"

Bobby nodded.

"You're the lucky ones. Sending half back to the London bank every month, eh? Salting it away. But bad in the Collectorate now. Going to be a lot of trouble there, I reckon."

"I don't know what you mean by trouble," Bobby said.

The ruined man became guarded. "No trouble up here." He nodded to the photograph of the president. "The witchdoctor's all right. Oh no. No trouble here. Tourism's going to be big business, and the African knows he can't manage it by himself. Say what you like, the African's no fool."

Bobby put the magazine down and began to move away. He didn't hurry; there was no need. The ruined man started after him, but couldn't pursue.

The African was still outside the office. The spaniel sat, old and blank, on the office steps. The woodpile outside the cottage door had been pulled down. Near it Bobby now saw lavender in bloom, an old bush. As he bent down to break off some spikes he saw, among the scattered logs, a lizard's tail, separate, dead. Then he saw Linda and Carter. Linda waved. It was a large gesture; her blue trousers and cream shirt, seen at a distance, against the gravelled path and the unsettled light of the open hillside, were vivid; and again, as at the start of the day, it was as though they had an audience and were all three in a film or play. Bobby turned: it was only the gaze of the African, cleaning his top lip with his tongue.

Linda said, "What have you got, Bobby?"

"Lavender." He passed a spike below her nose. "I love lavender. Is that effeminate of me?"

She laughed. For the first time he saw her poor teeth. "I wouldn't say effeminate, Bobby. I would say old-fashioned."

She was the brightest of the three when they went into the high timbered dining-hall.

THEY SAT AT the edge of the desolate room, next to the high fireplace. There was no fire, but logs had been laid. The boy was nervous and abstracted and kept on adjusting the cutlery on the table. His white shirt was less than fresh; his dusty black bowtie was askew.

Carter said, "You colonialists did pretty well."

"What a lovely word," Linda said. "One so seldom hears it in conversation. You make it sound very big and technical."

"Sitting here, I feel they must have been very big people. Giants in fact. I suppose that's why they haven't lighted the fire for us. We're too small."

Or too ugly, Bobby thought, breaking his roll.

The frightened boy brought in the soup plate by plate, pressing his thumbs on the rims. He walked with a stoop, raising his knees high; his big feet, loosely hinged at the ankles, flapped up and down.

"He almost looks like one of ours," Carter said.

"Carter says there's a four o'clock curfew in the Southern Collectorate, Bobby. The army's rampaging somewhat, apparently."

"That's what African armies are for," Carter said. "They are intended only for civilian use."

"So it looks as though we'll have to spend the night at the colonel's," Linda said. "Or stay here."

"The 'boy' might light the fire for you," Carter said to Bobby.

Something was wrong with Carter's molars, and he ate like a dog, holding his head over his plate and catching the food in his mouth with every chew, at the same time giving a slight hiss, as though every mouthful was too hot.

He finished a mouthful and made conversation. He said, "I can't get used to this word *boy*."

"Doris Marshall tried to call hers a butler," Linda said.

"Isn't that typical!" Bobby said.

"In the end she settled for steward. It always seems to me such an absurd word," Linda said.

Bobby said, "It offended Luke. He said to me afterwards, 'I am not a steward, sir. I am a houseboy.' "

"Who is Doris Marshall?" Carter asked.

"She's a South African," Linda said.

Carter looked puzzled.

"Luke is Bobby's houseboy," Linda said.

"I imagine," Bobby said, looking at Linda, "she thought she was bending over black-wards."

Linda cried, "Bobby!"

"We are on to my favourite subject," Carter said. "Servants."

Bobby said, "It always fascinates our visitors."

Carter ate.

"I can't," he said later, looking round the dining-hall, once more playing the visitor, "I can't get over the Britishness of this place."

"When I was in West Africa," Linda said, "everyone was always saying what rotten colonialists we were and how good the French were. And when you crossed the border it looked true. You saw all those black men just like ours sitting on the roadside and eating French bread and drinking red wine and wearing those funny little French berets."

"So at least," Bobby said, "we might be spared over here."

Carter looked at Bobby and said with direct aggression, "You do pretty well."

It began to rain. The dining-hall grew dark; the roof drummed.

"That stretch of mud," Linda said. "It's the one thing that makes me hysterical, skidding on mud."

"I wonder if it's true about the curfew," Bobby said.

"You don't have to take my word for it," Carter said.

"I don't have to take your word for anything."

Linda appeared not to notice. "Poor little king," she said, going girlish and affected. "Poor little African king."

After this there was nothing like conversation. They finished the bottle of Australian Riesling; and then, to the visible relief of the boy, lunch was over. Bobby seized the bill when the boy brought it. Carter became morose.

"Office," the boy said. "You pay office."

The African was still there, sheltering under the narrow eaves. Rain blurred the edge of the hill, dripped down the tiled roof of the cottages onto the flowers, washed the gravel path. It was almost chilly. Carter was alone in the dining-hall when Bobby went back. They didn't talk; Carter turned and looked out at the rain. Linda, when she came in, was as bright as before.

It was time to leave. Bobby began to fuss.

"I'll stay here for a little," Carter said.

"Will we be seeing you later perhaps?" Bobby asked.

"Let's leave it open," Carter said.

Bobby ran through the rain to the car and drove it up to the hall entrance. Linda got in. She looked at Carter; she seemed concerned now. There was some sort of movement in the shadows behind Carter, and the ruined man appeared, leaning forward, as if with exaggerated interest. As Bobby was driving off, the woman with the arm-sling came out on the office steps. She gestured towards the African with her uninjured hand and shouted through the rain.

Bobby stopped and rolled down the window.

"Can you take him down to the road?"

"Oh Lord," Linda said, leaning over the seat to clear her things away.

THE AFRICAN OPENED the door himself. He filled the car with his smell. Through the rain, the windows misting, they drove off, Linda rigid, Bobby wiping the windscreen with the back of his hand. When Bobby looked at the rear-view mirror he caught the African's smiling eyes.

"You work here?" Bobby asked, in the brisk, friendly, simple voice he used with country Africans.

"In a way."

"What you do? What your work?"

"Anyanist."

"Oh, you mean *trade* unionist. You *organize* the workers, you *bargain* with the employers. You get your members more money, better conditions. That right?"

"Yes, yes. Anyanist. What you do?"

"I work here."

"I don't see you."

"I work in the south. The Southern Collectorate."

"Yes, yes. South." The African laughed.

"I'm a civil servant. A bureaucrat. I have my in-tray and my out-tray. I also have my tea-tray."

"Civil servant. That is good."

"I like it."

They were driving slowly down the rocky slope, the rain washing against the windscreen, almost too fast for the wipers. An African came round the corner at the bottom of the slope, walking up to the Hunting Lodge. He saw the car and stood at the side of the road to wait for it to pass. His hat was pulled down low over his head and the lapels of his jacket were turned up.

"He is getting absolutely soaked," Bobby said, still in his friendly simple voice.

"That is obvious," Linda said.

"You stop," the African in the car said to Bobby.

When Bobby looked in the mirror he met the African's gaze.

"You stop," the African said, looking at the mirror. "You take him."

"But he is not going in our direction," Bobby said.

"You stop. He is my friend."

Bobby stopped beside the African. Rain ran down the sloping brim of the African's hat; nothing could be seen of his face. Still in the rain, he took off his hat; he looked terrified. The African in the back opened the door. The man came in. He said "Sir" to Bobby and sat on the edge of the plastic-covered seat until the first African pulled him back.

The Africans made the car feel crowded. Linda rolled down her window and breathed deeply. Rain spattered her scarf.

The level polo ground was awash and now, with the scattered

clumps of reeds and grass rising out of the water, looked more than ever like a swamp. Rain had darkened the ruined pavilion.

"Is your friend a unionist too?" Bobby asked.

"Yes, yes," the first African said quickly. "Anyanist."

"I hope you don't have too far to go in this weather," Bobby said.

"Not far," the first African said.

Rain splashed the frothing red puddles in the deep wheel-tracks. Sometimes the car slithered. The road began to rise to the high embankment of the highway.

"You turn right," the African said.

"We are going left," Bobby said. "We are going to the Collectorate."

"You turn right."

They were now nearly where the red dirt road turned to sand and rock and widened for the last sharp climb to the highway. The African was still looking at the rear-view mirror.

"Is it far, where you want to go?" Bobby said.

"Not far. You turn right."

"Christ!" Linda said. She leaned back and put her hand to the rear door handle. "Out!"

Bobby stopped. The wet African, behind Linda, at once jumped out. Almost at the same time the African who had been talking opened his door and got out and put on his hat. Immediately he was faceless, his smile and menace of no importance. Bobby moved up to the embankment, leaving them there, standing on either side of the dirt road, hats pulled down to the shape of their heads, soaking in the rain, two roadside Africans.

"What a smell!" Linda said. "Absolute gangsters. I'm not going to get myself killed simply because I'm too nice to be rude to Africans."

Just before he turned into the highway Bobby looked in the mirror: the Africans hadn't moved.

"I've had this too often with Martin," Linda said. "It's these damned oaths they're swearing. They feel that everybody's scared stiff of them as a result."

"But still, it makes me so ashamed. So cocky, and then going just like that. What I can't understand is why he should have hung around for so long up there. You don't have to be from a foundation to find that a little sinister."

"Sinister my foot. It's just stupidity, that's all. Let's open this window. You can smell the filth they've been eating."

The rain slanted in, big drops. Bobby, looking in the mirror, saw the Africans standing on the highway. Black, emblematic: in the mirror they grew smaller and smaller, less and less distinct in the rain and against the tar. They began to walk. They walked off the highway, back into the road that led to the Hunting Lodge. Bobby didn't think Linda had seen. He didn't tell her.

4

"IT'S SO PATHETIC," Linda said.

"I'm sorry. I should have been firmer."

"You feel sorry for them, and you keep on feeling sorry and saying nice things, nice encouraging things, and before you know where you are you have a Sammy Kisenyi on your hands. I'm afraid we shall have to close the window. The Marshalls talk about the smell of Africa – have you heard her?"

"I should have been firmer."

"This very special smell."

"I've never got on with people who talk about things like the smell of Africa," Bobby said. "It's like people who talk about, well, the Masai."

"You may be right. But I used to think I wasn't very sensitive, getting this smell of Africa that the Marshalls and everybody else said they so loved. But I got it this time, when we came back from leave. It lasts about half an hour or so, no more. It is a smell of rotting vegetation and Africans. One is very much like the other."

It was the smell, in a warm shuttered room, that Bobby liked. He said, "Perhaps it is time for you to go South."

"It's so damned pathetic. You remember when the president came to the Collectorate? All those thin and haggard white men, all those fat black men."

"I don't know why you have this thing about them being fat."

"I like to think of my savages as lean. You wouldn't believe it now, but Sammy was as thin as a rake when he came back from England. Martin showed the president round the studios. Sammy, of course, doesn't know a microphone from a door-knob. Do you know the first thing Martin said afterwards? It's so embarrassing to say. Martin said, 'I'll say this for the witch-doctor. He smells like a polecat.' Martin! Well, you know, that sort of thing makes you feel ashamed for everybody, yourself included. But then."

"Oh dear."

"Perhaps the word will get around and they'll deport me. I'd like that."

"Lunch wasn't a good idea."

"Perhaps not."

"Your views seem to have changed a good deal since the morning."

"I don't know whether I have any views really." Linda's voice was going lighter. "That's why it would be nice to be deported. We must tell Busoga-Kesoro."

Bobby didn't like the archness; he didn't like the innuendo. He began to drive fast, too fast for the wet road.

He said, "They say the animal is always sad afterwards."

"How romantic, Bobby."

He decided to say no more.

The rain thinned. The sky lifted. The road shone in a silver light.

AN OBSTRUCTION IN the road ahead defined itself as police jeeps, policemen in capes, and two zebra-striped wooden barriers.

Linda said, "I suppose this is what is known as a roadblock."

Slowing down, preparing a face for the policemen, Bobby began to smile.

"Please don't be too nice, Bobby. So English those policemen, with their black uniforms and their capes and caps. You can tell that the boss is the fat one, with the plain and fancy clothes."

It passingly enraged Bobby that the man Linda spoke about seemed to be in charge. He was young and big-bellied; a dark-brown felt hat sat lightly on his head; below a police-issue cape he wore a flowered sports shirt.

With two uniformed policemen he came down the centre of the road to the car.

Bobby said, "I am a government officer. I'm attached to Mr Ogguna Wanga-Butere's department in the Southern Collectorate."

The plainclothesman said, "Licence."

While he examined Bobby's driving permit his lips and tongue played together, and he held his elbows tight against his sides, giving his paunch a slight lift from time to time.

"My compound pass is on the windscreen," Bobby said.

"Bonnet and keys, please."

Bobby pulled the bonnet-release lever and handed over the keys. The uniformed men searched under the bonnet and in the boot, while the plainclothesman himself patted the upholstery on the doors and felt between the seats. He opened Linda's suitcase and pressed down the flimsy contents with a flat, broad hand.

"So' you been troubled," he said at last.

It was the formula of dismissal. Then hurriedly, when the car was moving off, like a man remembering part of the drill, he smiled and raised his hat. The hair on which the hat sat so lightly was extravagantly of the English style, scraped together in a high springy mound on one side, with a wide, low parting on the other side.

"It's a consolation anyway that he's one of 'ours'," Linda said, as Bobby drove between the zebra-striped barriers. "But I thought they were looking for the king in the capital, didn't you? The story last night was that he'd got away in one of those taxis."

"They were looking for arms. I happen to know that there's a lot of concern high up about people smuggling in arms to the Collectorate. Tourists and so forth. They say there's an absolute arsenal in the king's palace. Weren't they extraordinarily polite, though?" The roadblock, the policemen, the rain on the black capes, the open road, his own security: excitement was in Bobby's voice. "That's Simon Lubero's doing. He's very keen on good relations with the public and so on. Everybody says that Hobbes keeps him up to the mark, but I met him at the conference last year and was most impressed. There was an interview with him in the paper the other day which I found extremely good, I must say."

"In our own 'Two-Minute Silence'. Preparing us all. Simon's very British."

"That's not bad. With him."

" 'So' you been troubled,' " Linda mimicked. "I feel there must be a curfew, don't you? I know we are white and neutral, but I'm beginning to wonder whether we shouldn't be 'racing' in the other direction. We don't seem to have too much company."

He was in fact racing, half acting out, after the peculiar excitement of the roadblock, a make-believe of danger and escape on the empty African road, lined now on one side with the tall, bare, candelabra-like branches of sisal: the rain almost gone, the clouds high, the light shifting, the rolling land streaked with luminous green, bright colour going on and off on the distant mountains.

He looked at the petrol gauge and said, "We'll stop at Esher and fill up with petrol."

"At the time of the Asian boycott everybody in the compound always kept their tanks full, ready to dash off at any moment of day or night to the border."

"My dear," Bobby said. "Such excitement. Daily mentions

on the BBC, signing on for the airlift at the High Commission, laying in tins."

"I laid in my tins."

Linda was showing the effect of the lunch and the Riesling and the drive. Her face was white and strained, dark below the eyes, and the tan on her prominent temples looked like stains, yellow below brown.

She said, abruptly, "I love this dramatic light, don't you? And the sisal. It all looks so empty until you start seeing those little brown huts. You feel that nothing has ever happened here." Her voice was going mystical; she was listening to herself speak; Bobby could tell now. "No one will ever know what has happened here."

He said, "Some of us know what happened here."

"Twenty or thirty people were killed during the Asian boycott. And it wasn't only those Danish dairy experts who were made to double up and down in the sun. I wonder if these things that don't get into the papers or on the radio are reported in some special place, in some little black book. Or big black book."

Bobby thought: she is not concerned; she is concerned about other things; she is only trying, for no reason, to undermine me, and to transfer her mood to me. Thinking this, he found that his own excitement had gone, that he was waiting to be irritated by her.

"You weren't here for the earthquake," Linda said. "I'd just come. The houseboy came to me in the morning with tears in his eyes and said that his family lived in one of the villages that had been destroyed. I took him to the police station, to see whether they had a list of casualties. They didn't, and everybody was very rude. I tried every day for a week. There was no list, and even the houseboy stopped worrying. Nothing in the 'Two-Minute Silence'. Nothing on the radio. Everybody had just forgotten about it. Was there an earthquake? Did it matter? Perhaps all those people hadn't died, and it didn't matter if they had. Perhaps the houseboy was just trying to make himself interesting. Perhaps nothing that happens here is more interesting than any other thing that happens. Perhaps in a place like this there isn't any news. Sammy Kisenyi can put out the Lord's Prayer every day and call it the news."

Bobby thought he detected one of Martin's bitter *mots*. But he only said, "If you put it like that, perhaps there isn't news anywhere."

"I don't want to argue. I believe you know what I mean."

"We'll stop at Esher for petrol."

She said, in half-apology, "I have a slight head."

She took her bag from the floor and put it on her knees, looked at her face in her hand mirror and said, "Good Lord." Briskly, as though banishing the mood, she made up her face; without weariness, she rearranged her hair and retied her scarf, her arms still young, the short sleeves of her shirt opening to show the mole in her shaved armpit. Then she put on her dark glasses, sat back in her seat and looked quite composed.

Bobby was hating her.

ESH, THE MILESTONES HAD been promising every two miles, ESH. And now at last the board – of English design: it might have been imported from England – said ESHER. But there was still only wilderness.

Then old pine trees grew behind wire fences; tractor-marked dirt tracks met the highway in flurries of melting mud. And it was wilderness again. The hills rose in humps on one side; the highway twisted. A washed-out board gave insufficient warning of a level-crossing; the car was jolted. Tall eucalyptus trees made an open, dripping grove, tattered bark on straight trunks; and, against the great mountains in the distance, the rising hills showed a mixture of fenced pastures, hummocked open land, eucalyptus windbreaks, old forest patches: an unfinished landscape, a scratching in the continent.

The verges widened; a few tarnished villas were set in large gardens. There was a roundabout, its garden still maintained, and the highway entered the town. Cross-streets, each with a new black-and-white board bearing the name of a minister in the capital, could be seen to end in mud after two or three hundred yards. The town had been built to grow. It hadn't grown. It remained a collection of old tin-and-timber buildings, its pioneer flimsiness pointed by the small new bank building, the motor car and tractor showroom. The mud-splashed police barracks, low white concrete sheds flat to the ground, already looked like the hutments of the African quarter in the capital.

The filling station Bobby turned into belonged to an oil company that had come to the country after independence. A tall yellow-and-black board announced the amenities in bold international symbols. But one of the symbols, the telephone, had been partly covered over with a square of brown paper; and another symbol, the crossed knife and fork, had been crossed out, apparently by a finger dipped in engine oil. Along the lower edge of the yellow board, as on the white walls of the office, were the marks of oily fingers and sometimes whole hands that had tried to wipe or roll themselves clean. The covered part of the asphalted yard was black with oil; the exposed part, still wet after the rain, was iridescent.

Four Africans in old blue dungarees that looked like cast-offs watched the car come in. When Bobby stopped outside the covered area and sounded his horn, all four Africans started; but then, looking at one another, all four hesitated. One of the Africans was very small; his dungarees drooped low at the crotch and were thick with turn-ups at the ankles.

"I'll go and risk the Ladies'," Linda said.

She walked with fussy little steps, keeping her head down. Her trousers were baggy below the knee and there was a long blot of perspiration on her shirt between the shoulder blades.

The small African and another African came to the car, the small African kicking out at every step, fighting the encumbrance of his dungarees. The small African carried a bucket, a sponge and a metal-handled cleaner. Silently he began to clean the car windows.

Linda came back. "The place is locked."

The big African dipped into his pocket and held out a greasy Yale key between a greasy thumb and forefinger. Linda took the key without comment and walked away briskly again.

Oil, petrol, water, battery, tyres: Bobby anxiously superintended and encouraged the big African. He used his simple friendly voice and he laughed a lot. The African was too preoccupied to respond. When Linda came back, Bobby went silent. Self-possessed, hard to read behind her dark glasses, she stood at the edge of the asphalted yard, looking across the road to the hills and the mountains.

At last Bobby paid, and he and Linda got back in the car. While they waited for change they were aware of the small African, the cleaner, darkening one window, then another. Linda's forehead began to twitch; she sighed. The big African came with the change. If she sighs again like that, Bobby thought, I'll give her a piece of my mind. The African counted out the change coin by coin into Bobby's hand. It was too much; it was more than Bobby had given.

"It's pathetic," Linda whispered.

The small African moved from Linda's window to Linda's side of the windscreen. He pulled back the wiper in an alarming way and began to clean, his face level with Linda's and just a few inches away. He frowned, doing his work, making a point of not looking at her.

She looked down at her lap and whispered, "It's pathetic."

If she uses that word again, Bobby thought, I'll hit her. He was counting back the excess change into the patient cupped palm of the big African, and he was deliberately counting in his friendly simple voice. He paid out the last coin, which included a tip, and smiled at the African. The big African went away, and the small African came round with his bucket to Bobby's side of the windscreen.

Linda said, "Look what this one's been doing."

Bobby looked at Linda's side of the windscreen. Then he looked at the small African. The African was using a double-edged cleaner, one edge made of rubber, one edge made of sponge; but both sponge and rubber had perished, and he was rubbing the central bar of metal on the windscreen. He had left a complicated trail of deep scratches on the windows all around the car. Scratching away now, not looking at Bobby, he frowned, to show his intentness.

Bobby saw the fineness of the African's features, the special, dead blackness of the skin, and recognized him as a man of the king's tribe. Bobby was at once deeply angry. The African, aware of Bobby's scrutiny, frowned harder.

"What on earth do you think you're doing?"

Bobby pushed the door open so violently that the African was hit and thrown off balance.

The African recovered and scrambled away from the car. He said, "What?" and opened his mouth to say more. But then he just looked at Bobby with shocked, liquid eyes, the disintegrating large sponge in his left hand, the metal-handled cleaner still in his right.

"Look at what you've done," Bobby shouted. "You've ruined my windscreen. You've ruined all my windows. You've knocked several hundred shillings off the resale value. Who's going to give me that? You?"

"Insurance," the African said. And again he seemed about to say something else; but the words didn't come.

"Oh yes, you are very clever. Like all your people. You always know. Insurance? I want it back from you."

Bobby took a step towards the African. The African stepped back, awkward in his dungarees.

The three other Africans stood still, in their dingy blue dungarees, one next to the door of the office, against the white wall, one in front of the yellow board, one beside the petrol pump.

"I'm going to have you sacked," Bobby said. "Sent back to your people. Who's the manager here?"

The African standing against the white office wall raised his hand. He was the man with whom Bobby had dealt, the man who had given the change. He hesitated, then he came towards

Bobby. He stood a few feet away, held his hands behind his back and said, "Manager."

Company policy, clearly; but Bobby doubted whether this manager had it in his power to recruit and sack.

"I'll be dropping a note to your head office," Bobby said. He took out an envelope and ballpoint pen from the pocket of his native shirt. "Who's your superior? Who your boss-man?"

"Dis' sup'indant. Ind-ian."

"The old Asian trick of remote control. He come here today, your district superintendent?"

"Today no. Home. He live there." The manager waved towards that part of the town Bobby had just driven through.

"Oh yes, they're all hiding today. Give me his address. Boss-man, where he live?" And while he scribbled on the envelope, with such impatience that he almost immediately stopped writing words and then, deliberately, was just making marks, he said, "These people shouldn't be employed. They and their king have had it all their own way for too long. But their little games are over now. Look at my windscreen."

The manager looked, leaning to one side to show that he looked.

The small African had begun to relax within his dungarees. He was looking down penitentially at the oily yard, still holding his sponge and cleaner, his little mouth set.

Bobby resented this inattention. He said, "This is something for the police."

The African looked up, his eyes wide with terror. Again he opened his mouth to talk but said nothing. Then, making a gesture as if he was ready to throw aside the tools of his trade, the sponge and the metal-handled cleaner, he turned and began to walk, kicking out in his dungarees, to the edge of the yard.

"I'm a government officer!" Bobby shouted.

The African halted and turned. "Sir."

"How dare you turn your back on me while I'm addressing you?"

Native shirt swinging, crooking his right arm, pulling back his open palm, Bobby advanced on the small African.

The African was making no effort to dodge the blow. There was only expectation in his glittering eyes.

The other three Africans stood where they were, one in front of the yellow board, one next to the pump, the manager near the car.

"Bobby," Linda said, through the half-open car door. Her voice was neutral, without reproof; she spoke his name as though she had known him a long time.

"How dare you turn your back on me?"

"Bobby." She had opened the car door and was preparing to get out.

All four Africans stood just where they were as, yellow native shirt dancing, Bobby bustled back to the car. And they remained where they were while Bobby started the car and drove down to the edge of the yard. There he stopped.

"That damned address," Bobby said. "Where did I put it?" He acted out an angry search for the envelope on which he had written nothing.

"I think we can forget that," Linda said.

"Oh no."

"Drop a note to head office, as you said. I don't think we should go chasing any address that man has given."

He still searched.

Very quickly, then, with a revving of the engine, a burst of blue smoke and a squeal of tyres, he turned left, heading out of the town, giving up the district superintendent.

The four Africans stood where they were.

"The humiliation," he said, restless in his seat.

Linda said nothing.

The town was quickly past: three or four big concrete sheds and a foundry among the empty overgrown lots of an "industrial estate", a stretch of bumpy dual-carriageway, washed-out hoardings with their close-to-Caucasian pictures of laughing Africans.

the highway again, and then on a hillside rows and rows of unpainted wooden huts, relics of a failed colonial plantation.

"The humiliation."

Rainclouds darkened the far hills to the right, and the mountains in the distance were hidden. But to the left, where the land was open, the sky was still high, and when the sun struck through the clouds the wet road glistened and the fenced pastureland was the freshest green.

Suddenly Bobby braked, but with care, without skidding, and pulled in at the side of the road. The road was empty; the manœuvre was safe. The left wheels sank in soft grass and mud; but he had kept the right wheels on the tar. He bent over the steering-wheel and knocked his forehead lightly against it. Raising his head, resting his right elbow on the wheel, he jammed his palm against his mouth, held his forehead and looked down, and jammed his palm against his mouth again.

"Oh, my God," he said. "How awful."

Clouds raced in the sky. The fields darkened and lit up. Now it was like dusk; now it was afternoon.

"Awful," he said, hitting his mouth with the heel of his palm. "Awful."

He held the wheel with both hands and leaned right over it, the sleeves of the native shirt riding down his arms, pink from the day's exposure.

Linda said nothing. She didn't turn to look. Her dark glasses gave nothing away.

Bobby looked up. "I know the king's people," he said. "He probably is a Christian. He goes to church every Sunday. He keeps his clothes very clean. He washes and irons his own two shirts very carefully. His wife does a little teaching in the school in their village in the Collectorate. He reads. He had that foolish little paperback in the back pocket of those dungarees." Bobby was thinking of his own houseboy, who was also small and fine-featured and of the king's tribe: a churchgoer and a reader of devout or educational primers in the second, moneyless half of the month, a drinker in the first half, often tortured by hangovers, light and silent then, with an additional quality of delicacy. Bobby said softly, "God." Then, leaning again on the steering-wheel, he made himself think of the bar of the New Shropshire. "God. God." He looked up. "God." But now his voice had changed. "God, how beautiful." He was speaking of the play of sunlight in the green field.

At last Linda responded. She turned to look at the field.

Bobby said, "And now I've destroyed his pathetic little dignity."

"I don't think so," Linda said. She saw the tears in Bobby's eyes, and her manner altered. "I don't think he even knew what it was all about. And anyway they needed a ticking off. It certainly hasn't done them any harm. You should have seen that lavatory. You know, I believe I still have that key."

"Perhaps I should go back."

"Whatever for? That would really frighten them. They might even send for the police."

"I'll probably burst into tears." His eyes, already clearing up had just brimmed over. He smiled.

"I doubt it. I think it might get you angry all over again if you went back and found them laughing all over the place."

"I'll go back."

"I've been through this so often with my houseboys. You lose a dozen tins of powdered milk, and you tick them off. There is the most terrible scene, and you start walking about your own house on tiptoe. You expect suicide at least, but in the quarters they are having a high old time. They've called in all their friends and they are killing themselves with laughter."

"We misinterpret their laughter," Bobby said, his hand playing with the gear lever.

"That may well be. It's embarrassment or disapproval or something like that. Sammy Kisenyi was telling me. And some European probably told him. But I feel that some of it is good old-fashioned laughter."

Bobby turned on the ignition.

Linda gave a yelp, lifted up her shirt, twisted violently in her seat towards the door.

"I've been stung! See what it is. I can't bear to look."

Remaining twisted on her left hip, keeping her shirt lifted, she gazed up at the roof through her dark glasses, while Bobby looked. Just below her ribs he saw the red rising bump.

"What is it?" Linda called. "What is it?"

"I can see where it bit you. But I can't see it."

"Oh my God."

She remained rigid and Bobby studied the body which now, like a child, she displayed: the thin yellow folds of the moist skin, the fragile ribs, the brassiere, put on for the day's adventure, enclosing those poor little breasts, and below the waistband of her blue trousers the undergarments that looked as strapped and surgical as the brassiere.

He bent over and kissed the red bump. Linda dropped her eyes from the roof of the car to the top of Bobby's head. She was careful now to hold her shirt up to keep it from covering Bobby's head; and she was also careful to stay still, not to disturb him.

He kissed the bump again and asked, "Is it better now?"

"It is better."

He took his head away. She straightened up and dropped her shirt.

"I hope you don't misinterpret my intention," Bobby said.

"Oh, Bobby, that was one of the nicest things that's ever happened to me."

"Oh dear," he said, starting the car. "You make it sound like childbirth."

"Women can believe anything."

She spoke sharply. But it was what he was expecting. It gave the mood a balance; and it was as friends, personalities established, personalities accepted, that they started again on the road.

It became very dark. The black, over-charged clouds were low; the last streak of light on the green field faded. And the rain did come, hard, drowning the sound of the engine, spattering white on the tar. There was no longer a view; there was only rain. It was cosy in the car.

"THESE SCRATCHES," BOBBY said. "I suppose I'll get used to them. I was bitten by my mother's dog once. You can imagine the upset. For me, for my mother, and the poor dog. It was a pretty bad bite. It came out, curiously enough, as two perfectly parallel lines. Just below my calf. The dog is dead now. I still have the marks and, you know, I am rather pleased to have them."

A little later he said, "A doctor gave me some tranquillizers once. This was some years ago. I had a recrudescence of my old trouble and I thought I was going to get my breakdown all over again. I don't suppose you ever lose the fear, really."

"Tranquillizers. Oh dear. Don't tell me you're on those."

"Listen. He gave me the tranquillizers. Harmless-looking little white tablets. They had a very strange effect. After three days – do you really want me to tell you?" He smiled.

"Do."

"After three days they burnt the skin off the tip of my penis."

Linda didn't hesitate. "How awful for you."

"Absolutely scorched." He was still smiling.

THE RAIN CONTINUED.

"It's strange," Bobby said. "I never learned to drive until I came out here. But during my illness I always consoled myself with the fantasy of driving through a cold and rainy night, driving endless miles, until I came to a cottage right at the top of a hill. There would be a fire there, and it would be warm and I would be perfectly safe."

"Rain outside, fire inside. That's always romantic."

"No doubt. Very romantic. But it gave me much comfort." There was a hint of reproof in his voice. "And then there was this room I saw myself in. Everything absolutely white. White

6

curtains, blowing in with the breeze. White walls, white bed. Lots of tall windows, all open. Outside, the greenest of hills and, at the bottom, a very blue sea."

"It sounds like a hospital on some Greek island."

"I suppose it was just that. A wish to give up, to be nothing, to do nothing. Just watching yourself become a ghost. I used to spend hours every day in that room. And every night. I didn't have a bedside table. I used to put my watch on the floor. One morning I stepped on it and broke the glass. I was going to have it mended, but then I changed my mind and decided not to mend it until I got better."

"Now that is macabre."

"Walking around with a smashed watch. It's just the sort of sick thing you can do. But the most terrifying thing is how quickly you can adapt to having your whole life written off. At first I used to say, 'I'm going to get better next week.' Then it was next month. Then it was next year."

"Isn't there some kind of shock treatment?"

"Like the tranquillizers. I didn't know anything about anything. I thought psychiatry was an American joke and a psychiatrist was someone like Ingrid Bergman in *Spellbound*."

"It dates us. Wasn't that a gorgeous film?"

"Wasn't it. In a way, you are right about the shock, though. That was how I started to get better. This psychiatrist I used to go to, the one who cured his rheumatism by telling himself he was only frightened of dying, he said to me after one session, 'My wife will give you a lift into town.' I had never met his wife. I sat in the drawing-room and waited for her. He was that sort of psychiatrist. No surgery, just his house. Perhaps I should have waited somewhere else. I heard this woman talking to some other people. Then I heard her say in her bright voice, 'But I can take you in. I've got to take in one of Arthur's young queers.' She didn't know I was right there. I thought everything I'd told the man was confidential. I don't believe I've ever hated anybody so much in my life. I really wanted them both to die. It was unfair really, because he'd done a good job with me. I suppose without knowing it I was getting better. But this shock, as you say, give me the jolt I needed."

Linda looked through the scratched glass at the rain.

" 'One of Arthur's young queers.' " Bobby smiled.

Linda said nothing.

Bobby knew he had embarrassed and moved her. He said, with a touch of aggression, "I don't believe I've said anything to surprise you?"

"You do terrible things," he said after a while, the smile gone, his voice altered. "You do terrible things to prove to yourself that you are a real person. I don't believe I ever felt so exploited."

"The public attitude has changed a lot."

"I wonder why. I hate English queers. They are awful and obscene. And then, of course, I was arrested. On a Saturday night, in the usual place. The policeman was niceness itself. He tried to 'reform' me. It was funny. He tried to fill my mind with images of desire. It was like an incitement to rape. I thought at one stage he was going to pull out his wallet and show me pornographic pictures. But he did the usual things. He took my handkerchief off me, very carefully. My handkerchief! I could have died with shame. It was a very dirty handkerchief. My case came up early on the Monday morning. After the tarts. Guilty, guilty; ten pounds, ten pounds. I told the magistrate I acted 'in the heat of the moment'. This caused a little titter and as soon as I'd said it I knew I couldn't have said anything more foolish or damning. But I was discharged very quickly and was able to catch the fast train to Oxford. Oh yes, after my wild London weekend I was back in time for lunch in hall. But I thought Denis Marshall told you. I 'broke down' and 'confessed' to him some time ago. It always gets me into trouble, but I always break down and confess in the end. It's the effeminate side of my nature. What is it Doris Marshall says they do with people like me in South Africa? They shave our heads, classify us as natives, put us in dresses and send us to live in the native quarter?"

Linda continued to stare at the rain.

"I'm sorry. I've been blabbing as usual, and I believe I've depressed you."

"I was thinking about the road," Linda said. "Even if the mud isn't too bad, I can't see us getting to the compound before eight or nine. I think we should make up our minds pretty quickly whether or not to detour to the colonel's. I was beginning to feel there's something in the settler maxim about aiming to get where you're going by four. It is now half-past two."

"I haven't heard of anyone starving on the road to the Collectorate."

"We should make up our mind pretty soon. The turning's going to be on us any minute."

"No need to ask what your wishes in the matter are."

"I always think the old colonel's fun," Linda said. "And I would love to see the lake in bad weather."

"I'm glad at any rate that I haven't depressed you. It is nice, isn't it?" he said, speaking now of the landscape. "Even in the rain, as you say."

"Driving 'through the night' to your little house on the hill."

"Oh dear. I see that's been taken down in evidence against me. I can't say I'm sorry Denis Marshall's contract isn't going to be renewed. But I don't believe I'll get anyone to believe that it had nothing to do with me."

"I don't think it matters, Bobby."

"Busoga-Kesoro brought me the papers. What could I say? We talk so much about corruption among the Africans. And who are my loyalties to, anyway?"

"Doris Marshall can be very amusing. But no one pays too much attention to what she says."

"It makes me laugh. All the time some people are here they run down the country and criticize the people. As soon as they have to go it's another story."

"I suppose that's true of me."

"I didn't mean it like that. I'm sorry that you are going."

"Why should you be sorry?"

He couldn't say he was sorry because they were in the car together and because he had confessed to her and because she would now always have some idea of him as he truly was.

He said, "I'm sorry because it hasn't worked out for you."

"It's different for you, Bobby."

"You keep saying that."

"Look. I do believe they've closed the road."

AT THE ROAD junction, on the road itself, and in the fields about the road, uniformed policemen stood black in the rain with rifles below their capes. Just beyond the junction dark-blue police jeeps blocked the highway to the Collectorate. A red lantern hung from a white wooden barrier; and a black arrow on a long white board pointed down the side road that ran flat to the mountains.

The road to the mountains was clear. No policeman waved Bobby down. But Bobby stopped. Fifty feet or so behind the barrier and the jeeps two heavy planks were laid across the highway: the rain-surf danced about two rows of six-inch metal spikes. A hundred yards or so beyond that, just before the highway curved and was hidden by low bush, there were about half a dozen army lorries with regimental emblems on their tailboards.

Bobby prepared a smile and began to roll down his window. The window-frame dripped, the rain blew in. None of the policemen moved; no one came out of the jeeps. Then a man sitting in the back of a jeep, a fat man, quite young, leaned forward, a chocolate-and-yellow flowered shirt below his cape, and impatiently waved Bobby on; he appeared to be eating.

"Thank God for that," Linda said. "I was dreading another search."

"They're very good that way," Bobby said. "They have a pretty shrewd idea who we are."

"At least they've made up our minds for us," Linda said. "Now it will have to be the colonel's. I feel that Simon Lubero's writ ends right here, don't you? The army seems very much in control. I hope we don't run into any of their lorries. They're absolute fiends."

"I always show the army respect."

"Martin says that whenever you see an army lorry you must park off the road until it passes. They run you down for fun."

"I wish they could have kept it a police operation," Bobby said. "I'm sure it is what Simon himself would have preferred."

5

FOR SOME MILES the road to the mountains was asphalted and as wide and safe as the highway they had just left. But this road wasn't built on an embankment; it followed the level of the land which here, near the mountains, had flattened out into the gentlest slope, smooth and bare, without trees. In the openness fenceposts stood out, and the rain-washed road could be seen for some way ahead, empty, skimming the tilted land. The mountains were faint in the rain, but they no longer simply bounded the view; they led the eye upwards.

Fields, fences; a dirt cross-road with a washed-out signpost; a scattered settlement with concrete and timber the colour of wet adobe; trees and bush. The road began to twist and climb. It narrowed. And then there was no more asphalt, only a rough rock surface.

Climbing, they had glimpses of the high plain they had just left; and even through the rain there were suggestions of the land dropping away beyond that. But then, as they went deeper into the mountains, all they saw was the bush on both sides of the road. Curves were sharp around cuttings, wet rock shining below shredded overhangs of roots and earth. There were little, melting landslides in the shallow overgrown ditch and sometimes on the road.

"Really it's hard to know what one would choose," Bobby said. "A hundred miles of mud on the highway. Or this."

Soon they were well into the mountains. Every now and

then they saw peaks and further peaks rising above the rain and the mist; so that after only half an hour of climbing it seemed they were on the roof of the world, at the heart of the continent. The sunlight and the scrub, the straight black road, the hiss of the tyres, the play of light on brilliant green fields: that belonged to another country. The car bumped along the rocks; sometimes for stretches the road was strewn with cinders, which made a squelchy sound; the car was noisy, rattling, low gears always above the din of the rain. Not talking, listening for other motor vehicles, half expecting to see army lorries around every blind corner, Bobby and Linda concentrated on the shut-in road.

Occasionally now they saw huts beside the road and wild lilies in small rain-splashed ponds. Sometimes the land fell away on one side and the black trunks of roadside trees and the wet black lower boughs, leaves dripping, framed a view of a grey-green valley: inset terraced hills, red paths going up each hill to a little stockaded grass hut, paths winding away to other, hidden valleys.

"This was what I meant," Linda said. "I never expected there would be fields here or that they would terrace up all those hills, right to the very top. I never thought of those tracks, and never thought it would look so old and settled."

"It was the land we left them," Bobby said.

She leaned back in her seat and took off her dark glasses, and Bobby saw that he had said the wrong thing, had struck the wrong note.

"It's absurd to think of now," he said soon after, in another voice. "I knew nothing at all about Africa when I came here. I was surprised to find them working iron. Somehow no one had thought of telling me that. I was really surprised. But you know that if you leave any old piece of metal lying about – "

"And not so old. Overnight your car can disappear, with only the seats left to mark the spot. They'll pick a Boeing clean in a week."

Bobby knew the joke, but he laughed. "I suppose I vaguely felt when I came here that they would be hostile because I was white and English and because of South Africa and things like that."

"They don't care about South Africa."

"That's just it. This extreme sophistication. They laugh."

"Sammy Kisenyi was telling me that's because they're very angry."

"Sammy exaggerates, like the politicians. Sammy likes to do the racial thing from time to time. He's really just testing you. That can be a bit of a bore. I can't bear that sort of socialistic, third-world pose, can you? It's something he picked up in England. It's not typical. They say Sammy had a rough time in England."

"It's certainly left him with a thing about the white woman. The blind, the lame, the halt, no one's safe."

"That's rather pathetic. I wonder how many Sammys we are creating."

"Pathetic, it's frightening. Sammy believes he's irresistible because he's black and fat. He feels he learned how to 'handle' English people in England. Seriously. He's badly mixed up."

"Sammy's an exception. I suppose what I like about ordinary Africans is that with them there's none of this testing. They take you just as you are. Doris Marshall is right. I have a lot to be grateful to Denis for. He made me come over here. The things you do when you're young. Writing the LCC exam because everybody else was writing it, applying to Hedley's because everybody else was applying. I suppose it's a kind of hysteria. There are so many things you can do perfectly adequately. So many things that you know are not enough, but would do. You look steady, when in fact you're just drifting. I wasn't much of a fighter. After Oxford I was just content to be well again. It never occurred to me that I might want to use myself fully as a human being. It isn't easy to explain, I know, and everything one says can be twisted here. There are too many people around who know how to make the correct noises."

"You make it so difficult, Bobby."

"In what way?"

"People take jobs for all sorts of reasons. I wonder if people talk about the place they live in as much as they do about Africa."

"Oxford. People talked about nothing else except being up at Oxford."

"I suppose we did try too hard to make the correct noises. We should have known from the first day that the country wasn't for us, and we should have taken our courage in both hands and gone back home."

"But you've been here six years."

"As Martin says, the only lies for which we are truly punished are those we tell ourselves."

"And you're really going South?"

"It's only an idea. In four years Martin will be fifty. I suppose we could go back to England and Martin could go freelance. He is a hack who thinks he is, as Martin says. But you can't really make a fresh start at forty-six. And Martin isn't really the freelance type. He isn't much of a fighter either."

The car bumped and bumped. The trees dripped. Through black overhanging leaves they had a glimpse beyond far peaks of a small mountain lake, grey, like the sky. A roadside jacaranda had freshly shed its purple flowers, a brushing of delicate colour on the rock and mud of the road: they went over it.

"My life is here."

"Bobby!"

On a path on the wooded hillside just above the road about a dozen Africans in bright new cotton gowns were walking one behind the other in the rain, covering their heads with leaves. With the bright colours of their cottons, and the leaves over their heads, they were very nearly camouflaged. They didn't look at the car.

"That's the sort of thing that makes me feel far from home," Linda said. "I feel that sort of forest life has been going on forever."

6*

"You've been reading too much Conrad. I hate that book, don't you?"

"You mean they're probably just going to a wedding or an annual general meeting."

"Now you sound like Doris Marshall."

"All right."

"I loved Denis. I can never stop being grateful to him for what he did for me. My meeting with him at that college Gaudy changed my life. I began to feel I wanted to use myself again. He got me my job here, and I suppose he showed me how to look at the country. But he wanted me to keep on being help-less. He wanted to remain my go-between. He kept on saying that I didn't understand Africans and he would handle them for me. He didn't like it when I started to find my own feet and get around. Such a naive man, really. He wanted me to remain his property. He went insane when he discovered I didn't object to physical contact with Africans."

"You were neither of you discreet."

"He talked so much of service to Africa. I can't tell you how shattered I was. And then he started this campaign against me. I thought I was finished. But that was when I truly got to admire Ogguna Wanga-Butere and Busoga-Kesoro. They understood what Denis was up to."

"I don't want to hear any more."

"They are all like that."

All at once Bobby's excitement died down. He felt he had destroyed the mood of confession and friendship and had lost Linda. He had spoken too much; in the morning he would be full of regret; Linda would be another of those people from whom he would have to hide. He set his face, the silent man.

They passed more Africans on the hillside. Linda didn't exclaim or point them out. Bobby began to search for words that would restore the old mood. Half an hour ago he had so many things to say; now nothing new suggested itself. Feeling Linda sitting in reproach beside him, he wished only to go over what he had said, to recapture those passages where he had held her.

"I suppose," he said, "this is the sort of drive I used to dream of. The mountains, the rain, the forest. To me it is like Bergman country."

Yellow mounds of fresh earth began to appear at the road-side and sometimes on the road itself. Heavy vehicles had passed some time before, and their tyres had squashed the earth and spread it over the road; yellow rivulets ran everywhere. Below them there was a valley, grey-green and blurred in the rain. Within the valley there were many conical little hills, each terraced, each with its grass hut behind a grass stockade; and to the huts and along the bottom of the valley faint brown paths ran, like the paths in a fairytale.

"I used to drive day after day along this road and spend hours in that white room – "

"Bobby!"

THEY WERE SKIDDING, slithering first to the left, the back of the car slapping a mound of earth, the wall of the hillside coming at them, then to the right, the valley clear below them, and it was only the knowledge that the mounds of earth would prevent them going over the precipice that saved Bobby from panic. Then motion became absurd and arbitrary; the car suddenly felt fragile; at every swing it seemed about to overturn. And when at last the car came to rest, they were at a slight tilt in the ditch beside the hillside wall, facing the way they had come, deep in roadside bush, black twigs and wet leaves sticking to the left-hand win-dows. The engine had cut out; they were aware of the rain on leaves and the car.

Bobby restarted the car and put it in gear. The car bucked and they heard the whine of wheels spinning in mud. He tried again. This time the car didn't buck; they only heard the whine.

Bobby opened his door. Rain and leaves and wind racketed. Stooping, he climbed out onto the road. His yellow native shirt, at first dancing with his brisk movements, quickly became limp and dark with rain.

"There's no damage I can see," he said to Linda. "I think it just needs a little push. You take over."

"I can't drive."

"Someone will have to push."

"Can't we wait until some of those Africans we saw turn up?"

"That was miles ago. We'll be well and truly stuck by the time they get here.'

Linda came out through Bobby's door and stood in the gutter behind the spinning wheels. She pushed and then, on Bobby's instructions, she tried to rock the car; and then she simply beat her palms on it. Bobby decided to use the reverse gear. Linda pushed from the front. The reverse gear worked. The car was freed, and Bobby got it back on the road.

Some time later, while Bobby was working the car round to face the way they were going, with Linda moving from one side of the road to another to guide, muddy up to her knees, her shirt wet, her brassiere showing, her hair damp, her hands sticky with mud, some time later the exhaust rammed into a mound of earth and the car stalled. They both then abandoned the car to look for a length of stick to clear the exhaust: the empty car blocking the narrow road at an irrational angle, its occupants soaking and frenzied in separate parts of the bush, Bobby anxious again about army lorries, Linda in the end hysterical, tearing at bush at random and offering Bobby little twigs and sprays, like someone offering herbs.

When they were together again in the righted car they didn't talk. The view was as spectacular as before but they ignored it. The car felt wet and damp; there was mud on the plastic seats and the rubber mats, mud on the floors and dashboard.

"I don't know what idiot dumped this stuff right on the road," Bobby said.

Linda said nothing.

For miles, it seemed, the mounds of earth continued; and whenever they went over the squashed yellow spread they waited for the car to slip. Without comment they crushed purple jacaranda flowers into the mud. Then there were no more mounds of earth;

and then, too, the rain stopped. The sky lightened, became almost silver to the west; and they saw, after the dusk of forest and rain, that it was still only afternoon.

In the valleys there was that stillness that came after prolonged rain. The paths were empty; the depleted clouds, less dark, higher now, didn't move; plants and trees were still. The grey sky was settled: the sun wasn't going to come out again that day. Then, as they drove, they began to see people on the paths, people within the stockades. Smoke rose up straight from some huts.

Always the road followed the contour of a hill; always they had hill and woods on one side. For some time now, in those woods, on paths that had been stamped or beaten into brown-black ledges, they had been seeing Africans on the move, in bright new clothes. The Africans had never been easy to see, with their black skins and multi-coloured cottons. And now Bobby and Linda saw that the hillside along which they had been driving was alive with Africans. Wherever they looked they saw more. On a wide ledge cut into the hill was a low thatched shelter. With its rough leaf-thatch and black poles, trimmed tree-branches, it had at first looked just like part of the woods; but it was packed with seated Africans, all in new clothes. On zigzag paths above and below the shelter many more Africans were standing.

"It's not a wedding," Linda said. "It's those oaths of hate again."

"They're not the president's tribe."

"They're close enough. Somewhere up there they've taken off their nice new clothes and they're dancing naked and holding hands and eating dung. The president probably sent them a nice piece of dung. You could disappear here without trace. You know what happened on the other side, don't you? The rivers ran red. But that again is something that never happened."

"They were serfs over there," Bobby said, his own temper building up. "They were oppressed for centuries."

"It's so damned absurd," Linda said.

He concentrated on the road.

"Not absurd for them. Absurd for me. Being here."

They had been moving towards the crest of a ridge; the sky felt more open. They came out of the forest on to the bare ridge, and the valley on the other side opened spectacularly: a miniature country laid out below them, every corner filled with the same details of terraced hill and thatched hut, the smoke of cooking-fires, the wet winding paths: a view ending in miniatures of itself, dissolving in mist. The view called for exclamation.

But Linda only said, "Bergman."

Bobby set his face.

They began to go down; they lost the view. On this side of the ridge the vegetation was different, more grassy. Some hillsides were feathery with a fine bamboo. They had a glimpse of the lake they were making for, leaden in the dim light. Then, still going down, they entered woods again and were again in gloom. The road twisted; the ride seemed rougher downhill. There were no signs of men until a cluster of huts and then a villa in a clearing grown wild again announced the nearness of the lake town. By now, in the car, they had exhausted silence and irritation. They had dried out; the mud on the seats and the dashboard was drying fast.

Bobby said, "Does the colonel give a hot bath?"

"I hope so." Linda spoke gently.

It was like another turning in the rocky road. But then forest and gloom were abolished and they were out into openness and the light of late afternoon. The lake was before them, wide as the horizon, water indistinguishable from sky. And they were on asphalt again, on a short road that appeared to run right down the hill to the lake, but then turned to show the town and almost immediately became a two-lane boulevard, lamp-standards down the centre, and tall palms, an import, suggesting not the natural growth of the tropics but the nurtured sub-temperate planting of a resort in a colder country.

The boulevard was bumpy. A lamp-standard was broken. A park separated the boulevard from the lake: unlighted cafés on the front, a small, empty pier. On the other side of the boulevard were villas set in enormous gardens, full of colour, startling after the forest. Red bougainvillaea festooned a dead tree. There was an old filling station with one pump; the small window of a tourist shop was choked with ivory and leather objects; on a billboard outside a low, blank building white hand-written posters gave the names of films and actors.

And then, quickly, the town that had looked whole showed its dereliction. The drives of villas were overgrown, disgorging glaciers of sand and dirt through open gateways. The park was overgrown. The globes and imitation coach-lamps in walls had been smashed and were empty. Metal was everywhere rusty. The boulevard was more than bumpy. It was cracked and fissured; the concrete gutters were choked with sand and dirt and weeds; the sidewalks were overgrown. The roofs of some villas had broken down. One verandah roof, of corrugated iron, was hanging like a bird's spread wing.

The boulevard and park had been cut level in land that was uneven. Almost at the end of the boulevard there was a long mildewed concrete wall, sagging from the pressure of earth on the other side. Above the gateway a vertical board shaped like an arrow with a curving head said HOTEL. They turned in there and went up the concrete incline to the gravelled yard where, next to a strip of old garden that ran parallel with the concrete wall, a large two-storeyed timber building with a built-in verandah still appeared whole.

When they stopped they heard the sound of water. That came from the lake. From the building itself, from a little room near where they had stopped, they heard an English voice shouting.

"That is the colonel," Linda said. "He is in form."

6

THE SHOUTING CONTINUED, while Bobby and Linda got their suitcases out of the car and Bobby set the burglar alarm, which immediately cheeped, and then almost brayed as Bobby locked the car door. The shouting continued, but the African who came down the steps from the office, carrying his felt hat in his hand, was smiling; and when he saw Bobby and Linda he smiled more widely. When he put on his hat he became faceless, his smile vanished. His drooping, grimy European-style clothes looked damp; his battered army boots dragged on the wet gravel all the way out of the yard.

Bobby, going up to the office with Linda, set his face. The colonel had heard the car; in the dark office, in a disorder of ledgers and pads, paperbacks and calendars, he was waiting. Set face met set face. The colonel was shorter than Bobby had expected. He was in a short-sleeved shirt and his outstretched hands were pressed against the edge of the counter. The muscles on his arms had shrunk, but he was still powerfully built. He ignored Linda; his dark, moist eyes, full of the strain of his shouting and a rage that had taken him almost to tears, fixed themselves on Bobby.

The colonel wasn't going to speak first. Linda, unrecognized, was also silent.

"We would like two rooms for the night," Bobby said.

The colonel's gaze dropped from Bobby's face to Bobby's shirt.

A Belgian calendar hung from the pigeonholes on the back wall, above an old black iron safe. There was no photograph of the president, only a framed watercolour of the lake and the hotel, dated 1949 and dedicated by the artist "to Jim".

Without speaking, the colonel opened a ledger and turned it to Bobby. Silent himself, his face equally set, Bobby wrote. And it was only while he was writing that he began to understand that the colonel was an old man. The colonel's hands were blotched, the skin loose; they trembled as they pressed against the counter. Bobby was also aware that the colonel was smelling. He saw that the colonel's singlet was brown with dirt; he saw dirt in the oily folds of skin on the colonel's neck.

Bobby passed the ledger to Linda. The colonel stepped back from the counter, turned his head and shouted for the boy. His hands stopped trembling then, and when he turned to Bobby again his face had cleared up; his eyes were even touched with mockery.

He said, "I take it you'll be wanting dinner?"

"There may be a third person," Linda said. "He's probably stuck in those mud heaps on the road."

This was news to Bobby. And now the set face and the silence, which he had been addressing to the colonel, served for Linda as well.

They didn't talk as they followed the boy into the main building and up the staircase. The boy was young; the black trousers and red tunic he wore had become, on him, only a type of African clothes; at every step his bare heels popped out of his black shoes. Paint had peeled on the staircase; on the landing there was a stack of old unpainted boards, perhaps discarded shelves; in the dark corridor upstairs, where the jute matting smelled of damp and mould, a bed was stood up on its end. Still without speaking, Linda and Bobby went into their rooms, on opposite sides of the corridor. Linda was the lucky one; she had the room overlooking the boulevard and the lake.

Bobby's room was close and in near-darkness. The rain-spattered window showed the hotel's water-tower, trees and bush, the roofs of buildings in the next street and, in the yard below, the low whitewashed quarters of the hotel boys. Bobby heard the high-pitched chatter in the language of the forest, the banging of pans, the exclamations that were like squeals. No noise came from the rest of the town, over which there hung a faint blue haze, as from scattered cooking-fires.

The bed had been made up some time ago; the bedspread, in a small flowered pattern, had moulded itself to every ridge and hollow of the bedclothes. The top light was dim; on the timber ceiling the hard graining of wood, and knots, showed like burns through the white paint. In the bathroom the fixtures were old and heavy, the wash-basin minutely cracked, stained where taps had dripped. The brass fittings in the plug-hole were black. And the water, when Bobby ran it, spat out red-brown with mud: lake water, after rain. It didn't get lighter, but it presently ran hot. Bobby washed.

Downstairs someone turned on a radio. An African voice burred and boomed through the hollow wooden building, stumbling over the six o'clock news from the capital, or the comment that followed the news: a voice reading word by word, evenly, and sometimes syllable by syllable, often trapping itself and then impatiently eliding. "*Feu-dal . . . ter'rists . . . se'ssionist . . . Ab'am Lincoln . . . secu'ty forces . . . exte'm'nated . . . vermin.*" The words came up to Bobby like an angry stutter. Against the competition of the radio the hotel boys banged about more and laughed more shrilly and squealed harder and longer in their forest language.

The brown water gurgled away past the black brass outlet into the dark hole, past the flowing strands of slime that were like the ferns at the bottom of a brook; it sent up a rotting smell. The white towel was worn and thin and had a smell of mildew. All at once, drying his face, pressing the towel against his eyes, Bobby felt exhausted, dazed by the long drive; and in that resort town, which he hardly knew, at the edge of that lake, in this hotel room, at this time of day, his exhaustion turned to melancholy.

It was not a disagreeable melancholy. Solitary, he wished now to be alone; he enjoyed the idea of wishing to be alone. It had been a long day; he had talked too much and made many misjudgments. He wished to be absent, to be missed. It was the beginning of one of his sulks; it was so that he punished and refreshed himself.

He didn't change his trousers. He put on the grey shirt he had worn for the buffet lunch in the capital the day before, and went downstairs. In the bar, where the radio was on, the commentator still angrily entangled in his violent words, there was no light. Above the long concrete wall, on this side no higher than a parapet, the broad spiked palm fronds on the boulevard were black against the lake and the unmoving clouds. In the park, bush hid the wall against which the lake slapped and thumped. Smoke hung faint in the air. The light had almost gone.

Bobby stood in the hotel gateway: he was unwilling to go out on the boulevard. He walked about the yard. He glimpsed cooking-fires in the boys' quarters; women and children looked up; he hadn't expected such numbers. He went and stood in the gateway again. He felt observed. He turned and saw the colonel leaning in a doorway of the unlit bar, looking at him. Bobby went out on the boulevard.

He walked past the hotel's concrete wall; past an empty house, green with damp below a great tree, clods of earth and bits of brick and mortar strewn about the verandah, weeds binding the sand and earth that had flowed out from the drive; and he turned up a side street. The side street was short; the town was only three blocks deep. In the verandah of a villa some Africans were stooped around a cooking-fire. One man, in a tattered army tunic, stood up as Bobby passed. Bobby looked away. But the man had stood up only to throw something from his pocket into the pot.

The town was inhabited. Many of the houses that looked abandoned were occupied, by Africans who had come in from the forest and had used the awkward, angular objects they had found, walls, doors, windows, furniture, to re-create the shelter of the round forest hut. Within drawing-rooms they had built shelters; they had raised roofs on verandah half-walls. Fires burned on pieces of corrugated iron; bricks were the cooking-stones. Many of the men wore ragged army clothes, still wet from the rain, pockets stuffed and drooping. A bicycle leaned in a doorless doorway, as within the stockade of a hut.

On the sidewalks grass had grown around rubbish from the houses, things that couldn't be used and had been thrown out: cracked squares of picture glass, fragments of upholstered chairs, mattresses that had been disembowelled for their springs, books and magazines whose pages had stuck together in solid, crinkled pads. Once Bobby saw a flattened cigarette packet, black on faded red: *Belga*. It recalled European holidays: as though Belgium and Europe had once lain across the water, and the lake had only been a version of the English Channel. This resort hadn't been built for tourists in Africa; it had been created by people who thought they had come to Africa to stay, and looked in a resort for a version of the things of home: a park, a pier, a waterside promenade. Now, after the troubles across the lake, after independence and the property scare, after the army mutiny, after the white exodus South and the Asian deportations, after all these deaths, the resort no longer had a function.

Faintly now, in the distance, there was a rhythmic sound, as of dancing, but so faint that even when Bobby stood still he couldn't be sure. He walked on. At the bush end of a side street he came upon a row of what had once been shops. He heard then the sound of an engine; and a little later a car came banging up the broken street. It was a Chevrolet, driven by an Indian girl. She stopped outside one of the shops. She barely looked at Bobby and hurried in, her high-heeled shoes tapping on the road and the concrete. The shop was in darkness, but it still worked, and was open for business. The shelves were bright with tins; there was a middle-aged man behind the counter.

The rhythmic sound persisted. It became clearer; above it now could be heard a man shouting. Bobby turned back towards the openness of the lake, dead silver through the black of bush and trees and hedges that had begun to grow into trees. But he was walking towards the sound, and the sound itself was coming closer. When he got to the boulevard he saw a company of soldiers coming out at the double into the boulevard from a tunnel of trees. In the dark, and against their shining black skins, the soldiers' white vests glowed like so many white shields; their white canvas shoes were like a separate flutter of pigeon wings. The moustached man shouting at them, and running with them, was in the fatigues of the Israeli army.

Three abreast the soldiers came, khaki trousers, white shoes, white vests, faceless. They had fallen into an easy rhythmic jog. The Israeli, calling time, was running up to the head of the column. There he turned and, continuing to shout, lifting his own legs high, he reviewed the company as they jogged past. But the Israeli was doing one thing, the Africans another. The Israeli was using his body, exercising, demonstrating fitness. The Africans, their eyes half closed, had fallen into a trance-like dance of the forest. Their knees hardly rose; their faces were blank with serious pleasure; they went blinking past the Israeli, blinking away the sweat that rolled down their shaved heads to their eyes. When they had all passed, the Israeli swivelled, still calling, "Ah! Ah!" Then, like a sheepdog, he scampered to the head of the column on the other side, calling to the Africans in vain. The Africans had grown fat and round-armed on the army diet; the Israeli instructor was small, slender, fined down.

Instructor and soldiers continued down one lane of the boulevard; and Bobby, on the other lane, followed them, walking towards the hotel. The jogging white vests came together in the gloom; the white shoes fluttered; then they were hidden by the dark vegetation in the centre of the boulevard. Slowly the tramping receded. But it was always clear, with, above it, the instructor's shout.

And then the tramping and the shouts grew louder again. The soldiers had turned, and were coming down the other lane of the boulevard. A disturbance in the gloom, white growing out of blackness: Bobby stopped to watch. But as the soldiers came near, and shaved heads appeared above bobbing white vests, Bobby became uneasy. It was wrong to stare; he would be noted. So, looking straight ahead, resisting the rhythm of the dance, he walked past the sweating, blinking soldiers and their instructor, who scampered by, inches away, shouting, "Ah! Ah!"

The night had now fallen. In one or two verandahs African campfires burned low. Some of the street lamps came on, blue, fluorescent. A dim light showed in a villa. On the other side of the boulevard the overgrown park had become the colour of the lake, a flat blackness. Bobby came again to the house with the great tree, its mass suggested by the pale glow of the hotel yard. It was very dark below the concrete wall. Light fanned out through the gateway; the gravelled yard was crisscrossed with shadows. The bar lights were on. Linda was silhouetted in the verandah.

"Bobby?"

He had been missed: she sounded lonely and waiting. She had changed; she was in trousers that were white or cream.

She said in a whisper, "I feel like a port and lemon."

But the bar was silent and desolate; and the joke, which had to do with the colonel and Doris Marshall, didn't work.

They sat without talking, sipping sherry, studying the photographs and watercolours on the panelled walls and the dusty Johnny Walker figure on their table. The colonel, now wearing silver-rimmed glasses, sat below one of the ceiling lamps and read a paperback; he was drinking gin. The boy with the red tunic drooped behind the counter, looking down at the counter.

THERE WERE FOOTSTEPS on the gravel, on the concrete steps, on the verandah, and a tall, thin African stood in a doorway of the bar. Below a ragged army raincoat he wore a black suit, a dirty white shirt and a black bowtie; his army-style boots were caked in mud. He stood in the doorway until the colonel looked at him. Then he bowed and said, "Good evening, Colonel, sir."

The colonel nodded and went back to his book.

Tiptoeing in his boots, moving swiftly, not looking at anything in the room, the African went and stood at the bar. The boy poured him a whisky and soda. The African curled thin, long fingers around the glass. As he raised the glass, he rolled his eyes to one side to look at Bobby and Linda.

The colonel went on reading. The silence in the room was like the silence outside.

A motor vehicle hummed in the distance, and then it was in the boulevard. It came closer, its lights lit up the boulevard; it was just outside, it turned into the yard. Two doors banged. Linda, Bobby and the barboy looked at the verandah. It was two Israelis, small, slender men in civilian clothes. They acknowledged the colonel but didn't look at Bobby or Linda. When the barboy went to their table they gave their order without looking up at the boy; and then they spoke softly, almost in whispers, in their own language, like people under orders not to fraternize, comment or see.

One hand in his pocket now, the African finished his drink.

Carefully, with thumb and forefinger he placed a coin at the far end of the counter. He stopped near the colonel's table, again waited to be seen, bowed and said, "Good night, Colonel. Thank you, sir."

The colonel bowed.

When the African had gone the colonel looked at Bobby and Linda over his glasses and said with what might have been a smile, "Well, at least some of us still dress."

Linda smiled.

Bobby set his face, and he had the satisfaction of seeing the colonel give up his attempt at a smile.

"You don't have to tell me what your rooms are like," the colonel said. "I haven't been up those stairs for three or four months." He put one hand to his hip. "Peter looks after that now. Head boy. You should see his quarters. Used to inspect the quarters once a month. Gave that up years ago. Couldn't bear it. What's the use, what's the use?" Holding the paperback in both hands, flexing the spine, he began to read again.

A tall liveried boy came in from the adjoining room and said to the colonel, "Dinner, sir."

The two Israelis got up at once and went in with their drinks.

Linda said, "I'll go upstairs for a moment."

Bobby didn't wait in the bar. He went into the dining-room. It was a large open room with two square pillars in the middle and wide wire-netted windows in the wall that faced the lake. The panelled side walls were hung with more watercolours. There were about twelve tables and all were laid. Half a dozen sauce bottles, a tall silver cruet-stand and a stack of books and magazines marked the colonel's table. The table to which the boy led Bobby was laid for three.

The boy was big and he moved briskly, creating little turbulences of stink. The cuffs and collar of his red tunic were oily black; oil gleamed on his cheeks and neck. The menu he gave Bobby was written out in a strong old-fashioned sloping hand: five courses.

Linda came back.

"That was quick," Bobby said.

She took the menu and frowned hard at it. "I saw someone in your room."

She continued to frown, and Bobby understood that she wasn't just giving him news; she expected him to go and look. He was irritated by the casual feminine demand. But temper left him as soon as he was out of the dining-room.

A dim light burned above the stairwell. There was no light in the corridor upstairs. When he put on the light in his room the window threw back a dark reflection. The bed hadn't been turned down; his open suitcase was as he had left it; the yellow native shirt hung on the back of a chair. Nothing had been disturbed; nothing had changed. Only the smells seemed sharper.

He went across the corridor to Linda's room: a smaller room, but lighter and fresher: the colonel had shown Linda favour. On an armchair he saw the brassiere of the day, the shirt, the mud-spattered blue trousers with their intimate creases and still, around the crumpled waistband and smooth hips, retaining something of the shape of the wearer. A bright silver object shone on the bare bedside table: a bit of foil, a sachet torn open by clumsy fingers. It wasn't a shampoo. It was vaginal deodorant with an appalling name.

The slut, Bobby thought, the slut.

Walking across the dining-room again, he smiled down at the floor. But when he sat down at the table he had stopped smiling and his face was set. He saw that the third place-setting had been cleared away. And again it was a little time before he understood the nature of Linda's stare, which he had been ignoring. He had resolved to be silent; now he found himself saying, in a conspiratorial whisper that matched Linda's, "I didn't see anyone."

Linda was less than satisfied. Her forehead twitched; she gave an impatient sigh and shifted away.

Bobby was hating everything.

PRESENTLY THE COLONEL came in, with his stiff, halting step. He had a finger between his book. He was flushed; the gin was working on him. He looked about the room with satisfaction, as though it was quite full. He looked benignly at Linda.

"Have you read this?" He lifted the book: it was by Naomi Jacob: Linda couldn't read the title. "It's very good about the mentality of the Hun. Don't show me the menu," he said to the boy. "I wrote it. I'll have the soup. Used to get them here. Those package tours from Frankfurt. Had to drop them."

You mean they dropped you, Bobby thought.

"They would eat up your profits," the colonel said. "Literally eat them up. We used to do a buffet lunch for them. Terrible idea. Never offer the Hun a buffet. He isn't happy until he's eaten every last scrap. He believes the new ham on the buffet is for him alone. There used to be a stampede. I saw two women fight. No, no; clear away the buffet as soon as you see the Hun coming. Meet the horde at the door and say, 'It's strictly fixed portions today, gentlemen.'"

"They are tremendous eaters," Linda said.

"Like the Belgians. Now there's a crowd. We used to get lots of them here from the other side. The only thing you can say for the Belgian is that he knows a good bottle of burgundy. Little of that sort of thing here now, though. Of course a lot of this" – he waved at the wire-netted windows, at the darkness, at the lake – "a lot of this is their doing. They thought they would just come from little Belgium and start living the good life right away. No work. Nothing like that. Just the good life. There was this woman just before the troubles, she said to me, 'But it's our estate. The king gave it to us.' You should see what they got up to over there. Mansions, palaces, swimming pools. You should have seen. There's these two tribes among them – "

"The Flemings and the Walloons," Linda said.

"They sound the opposite of what they should be. The Walloons should be the fat ones, but they are rather thin and refined. The Flemings should be thin, but they are fat. Ever seen a party of Flemings at the trough? They would order dinner for ten o'clock and get here at seven. At *seven*. They would start drinking. Just to make themselves hungry. By eight they would be hungry and nibbling at everything and getting the boys to run back and forth with more and more savouries. You've got to watch the savouries when the Belgians are around. And they would keep on drinking and drinking, getting themselves hungrier and hungrier. The food's in here, the boys are waiting. But they said ten, and they're not coming in until ten. Until ten o'clock they're just building up their appetites. Quarrelling, shouting, playing cards. Children screaming. Everybody shouting at the boys for more savouries. There would be pandemonium in that bar, from one little Fleming family party. Then at ten they would come in and eat solidly for an hour and a half. Grunting and snorting together. Mother, father, child. Everyone a little ball of fat. That was the sort of example they were setting. You can't blame the Africans. The Africans have eyes. They can see. The African's very funny that way. You can drive him hard for weeks on end. But one day he'll gallop away with you."

There was a crash in the kitchen, and a burst of high-pitched chatter. One voice rose quickly to a squeal which sounded like laughter; and then all the voices in the kitchen squealed together.

The colonel became abstracted; he was no longer looking directly at Linda. The Israelis talked softly. The tall boy came to clear away Bobby and Linda's plates and left a little of his stink behind.

"You saw that chap in the evening dress?" the colonel asked.

Bobby frowned. Linda was about to smile, but she saw that the colonel was not smiling.

"He's been coming here for a month or so. Ever since he picked up those clothes. I don't know who he is."

Linda said, "He was awfully polite."

"Oh yes, all very polite. But he comes to put me in my place, you know. Isn't that so, Timothy?"

The tall boy stood still and raised his head. "Sir?"

"He would like to kill me, wouldn't he?"

Timothy remained still, the tray in his hands, and tried to look serious. He said nothing. He relaxed only when the colonel went back to his food.

"One day they'll gallop away with you," the colonel said.

With quick, long strides Timothy went to the kitchen. A fresh voice was added to the squeals there; and then, the voice abruptly withdrawn, an aggrieved squealing going on, Timothy came out again, still brisk, still serious, and went to the table of the Israelis.

"I remember how we'd train men for Salonika, India, and places like that," the colonel said. "Sometimes we had to strap them to the horses. *Ah-wa-wa!* You'd hear them bawling at the other end of the ground. Some of them would develop rashes an inch thick. But we'd make riders out of them. We'd get them off to Salonika, India, or wherever it was." He looked directly at Linda again. "These names must sound strange to you. I suppose the name of this place will sound strange soon."

The squealing in the kitchen died down.

The colonel became abstracted again, busy with his food.

A tall, slender African, dark-brown, not black, came out into the dining-room from the kitchen. He moved lightly, like an athlete. He nodded and smiled at the Israelis, at Bobby and Linda, and went to the colonel's table. The mobility and openness of his face made him look less like an African than a West Indian or American mulatto. He wore simple clothes with much style. His well-tailored khaki trousers were clean and ironed; the collar of his grey shirt was clean and firm. His cream-coloured pullover suggested the sportsman, the tennis-player or the cricketer. There was a parting in his hair, and his brown shoes shone.

He stood before the colonel and waited to be seen.

Then he said, "I come to say good night, sir." His accent had echoes of the colonel's accent.

"Yes, Peter. You're off. We heard the crash and we heard you squeal. Where to this time?"

"I go cinema, sir." The pidgin was a surprise.

"You've seen our local bug-house?" the colonel asked Linda. "I suppose that will close down when the army goes. If the army goes."

The Israelis didn't hear.

"And what are you going to see, Peter?"

The question confused Peter. He continued to look at the colonel. His face held a half-smile and then went African-blank.

He said, "I can't remember, sir."

"That's the African for you," the colonel said. The words were spoken at Linda but not addressed to her.

Peter waited. But the colonel was occupied with his food. Peter became composed again; the half-smile returned to his face.

He said at last, "I go, sir?'

The colonel nodded without looking up.

Peter moved away with his light athlete's step. His leather heels sounded on the floor of the bar, the verandah. As soon as they touched the concrete steps, the colonel slammed a sauce bottle down and shouted, "*Peter!*"

Bobby jumped. Timothy held his face straight as though he had just been slapped. Even the Israelis looked up. It was silent in the dining-room, the bar, the kichen.

Then, as lightly as his leather heels permitted, Peter came back to the dining-room and stood before the colonel's table.

The colonel said, "Give me the keys for the Volkswagen, Peter."

"Keys in office, sir."

"That's a foolish thing to say, Peter. If the keys were in the office, I wouldn't be asking you for them now, would I?"

"No, sir."

"So it's a foolish thing to say."

"Foolish thing, sir."

"So you are very foolish."

Peter was silent.

"Peter?"

"Foolish thing, sir."

"Don't say it with so much pride, Peter. If you are foolish, you are foolish and you do foolish things. No witchdoctor is going to cure that."

Peter no longer glanced about the room; his eyes were fixed on the colonel. His bony shoulders were hunched; he appeared to stoop.

"Oh, he looks so fine," the colonel said, as though speaking to Linda again; but he wasn't looking at her. "So polished." He held out his open palm and raised it up and down. "Pass by the door of his quarters, and it's all you can do to keep yourself from being sick."

In his thin face Peter's eyes had begun to stare and shine. His mouth was loose.

"Give me the keys, Peter."

"Keys in Volkswagen, sir."

Bobby pushed his plate aside. Linda kicked him below the table. He settled back. The colonel saw. He looked away from Peter to the floor near Bobby's feet, and he seemed to grow abstracted.

He made a gesture with his index finger. "How wide is the hotel lot, Peter?"

"One hundred and fifty feet, sir."

"And deep?"

"Two hundred feet."

"And in those thirty thousand square feet *I* am in charge. I don't care what happens outside. I am in charge here. If you don't like what I do you can get out. Get out at once."

Bobby pressed a finger on the tablecloth and picked up a crumb.

"What do you think of me, Peter?"

"I like you, sir."

"He likes me. Peter likes me."

"You take me in when I was small. You give me job, you give me quarters. You look after my children."

"He has fourteen. He's living with three of those animals right now. So polished. So nice. So well-spoken. You wouldn't believe he doesn't even know how to hold a pen in those hands. You wouldn't believe the filth he comes out of. But you like dirt, don't you, Peter? You like going in to some black hole to eat filth and dance naked. You will steal and lie to do that, won't you?"

"I like the quarters, sir."

"While I live you will stay there. You won't move in here, Peter. I don't want you to bank on that. If I die you will starve, Peter. You will go back to bush."

"That is true, sir."

"And you like me. I am good to you. But I haven't been good to you. In this room we've had people talking about exterminating you. Don't you remember?"

"I don't remember."

"You're a liar."

"I like you, sir."

"What about the boy who was locked in the refrigerator?"

"That was somewhere else."

"So you remember that."

"I never talk about these things, sir."

"The whippings? There was a lot of that. What about the crops you weren't allowed to grow? You remember that? You say you like me?"

"I hate you, sir."

"Of course you hate me, and I know you hate me. Last week you killed that South African. Old, helpless. Didn't you? Lived here for twenty years. Married one of your women."

"Thief kill him, sir."

"That's what they always say, Peter. But we know who killed him. It was someone who hated him."

"No, sir."

"Do you remember when your woman was sick, Peter?"

"You know about that, sir."

"Tell me again."

Peter's staring eyes were inflamed, moist with tears of irritation. His half-open mouth was collapsed, the upper part of his face taut.

"It's a story you always tell," the colonel said. "People always listen."

Timothy was leaning against one of the square pillars in the middle of the room, head back, slightly to one side, looking on.

"My wife was sick," Peter said. He stopped, choked with irritation.

"You had three others. Go on."

"She cry every night in the quarters."

"Black with filth and stink."

"One night she was very sick. I get car and take her to hospital. They say no. Hospital for Eu'peans only. Huts for natives. Indian doctor take her. Too late, sir. She die."

"And you went out the next day and got other women and sent them to the forest to chop wood. And they loaded up the wood on their backs and came back to you in the evening. It's a good story, especially for visitors."

"I never talk about these things, sir."

"Who do you hate more? The Indian or me?"

"I hate the Indian."

"You are ungrateful. Who do you hate more? The Indian or me?"

"I will always hate you, sir."

"Don't you forget it. Your hate will keep me alive. One night, Peter, you will knock on my door – "

"No, sir."

"You will be wearing a raincoat or you will have a jacket. You will be holding your elbows close to your side – "

"No, sir. No, sir." Peter was closing and opening his eyes.

"I won't behave like the South African, Peter. When you say, 'Good evening, sir,' I won't say, 'Why, it's Peter, my own boy. Come in, Peter. Have some tea. How are you? How's your family?' There'll be no cups of tea. I won't behave like that. I'll be waiting. I'll say, 'It's Peter. Peter hates me.' And you won't come past that door. I'll kill you. I'll shoot you dead.' "

Peter opened his eyes and looked at the top of the colonel's head.

"This is how I swear my oath," the colonel said. "Under these lights, in the open, before witnesses. Tell your friends."

For some time Peter stood looking at the top of the colonel's head. His mouth closed, became firm again; there were no tears in his inflamed eyes. He put his hand in the pocket of his khaki trousers and took out a key-ring with two keys. He was going to place it on the table, but the colonel held out his hand and Peter put the keys in the colonel's palm. There was nothing more to keep him; and with a step as light and springy and athletic as before he walked through the dining-room to the kitchen.

The colonel didn't look at anyone in the room. He took up a glass of water, but his hands trembled and he put the glass down. His face went pale.

Timothy left the pillar and made himself busy.

When the colonel recovered, and colour came back to his face, he looked at Linda and said, "It's their big night. They've been building up to it all week. Mister Peter was going to turn up in the hotel Volkswagen. A lot of them believe he's already taken over. Oh, out there he's quite a politician, Mister Peter. Well, that's his problem. Isn't it, Timothy?" He had stopped trembling; he smiled at Timothy.

Timothy smiled back, in relief.

There was chatter in the kitchen again. A high-pitched voice began to squeal, and there was laughter.

"Do you hear him?" the colonel said to Linda.

Taking a fork to her mouth, she nodded.

"That's Peter, although you wouldn't believe it. Do you know what they're saying? It sounds as though they're having the most fantastic argument, but they're saying *nothing*. They're like the birds when it comes to chattering. You should hear Timothy here when he gets going."

Timothy, clearing away the Israelis' last plates, smiled at the compliment, but remained correct. He creased his forehead and pulled back the corners of his closed mouth.

There was a peal of laughter from the kitchen.

"That's Peter all right," the colonel said. "They can go on like that for hours. It means nothing at all. What did you think of the dinner?"

"It was very nice," Linda said.

"Nothing to do with me. Cookboy does it all. Just tells me and I write the menu. You would laugh if you saw him." The colonel smiled. "Fresh from the bush. Never sat on a chair until he came here. I wonder what will happen to him when I go. But what's the use?"

"Are you thinking of going?"

"I think of nothing else. But it's too late now. Can't wait for the Americans to come and buy us all out. That'll come. But it'll be too late for me."

The Israelis, by signs alone, called for their bill. Timothy took their money and gave them change. The colonel made a point of not looking. When the Israelis went past the colonel's table they hesitated and bowed briefly. The colonel said nothing. He raised his eyes to acknowledge them and then he stared into space, as though their passage had disturbed the train of his thoughts. He kept on staring until the Israelis, in the gravelled yard, began to talk more loudly.

"These people don't know how *lucky* they are," the colonel said.

A car door banged, once, twice. An engine started.

"If the Europeans had come here fifty years earlier, they would have been hunted down like game and exterminated. Twenty, thirty years later – well, the Arabs would have got here first, and they would all have been roped up and driven down to the coast and sold. That's Africa. They'll kill the king all right. They'll decimate his tribe before this is over. Did you know him? Have you been listening to the news?"

"I only saw him," Linda said.

"Came here for lunch once. Very polished. If I were a younger man I would go out and try to rescue him. Though that wouldn't have made much sense either. He's no different from the others. Given half the chance, he'd be hunting the witchdoctor. They say there's good and bad everywhere. There's no good and bad here. They're just Africans. They do what they have to do. That's what you have to tell yourself. You can't hate them. You can't even get angry with them. Really angry."

Dinner was almost over. Timothy was clearing the tables that had been laid and not used.

"Too late," the colonel said, straightening the magazines and

7

books on his table. "Too late for that South African. He used to come here, until he had that last stroke. That was his great mistake. A real old Boer. They found the teapot half full, the two cups on the floor, and tea and blood everywhere. Once or twice he brought his wife. The ugliest woman you ever saw. Like a wrinkled and very happy old ape." He paused. "These past few years I've seen *things* here that would make you cry."

At the sudden falseness, the tone of a man saying what he thought was expected of him, Bobby looked up. He saw the colonel looking at him. Bobby, sipping coffee, blew at the steam. The colonel looked away.

The squealing and chatter in the kitchen stopped.

It was like a signal for the colonel. He stood up. "Not the sort of thing you read in the papers. Not the sort of thing the people in the High Commission want to hear about either. For them it's all sweetness and light now. Mustn't offend the witchdoctor." Steadying himself on his feet, he straightened the magazines again, rearranged his sauce bottles, took up his book and held it against his chest. "Not many votes in this quarter now."

He spoke it like an exit line. Walking off, he held himself exaggeratedly upright, but he couldn't hide his injured hip. In the bar, and then down the verandah to his room, his footsteps were slow, one light, one flat and heavy.

Timothy, moving with a new, almost playful, looseness, swiftly gathered up tablecloths. He made large and rapid gestures; he took long, stretching strides, each ending with a little skid, as though he was demonstrating his great height and reach. His smell swirled about the room.

It was not quite half past eight.

"I'm beginning to feel there's something to be said for the Belgians," Linda said. "Never eat before ten."

"The Flemings," Bobby said. "The fat ones."

Timothy switched off two of the three lights.

"You are the expert on the local amusements," Bobby said.

"Wait for me in the bar," Linda said. "We might go for a walk."

Bobby didn't care for her confident, confiding manner. It was as though disappointment, and darkness, had brought out the wife in her and she was casting him in the role of Martin. But he didn't want to be alone either. He went into the bar. Timothy switched off the last light in the dining-room and could be heard squealing with someone in the kitchen. The barboy was behind the bar, still drooping, still apparently studying the bar; it turned out now that he was reading a book. Presently Linda came down, a cardigan hanging on her shoulders. She gave a comic shiver, as though shivering at more than cold.

IN THE BOULEVARD they couldn't hear the voices from the kitchen or the quarters. They heard only the sound of their shoes on the sand and loose gravel of the broken road and the occasional slap of the unseen lake against the lake wall. The glow from the quarters at the back gave depth to the hotel building; the light from the bar, spreading out into the yard on one side, and show-ing faintly through the open windows of the unlit dining-room on the other side, outlined the hotel's concrete wall. Beyond that was the darkness of the great tree and the empty house.

Linda said, "I wouldn't like to be by myself here."

Ahead of them was one of the street lamps that worked, a splintering, fluorescent circle, smoky after the day's rain. Objects began to define themselves; shadows grew hard. Light fell on the stepped line of a broken brick wall. Wet palm fronds shone; there were glitters in the park.

"It's funny," Linda whispered, "how you can forget the houses and feel that the lake hasn't even been discovered."

"I don't know what you mean by discovered," Bobby said, not whispering. "The people here knew about it all the time."

"I've heard that one. I just wish they'd managed to let the rest of us know."

They came to the house with the broken corrugated-iron roof that hung down like a bird's spread wing. In the verandah there was a group squatting around a small fire.

Linda said, "They hadn't moved into the boulevard when I was here the last time."

As she spoke, she stumbled. A pebble skidded away. An African stood up in the verandah, thin bare legs and ragged jacket silhouetted against the fire. Linda and Bobby looked straight ahead.

When they had passed the house, Linda said, "He's right. They'll kill him."

They passed the filling station; the tourist shop; the cinema, still blank and closed. They came to the end of the boulevard and continued into the tree-hung lane from which the running soldiers had come out earlier that evening. There was no asphalt surface on this lane; their feet fell on wet sand, pebbles, leaves. The blackness grew intense very quickly. The pale walls of villas set far back in gloomy overgrown gardens were barely visible; verandahs were like part of the surrounding blackness. There were no fires here. The trees were low above the lane; the sense of openness had gone.

A dog barked, a low, deep sound; and then it was beside them, big and growling. They walked on, the dog shepherding them angrily past his lot. Dogs barked on either side of the road ahead. And soon they were walking between dogs that obeyed no boundaries. A faint electric light, not a campfire, burned in an inside room of a villa. From that villa, too, dogs came bounding, without a bark, paws ripping through undergrowth and then, over the low twisted wooden fence, beating lightly on the sand of the road, scattering small pebbles. And always, from the black road ahead, came the sound of more dogs. No voices called to the dogs.

"This is nonsense," Linda said.

They turned back. But where before the dogs had only been keeping them to the centre of the lane, now the dogs crossed in front of them and behind them. Paws pattered on the sand and made an almost metallic sound; growls were deep, abrupt, never loud. Always there was barking in the distance. The pack grew.

"Oh my God," Linda said. "These dogs don't have any owners. They've gone wild."

"Don't *talk*," Bobby said. "And for God's sake don't stumble."

And their speech did madden the dogs more. Now the dogs occupied the lane completely and their movements were thick and flurried. They were waiting for a signal: the first leap by the bravest in the pack, a sudden gesture from Bobby or Linda, a dislodged pebble. But, steadily, the boulevard and the light came nearer.

"You said your mother's dog left those two parallel lines on your calf?" Linda said.

Rage overcame Bobby. "I'll kill them. I'm wearing these steel-tipped shoes. I'll kill the first one that attacks me. I'll kick its skull in. I'll kill it."

The anger stayed with him and was like courage. And it was as if the dogs responded to his anger. They began to keep to the edge of the lane; they began to fall behind. But the boulevard was near; the darkness was thinning in the fluorescent light; and the boulevard was the boundary the dogs recognized.

Bobby was trembling. Slowly on the boulevard the sense of time came back to him.

Linda was saying, "They say you have to have fourteen injections for tetanus."

"They brought these dogs here to attack Africans."

"All right, Bobby. They're attacking everybody now."

"They trained them to attack Africans."

"They didn't train them very well."

"It isn't funny."

"How do you think I feel?"

They walked back to the hotel without talking. They didn't look at the campfires they passed. In the hotel the bar lights were still on; there was no light in the colonel's room, next to the office. In the verandah Linda appeared to wait for Bobby to say something. He said nothing. He set his face, turned away from her, and went alone into the bar. She went down the verandah to the passage; he heard her go up the stairs to her room. It was just past nine. The adventure had lasted less than half an hour.

BOBBY SAT ON a barstool and drank Dubonnet. The fear drained out of him; the moment of panic in the dark lane become remote. The anger turned to exhaustion, and melancholy at his own solitude, in that bar, beside that vast African lake. Vacantly considering the dusty head of the barboy in the red tunic, Bobby thought: poor boy, poor African, poor African's head; and tears began to come to Bobby's eyes.

"I read French book," the barboy said, showing a tattered book in very limp covers.

Bobby heard but didn't understand. He looked at the boy and remembered the dogs and thought: poor boy.

"I read geometry," the barboy said, lifting another tattered book from below the bar.

And Bobby understood that the barboy was trying to start a conversation. It was what some young Africans did. They tried to start conversations with people they thought were visitors and kindly; they hoped not only to practise their English but also to acquire manners and knowledge. It moved Bobby to be singled out in this way; it moved him that, after all that had happened, the boy should show such trust; and it distressed him that he had allowed himself to be influenced by the colonel and had so far not looked at the boy, had seen only an African in uniform, one of the colonel's employees, part of the hateful hotel.

"You read geometry," Bobby said. "You show me where you read."

The barboy smiled and danced up and down on his toes. He pressed his elbows on the bar and at the same time turned the first few pages of the book, gathering up each page with the whole of his palm. The pages he turned were black and furred, the edges worn.

"I read here," the boy said. Still hopping, he placed a palm across two pages and shoved the book towards Bobby.

Bobby put the book in the middle of the bar. "You read here? The three angles of a triangle together make one hundred and eighty degrees?"

"I read here." The boy leaned sideways across the bar. "You teach me."

"I teach you. You give me paper."

The boy brought out a chit-pad.

"Look, I teach you. I draw straight line. That straight line make one hundred and eighty degrees. Hundred eighty. Look now. I draw triangle on straight line. Like that. That angle here and that other angle here and that angle up there, all that make hundred eighty degrees. You understand?"

"Hundate."

"You no understand. Look, I teach you again. I draw circle here. Circle make three hundred and sixty degrees."

"Hundate."

"No. No hundate. Three hundred and sixty. Three hundan-sixty. I show you hundate. I draw line through circle. Hundate up there. Hundate here."

"I read French."

"You read plenty. What for you like read so much?"

"I go school next year," the boy said, showing off now, look-ing down his nose, sticking out his lower lip, and pulling back the geometry book with the fingertips of both hands. "I buy more schoolbooks. I get big job."

The words had echoes: Bobby understood that someone must have passed this way before. Adventure was not in Bobby's mind; adventure was what he had ceased to hope for that day. But now, with sadness for the boy who might have had a previous teacher, he saw that adventure was coming; and, as so often, it was coming when it was least expected, so that it seemed just, like reward. Teaching the boy, he had not studied him. Now he looked at the boy's head, dust adhering to oil; he looked at the lean, tough neck. And the boy, knowing he was being appraised, looked down gravely at his French book, moving his swollen lips.

"What your name?" Bobby asked, looking at the boy's ears.

"Carolus." The boy didn't look up.

"You have nice name."

"You teach me French."

The French grammar, its limp red cloth cover stained and sticky and bleached and curling, had been written by an Irish priest and printed in Ireland.

"How far you reach? You reach here? Partitive article?"

"Partitive."

"In English you no have partitive article. You no say, 'Bring me some ink.' " Bobby paused: language teaching had unexpected difficulties. "In French you always say, 'Bring me *some* ink.' "

"*Some* ink."

"That's it."

Bobby looked at the boy, and the boy looked down at the book and moved a thick tongue slowly between his lips.

"What time bar close?" Bobby said.

"You teach me *English*," the boy said. "You no teach me French. You no know French?"

"I know French. Look, I teach you. In English you say ink."

"Ink."

"In French you say *l'encre*."

"Link."

"What time bar close?"

"Any time. Link. You teach me more."

"Bring me some ink. Bring me *de l'encre*. *De l'encre*. How you mean, any time?"

The boy went coy. He hung his head low over the disintegrating Irish book, so that Bobby saw the top of his head: particles of fluff trapped between the springs.

"Bar close ten o'clock," the boy said.

"You bring me tea ten o'clock."

The boy hung his head lower. "Kitchen close."

"You bring me tea. Room four. I teach you more." Bobby folded the fingers of his hand and rubbed his knuckles through the oily springs of the barboy's hair. "I give you shilling."

"Kitchen close," the boy said.

Bobby placed his palm on the boy's taut neck, half on the springy hair, half on the warm skin. "What a little bargainer it is," he said; and, suddenly pulling the boy's face across the bar to his own, he whispered into his ear, "I give you five."

The boy didn't pull his head back and Bobby, still holding the boy's head close and feeling the boy straining to be still, began rubbing his thumb behind the boy's left ear, feeling the bone below the smooth African skin. The boy became very quiet. Tears came to Bobby's eyes; and though he was looking at his own thumb and the intricate modelling of the boy's ear and the coarse little springs of hair, he was not thinking of the boy or the dogs or the intimacies to come; he was surrendering only to his own tenderness and melancholy, which at such moments overflowed.

Suddenly the boy jumped away.

The burglar alarm on Bobby's car was shrieking. The sharp metallic vibrations rose and fell around a central, persistent wail. The hotel yard jumped with light, bright bulb after bright bulb, everywhere. The quarters broke out into high-pitched chatter, which instantly developed into a general squealing.

"Peter!" the colonel called. "Peter!"

From the quarters women wailed. Footsteps were everywhere, in the yard, in the hotel itself.

The boy was looking at Bobby with eyes of terror.

The burglar alarm continued to shriek. It would not subside until the car ceased to rock and became still again.

"Peter!" the colonel called.

Bobby went out to the verandah. The colonel's room at the end of the verandah was lit up. The door was open; the window at the back of the room showed the brightly lit yard.

The garage was an open shed. A naked bulb burned there now and threw deep shadows. The rocking of the car was not perceptible, but the alarm was still going, the central wail broken.

Bobby saw that no wheel was missing from his car, no hubcap taken off.

The silences between the wails grew longer, the wail itself fainter. The alarm became a series of cheeps, pips, and then finally died. And then the brightness of the awakened yard was as startling as the alarm had been.

7*

Bobby went back to the bar. The boy still looked at him with eyes of terror. He had put on all the bar lights.

"Peter," the colonel was saying.

At last the quarters went quiet.

"Dog or cat jump on car, sir."

"Were you sleeping?"

"Sleeping, sir."

"You are very foolish."

Women wailed.

"I'm going to have you tied up. Timothy! Carolus!"

The barboy jerked his head. But he didn't move.

The wailing continued, drowning the colonel's questions, the soft responses.

"Carolus!"

Now Carolus moved. His mouth, half open, had grown thick and immobile. His movement was awkward, his limbs heavy. He opened the back door of the bar and stood for a little with his back to Bobby, his hand behind him on the doorknob. Across the dark wide passageway half a panelled door was ajar, and Bobby had a glimpse of the bright yard: the unshaded bulbs on the cylindrical metal legs of the water-tower, the glare of the whitewashed quarters, the bush at the back that glittered in black shadow and looked artificial.

"Carolus!"

He pulled the door shut, and Bobby was alone in the bar. With all the lights on it seemed a bigger room.

Outside, the women wailed in relay, no two drawing breath at the same time. It was impossible to pick out what the male voices were saying. The wailing became simple sound, part of the background.

In a framed signed photograph behind the bar, the photograph enlarged, imprecise, a man in a boat held up a big fish and smiled in strong sunlight: the weather and the mood, and all the implied order, of a particular day. There was a calendar, with an African landscape, from a Belgian brewery, the names of towns in Belgium and Africa printed in the same red type. The paint on the half-empty shelves was old and scratched, cream below brown; in one corner half a dozen nearly empty liqueur bottles had old, dry, stained labels.

The wailing outside grew weaker, was no longer background. Bobby heard the colonel's voice. The wailing grew loud again, subsided again, and then there was almost silence.

Bobby left the bar and went quickly down the verandah to the enclosed passageway. The door that gave on to the yard was ajar. He didn't look. He was aware of brightness, movement. He also knew he had been observed.

Upstairs, as he was opening his door, he heard Linda open hers. She was in a short cotton nightdress; her shiny shins looked as sharp as her elbows.

She whispered, "Peter? I knew it, I knew it."

Again he felt that she was involving him in a neutral marital intimacy. And though he half wanted the company, he was perverse. He set his face, as though he had been especially affronted by what had happened downstairs, turned away from Linda and without a word pushed his door open.

It was unexpectedly bright with the glare from the yard. He closed the door, deciding at the last moment to give a little slam. He kicked something across the floor. He didn't need to turn on the light to see that it was the key of his car.

IT WAS ONLY when he was undressed that he became disquieted. Intruders: there might have been a crisis, and he might have been without his car, trapped. He decided then to pack, to be ready at any time for a swift getaway. He arranged, around a chair, everything he would need: packed suitcase, trousers, the yellow native shirt, shoes and socks. He went to bed in his vest and underpants. It was pointless, even a little deranged; it was the behaviour of the compound. But when the lights in the yard went off, and he felt himself alone in the darkness, he was glad he had done what he had done.

There was a knock on the door, but so gentle he couldn't be sure. He waited. The knock came again. He sat up; he didn't put the light on. The door opened, the ceiling light was turned on. It wasn't Linda. It was Carolus, with a tea-tray. The world was normal again; the hotel was the hotel.

"You close door," Bobby said.

Carolus closed the door.

"You bring tea, Carolus? You very good boy. You bring tea here."

Carolus set the tray on the bedside table. Just as his limbs had lost their lightness, and he moved clumsily, so his face had altered. His eyes had gone red, his lips thick, creased and dry, with a white bloom; his whole face appeared inflamed with apprehension and mistrust.

"You sit here. You talk with me. I teach you."

Carolus was taking out a piece of paper from the tight pocket of his red tunic.

"I teach you French? I teach you hundate?"

The paper was a chit for the tea. It was made out in soft pencil, in the colonel's firm handwriting.

Anger swept through Bobby; and his anger grew at the sight of Carolus's heavy face.

He ordered: "Pencil."

Carolus had one waiting.

"Now get out!" Bobby said, handing back the pencil and the chit.

Carolus didn't move. His expression didn't alter.

"Go!"

"You give me."

"Give you? Give you nothing. Give you whip."

It wasn't even true; it was someone else's words; he was violating himself. Sitting up in bed, looking at the inflamed African face coming nearer to his, he saw it invaded by such blank and mindless rage that his own anger vanished in terror, terror at something he sensed to be beyond his control, beyond his reason.

He said, "I give you. I promise you. I give you."

He took up a shilling from the change he had put out on the bedside table.

"You give me five."

"I give you, I give you."

Even when he had the money, Carolus looked at it suspiciously, and then he looked from his palm to Bobby's face. And as soon as Carolus began to walk to the door Bobby understood that Carolus was only "fresh from the bush"; and Bobby knew that he had misread the boy's face, had seen things in it that were not there.

He said, "Boy."

Carolus stopped. He started to turn to face Bobby.

"You take off light, boy."

Carolus obeyed. And when he left the room he shut the door quietly behind him.

Bobby turned on the bedside lamp. He poured a cup of tea. It was weak and full of leaves; it had been brewed in water that was barely hot. It was awful.

7

HE WAS IN a car with a woman whose identity he couldn't be sure of. They were quarrelling. Everything she said was accurate; everything was wounding; and though to everything there was a reply, he couldn't explain himself. He had to shout above her shouts; he was screaming; and as they sped along the empty road, dangerously, the wheel jumping in his hands, she wounded him and wounded him, more and more deeply; and there was rage and ache in his head, which seemed about to explode. He was no longer in the car. He was standing beside a table in a room full of people and chatter; and his exploding head made him collapse and stretch out right there, before them, on the floor.

When he awoke there was only the memory of the head. The woman and her arguments had vanished; but the wound remained. It was dark, but there was a quality about the darkness which suggested that it would soon be light. He reasoned: it was his early night, the events of the evening, and anyway he had packed for a quick getaway. Just the trousers and the native shirt, and he would be off. But petrol: he didn't have enough, his tank wasn't filled: again and again he panicked as in his dream. And then it was daylight: a faint chattering from the quarters, a glimpse of trees at the back which he hadn't seen the previous evening, and the radio downstairs, the African announcer stumbling over the violent words of the news bulletin from the capital.

It was the light, the openness, the lake, that surprised him when he went down to the dining-room. The sky was high and blue; beyond the ornamental palms on the boulevard the lake stretched to the horizon. The previous evening the wire-netting on the dining-room windows had appeared to enclose the room; now it offered no barrier to the light and was scarcely visible. So sodden and heavy and gloomily tropical the previous evening; but now the air was fresh. The hotel, the boulevard, the park, the lake: something of the resort atmosphere survived. And this morning there was activity on the boulevard. Above the hotel's concrete wall an army lorry could be seen moving slowly from left to right.

The colonel, dressed as before, was at his table. He had almost finished breakfast; he was drinking tea and reading his book. Bobby, in his yellow native shirt, forgot about the lake and the light; and, left hand at his side, right hand swinging, made his swift, grim passage to the only other table that had been laid. Seated, his face set, he looked at the colonel; but the colonel was reading. Crumbs on the tablecloth, disorder in the butter-flecked marmalade: Linda had been down already. Grimly, Bobby buttered a piece of cold toast.

"News not so good this morning," the colonel said. His voice was relaxed and casual. "Still, I suppose the sooner this thing's over the better for all of us."

Bobby, biting on his hard toast, gave a brief, blank smile. The colonel didn't see; he was turning the page of his book.

Timothy, his smell sharp in the light morning air, offered the breakfast card. The card was as dingy as the red-checked waiter's rag Timothy flicked about the table. His gestures were freer this morning. He was almost skittish, almost familiar, and he appeared anxious to talk. With every friendly flick of his rag he released a little more of his smell.

Another lorry went grinding past the hotel.

"Army's on the move this morning," the colonel said. "Not a time to be on the road, when our army's on the move. I always give them a wide berth myself."

"I imagine the road's still wet," Bobby said.

"Oh, one or two of those lorries are going to come to grief down some precipice or the other."

The colonel smiled directly at Bobby. The colonel looked older this morning; but there was no strain in his face; the flesh around his eyes and mouth looked softer and rested.

Bobby was uncertain about the joke.

The colonel noticed. "They're going to leave the road in an awful state."

"But I imagine it'll dry out pretty quickly," Bobby said. "With this sun."

"Oh, with this sun it'll dry out in no time at all. No time at all. By lunchtime, I'd say."

It was like an invitation to linger; it was unexpected. But Linda had been down; she and the colonel had no doubt talked.

A car came into the yard. A door slammed. The colonel put a marker, a polished strip of bamboo shaped like a paper-knife, clearly an old possession, in his book; and waited. He appeared to know who the visitor was.

It was Peter, coming in from the bar with his light athletic steps. He was in khaki this morning: the khaki trousers of the previous evening, an ironed khaki shirt with epaulettes and button-down pockets. His sleeves were rolled up; there was a big wristwatch with a shining stainless-steel strap on his left wrist. His arms were bony, the muscles slack; the crinkled loose skin around his elbows showed that he was older than he looked. He carried two or three handwritten lists; he must have been out shopping.

When he saw Bobby, Peter paused, bowed and smiled and said in his English accent, "Good morning, sir."

There was no irony in the smile. It was like the smile of an old acquaintance. It didn't go with the bow; it was part of Peter's disjointedness. Like his clothes, like the bow, like the accent, Peter's smile was only one part of his training, and it was separate from the other parts. Like Carolus and Timothy, Peter belonged to the hotel and the boys' quarters of the hotel. It was disturbing; as always in former settler haunts, Bobby felt he was trespassing.

Peter stood easily by the colonel's table while the colonel went through the lists. When Peter went away, after bowing again to Bobby and smiling, the colonel stood up, holding his book against his chest. He steadied himself and threw back his shoulders. Then he hesitated, as though listening to the whine of the army lorry on the boulevard.

He smiled at Bobby and said, "At times like this I always feel that the nearer you are to an army camp the safer it is. They're more under control. I don't know whether you were here for the mutiny. Even the witchdoctor ran away. Nobody knew where he was for a week. But it was perfectly all right here."

Again Bobby was uncertain.

"Of course it'll all blow over in a day or two," the colonel said. "Everybody'll be calmer. Day or two."

Bobby wasn't sure, but he thought the colonel was asking for company. He said, "We're a day late as it is."

"We'll give you an early lunch. You'll get to the Collectorate well before the curfew."

"So that's official, the curfew?"

"Four o'clock. We'll get you off in good time."

LATER, BOBBY CAME downstairs to find Linda in the verandah. She was looking at the bright lake through her dark glasses. She had changed her shirt but was wearing yesterday's blue trousers; there were faint dusty stains where the mud had been brushed off.

She said, "Has the colonel told you?"

She moved away without waiting for his reply. They were still quarrelling.

Bobby was in no mood to talk; he especially wished to be spared the colonel's disquieting company; and he decided, with relief, to go grim. Grim-faced, he looked through the paper-backs in the office, war stories, historical romances; made a selec-tion; and settled down in a red-painted wicker chair in the verandah to a sulky read.

Linda attached herself to the colonel. They sat in the open office and Bobby heard the colonel talking. They walked about the yard, the garage, the garden, the quarters, and Bobby heard the colonel talking. They sat in the colonel's open room; they came out and stood in the hotel gateway. The colonel appeared to recognize this gateway as a boundary. He kept within the gravelled yard and never stepped on the concrete that sloped down to the asphalt of the boulevard.

At intervals the army lorries rolled slowly by. Below green forage caps the fat faces of the soldiers were expressionless and still matt-black from their morning wash.

The air lost its morning freshness; the light became hard; and Bobby, not held by the paperbacks, began again to feel something of the desolation of the derelict resort. Carolus came into the bar, dusty-headed, oily-skinned, in his old black trousers and tight red tunic, as though he hadn't taken off his clothes or washed since the previous evening. He moved noisily about the bar with broom and rag, taking long, skidding steps, as if in imitation of Timothy. Then he saw Bobby in the verandah. Carolus didn't come out to the verandah. He retreated with his broom and rag and stayed in the bar, out of sight. Bobby didn't move. He put his book face down on his knees, looked at a point in the yard, and frowned. He heard Carolus moving quietly in the bar, trying not to draw attention to himself.

The colonel and Linda were still together, but there were now passages of silence between them. When they came and sat at Bobby's table, for coffee, Bobby saw that they had done so because they had exhausted the mood that had been created by their conversation.

Bobby, still grim, made no effort to talk. Neither did Linda, half smiling behind her dark glasses. And the colonel seemed to have nothing more to say.

Bobby thought: he'll start talking about Africans.

Carolus stood in a doorway with the coffee-tray.

The colonel said, "It looks as though the lorries have stopped."

Bobby looked at Carolus and then stared into space, demonstrating his capacity for sternness, even in the colonel's company. Carolus became quite stupid and heavy with fright.

"What gets me, you know," the colonel said, setting out the cups with his firm, square hands, "is the way those Africans manage to look so downtrodden as soon as they're obeying orders. Did you see those drivers? Driving very, very slowly, and looking very, very downtrodden, as though they'd all had the rod this morning. It's only because those instructors are looking on."

Bobby, not talking, tilted his empty cup to study a flaw in the glazing.

"You can train them so far and so far only," the colonel said, taking the cup from Bobby. "Carolus. Soon they are going to be driving those lorries like madmen, and those same downtrodden faces are going to look very nasty. Carolus."

Carolus was standing in the doorway, looking in terror from Bobby to the colonel.

Bobby stared at Carolus.

"Carolus," the colonel said, irritation breaking into his voice for the first time that morning, "this cup is absolutely filthy."

Carolus brought another cup. They had coffee. But the colonel's irritation, which had at first seemed only assumed, remained. The calm of the morning had gone; his face was becoming strained again. Linda was silent, smiling behind her dark glasses, as if with inner content. Bobby continued to be grim.

After coffee the colonel left them. And though they heard him talking to the kitchen about their lunch, he behaved afterwards as though they had already left. He didn't come to the bar or the dining-room while they were having their lunch. Timothy, his own manner less skittish now, brought their bill and took their money.

The colonel was in the yard when Bobby and Linda came down with their suitcases, but he didn't appear to see. He didn't appear to hear when Bobby unlocked the car door and the burglar alarm brayed. Hands in pocket, the colonel stood in the gateway. He looked at the boulevard and the lake; sometimes he looked at the hotel building, remotely, as though considering a picture. He didn't hear the car start; he didn't notice it coming close. But suddenly, as Bobby slowed down, the colonel leaned forward and smiled at Linda.

He said, "If you run into the army, play dead."

As Bobby moved off, a group of eight men began coming up to the yard from the boulevard. Two were Indians in turbans; the others were young Africans in white shirts and dark trousers, trainee-surveyors perhaps, builders from the army camp, or employees of the Works Department. One of the Indians spoke to the colonel.

"*Lunch!*" the colonel shouted. "This isn't a roadhouse. You can't just walk in here at any hour you choose and demand *lunch*."

Down the concrete incline, Bobby and Linda turned into the boulevard, whose ruin, in daylight, the colours so bright, so new, startled them afresh. The thin asphalt surfacing was swollen and cracked like the crust on a cake.

"No!" the colonel was shouting. "No! No!"

"That was for your benefit," Bobby said to Linda. "You made a great hit there."

"Oh dear. He could do with the money too. Eight fifteens, that's a hundred and twenty shillings. Not counting the drinks."

"I shouldn't worry. They'll get their lunch. Shall we come back and check, after we get our petrol?"

She lifted her chin, gave an impatient little sniff, and turned to look at the green damp walls of the empty house which the previous evening she hadn't been able to see.

8

THE PETROL STATION worked. They got their petrol; that secret anxiety of Bobby's was stilled. To avoid passing in front of the hotel again, he turned down a side street and drove out of the resort by a street that ran parallel to the lake boulevard. Soon the scattered villas on the edge of the town were left behind, and they were on the mountan road.

The soft shoulders of the road had been churned up by the army lorries, but the central surface was firm and dry. Here and there, especially at corners, rain and the lorries had dislodged rocks and created muddy potholes; in some places, where the road had subsided, large rocks stuck out; but the road was generally easy. The roadmenders hadn't been at work on this side of the resort; no one had dumped mounds of earth.

They climbed higher. They entered forest, still wet, with soft spots of sunshine on the road and the dark tangled hillsides. The light and openness of the lake were shut out. Sometimes they had a view of the lake below them, no longer glittering, indistinguishable from the sky; and when they came out of the forest into the damp valleys of ferns and bamboos the sky seemed lower and more oppressive, and the light had a different quality, settled, dead, holding no reflection from a water surface.

They hadn't been talking.

Now Linda said, "You wonder how they ever managed to find the place."

She was being provocative; their quarrel was still on. Bobby didn't reply, and she said nothing else. After some time she carefully changed her position in her seat.

Bamboos and ferns dropped away. At the top of the ridge the land was quite bare. Then they began to go down again, past a valley which was like the valleys they had seen the day before. Again there were fields, terraced hills, huts. In the rain the day before the colours had been soft, green and grey; the paths had meandered into mist; the fields had been empty. Now in the dead sunlight the colours were harsher. Mud was black, vegetation was shining green. The huts that yesterday in the rain had looked such comforting shelters were now seen to be rough structures of grass standing in fenced yards of trampled black mud. Women and children in bright clothes were at work with simple implements in little patches of wet black earth. The women maintained a fixed stoop on straight, firm legs, their broad hips rigid, exaggeratedly humped; so, doubled up, flexible and curving only from waist to head, they hoed and weeded and stepped along their row. All over the valley, among the women and the children, there were little smoking bonfires of damp weedings. It was the immemorial life of the forest. The paths were simple forest paths, leading to nothing else.

At a twist in the road ahead, where the bare verge widened and rose and fell away, half a dozen small domestic animals stood together silhouetted against the sky. But two turned out to be naked children. Dull-eyed, disfigured with mud, they stood where they were and watched the car pass.

Linda said, "I was hoping to buy some of those White Fathers cigars for Martin. Do you know them? You could get a great big bundle for a few shillings. Wrapped in a sort of dry banana-leaf box."

Martin, Bobby thought: they were getting near home. He said, "I thought Martin was a pipe man."

"He loves these. They're absolutely vile, but he likes to puff away and fill his room with the smoke. Just puffing away. Into curtains, bookshelves, under cushions. Just to get the smell everywhere. You used to be able to get them at the colonel's. But I didn't see them this time, and I forgot to ask. I imagine they used to come from the other side of the lake. But I suppose the poor old White Fathers now have other things to think about instead of cigars."

"I don't know. I wonder why we always think when things are not going well for us that it's all coming to an end."

"The colonel's under no illusion on that score. Oh dear, it was awful."

"I'm in no position to judge," Bobby said. "I've never been one for settler grandeur."

"It's gone down so much. I suppose since he had that accident and damaged his hip. The rooms are so awful and the boys are so dirty, and he's stopped looking after himself."

" 'That's what happens the minute you take your eyes off them.' "

Linda missed the irony. Her silence was like simple agreement.

Bobby tried again. "I thought only Africans smelled. What is it that Doris Marshall says? That little bit of settler wisdom about civilization and cleanliness?"

"Oh goodness," Linda said. "That Timothy."

Bobby let the subject drop.

Linda said, "I suppose there must be hundreds of people like that all over the world, in all sorts of strange places."

"They've had a good life."

"That's not the point."

"What is?"

"I don't believe you want to understand. It's so awful." Her voice broke; it took Bobby by surprise. "The foolish man is trying to live on his will alone. Oh dear. And the shirt he was wearing was so dirty. He wanted the company. And he's right. They're waiting to kill him."

"I'd kill him myself if I stayed there."

"I don't trust that Peter one little bit. A little too fawning and smooth, with that fancy wristwatch."

Bobby said, "Peter is a little too clean, I must admit."

"The colonel was shell-shocked in the Great War. He told me. He said that if anyone scolded him he became unconscious. Scolded, that was the word he used. Then he said he pulled himself together."

Bobby suppressed his unease. "He can go South." He paused. "Still a lot of blacks there he can take it out of."

"If you put it like that. But it doesn't matter where he goes now. He took Peter in as a boy, fresh from the bush – "

" – and trained him. I know.'

"I suppose they had a good life, as you say. But what strange places they landed themselves in. Salonika, India."

"How quickly we pick things up. I wasn't aware that we sent settlers to Salonika."

"I don't even know where Salonika is. He's sick of the sight of the lake, sick of the hotel and the quarters, sick of his own food and the table he goes to three times a day. But he won't leave. He told me he hadn't been outside his gate for months."

"That doesn't sound like will to me. I used to have an aunt like that, in darkest England."

"And he's still so damned fair. He still gives you a five-course dinner."

She had been talking slowly; he thought she was only growing "mystical". But then he saw a thin trickle of tears below her dark glasses. He wanted to say: I know why you're crying. But he decided to let her be, to do nothing that would feed her mood.

He concentrated on his driving. Always, on the rocky road, there were signs of the army lorries that had gone before: the churned-up soft edges, massively embossed with tyre-treads, the muddy potholes at some corners, and occasionally a dislodged boulder, white where it had been buried, earth colour above that. The road continued to be reasonably easy, and empty.

"I suppose you're right," Linda said. "Let the dead bury the dead."

VALLEY LED TO valley. The road climbed and dropped. But they kept going lower. The valleys became wider; the earth became less black, rockier; the light became more tropical. The dwellings were no longer all of grass; not all had fences and trampled yards. There were little clusters of timber-and-corru-gated-iron shacks; and sometimes now there were even ruins, of weathered boards and rusting corrugated iron.

Something like a monument appeared beside the road. It looked like a war memorial or a drinking fountain. It turned out to be a standpipe: a black nozzle sticking out of a large concrete wall with bevelled edges and cut-away corners, PUBLIC WORKS AND WELFARE JOINT ADMINISTRATION 27–5–54 roughly picked out in a stripe of blue-and-white mosaic at the top of the wall. It was the first of eight monumental standpipes. Then once more there was only the road.

From the car they had intermittent glimpses of a rocky river, widening as the land grew flatter. And then the road came out from a cutting in the bush and ran on a high concrete-walled embankment beside the sprawling riverbed: narrow muddy channels between islands of sand and half-stripped shrubs and heaped rocks white in the sunlight. There was no barrier on the embankment, and the openness gave a sense of hazard.

The road turned away from the river and entered bush again. But the river remained close; and when the road next twisted down out of the bush, to run beside the river once more, Bobby and Linda saw a soldier in a crimson beret standing in bright sunlight on the wide concrete wall of the embankment, the khaki of his uniform and the shining black of his face, contrasting textures, clear and sharp against the openness of the riverbed.

He waved at the car, leaning forward slightly, keeping his polished black boots together. African labourers in the valleys were thin, their clothes ragged. The soldier's ironed uniform was tight over his round arms and thighs and his soldier's paunch. He was conscious of his difference, of the army clothes, the evidence of the army diet. His wave was heavy and awkward and looked frantic, but it held authority; and there was confidence in the round, smiling face.

Bobby was driving slowly on the rocky road.

Linda said, "He's a nice fat one."

The African continued to smile and wave, his hand flapping from the wrist. The car didn't stop. The African's hand dropped; his face went blank.

Bobby, glancing at the shaking rear-view mirror, had a momentary, confused sense of openness and hazard: the barrier-less high embankment tilting behind him, racing beside him. He looked down from the mirror to the road.

"I don't like that look he gave us," Linda said. "Now I imagine he's going to telephone his other fat friends, and they'll be waiting for us at some roadblock. I imagine he's running to beat out the message on his drums right at this moment."

"I always give Africans lifts."

"I didn't stop you."

"How do you mean, you didn't stop me?"

"Just what I said. They'll pick you out anywhere, in that yellow native shirt."

"For God's sake."

He had been slowing down. Now, a little too wildly, he accelerated.

"I suppose it's because they can't read," Linda said, "but they're very sharp. You know that sort of common near the compound. Martin and I were driving past that one day, when we saw Doris Marshall's houseboy, or steward, I suppose we should say, rolling about on the grass, dead drunk as usual, in the middle of the afternoon. As soon as he saw us he ran out right into the road to wave us down. Martin was for stopping. I wasn't. Well, that drunken houseboy *saw* that conversation from fifty or a hundred feet away, and repeated it word for word to Doris Marshall. Doris didn't like it. Suffafrican ittykit. I'd wounded her steward's feelings."

Bobby braked. When the car stopped he held the steering-wheel hard and leaned over it.

"Oh, Bobby. I wasn't being serious."

He closed his eyes, then opened them.

"Really, I wasn't being serious. You weren't thinking of going back for him?"

It was, vaguely, what he had in mind.

"That would be too ridiculous."

"I knew there was something I should have done this morning," Bobby said. "I should have telephoned Ogguna Wanga-Butere or Busoga-Kesoro. It's just occurred to me."

She accepted the explanation. "I doubt whether either of them's at work today."

Bobby put his hand to the ignition switch.

In the distance, from the direction of the plain, there was the sound of a helicopter. It was a faint sound, now coming on the wind, now vanishing, then at last steady. When Bobby turned on the ignition, the helicopter couldn't be heard.

THEY DROVE TOWARDS the plain and the sound of the

helicopter, approaching, receding, always audible above the beat of the engine and the rattle of the car on the rocky road. They lost the river; but all the land now had the bleached quality of a river-bed. There were a few scattered huts on stilts. Cactus bloomed and threw black shadows. The road became sand, with sunken wheel-tracks; at corners there were drifts of dry loose sand in which the car wheels slipped. It was an old, exhausted land. But it was inhabited.

Two men ran out into the road. But perhaps they were only boys. They were naked, and chalked white from head to toe, white as the rocks, white as the knotted, scaly lower half of the tall cactus plants, white as the dead branches of trees whose roots were loose in the crumbling soil. For four or five seconds, no more, the white figures ran with slow, light steps on the stony edge of the road and then ran back from the road into the field of scrub and stone.

Their steps might have been normal. Perhaps they had only been frightened by the car. Perhaps it was their colour, robbing them of faces and even of nudity, that had made them seem light-footed and insubstantial. Perhaps it was the noise of the car, killing the cries they might have made and the sounds of their feet.

So brief an apparition, so abrupt and without disturbance: still listening for the helicopter above the beat of the engine, Bobby didn't look to see where in that bright rubbled landscape the chalked boys or men had gone. Linda didn't look. Neither she nor Bobby talked. And it was a little time before Bobby realized that the helicopter, for which he was listening, was no longer to be heard.

And now they were altogether out of the mountains, which began to show in the rear-view mirror as a blue-green range rising out of the bright plain. Farms appeared again, and fenced fields; little shack settlements at crossroads: houses and huts in dusty yards, two or three wooden shops: flaking distemper on old timber, faded advertisements on doors, twisted frames, dark interiors. They slowed down for a petrol tanker driven by an Indian. It was the first motor vehicle they had seen since leaving the hotel. But there were others now: old lorries, old cars driven by Africans. The road was tarred again. They were entering a market town.

Small ochre-and-red official buildings were scattered about the winding main road. But the gaps between the buildings had not been filled; much of the town was waste-ground, as eroded and full of glare as a riverbed. The buildings were in a type of Italian-ate style, with a touch of the South American. Walls went right down to the ground and were mud-splashed; roughly plastered concrete looked like adobe. Crooked telegraph poles, sagging wires, the broken edges of the asphalt road, scuffed grass side-walks, dust, scattered rubbish, African bicycles, broken-down lorries and motor cars outside the bus-station shed: the town had failed to grow, but it still worked.

Africans sat and squatted in a dusty park where eucalyptus had grown tall. There was a market with a little clock-tower. One stall was entirely hung with clothes for Africans, each garment on a hanger, the hangers staggered down and across, so that the stall appeared to be hung with a fluttering rag carpet. Below the clock on the tower there was, in raised concrete letters, red on ochre: MARKET 1951.

Then the town was past and the road was empty again. The road was so empty and the air so clear, the land so flat and stripped, that miles before they reached it they could see the embankment of the main highway to the Collectorate. And that too was empty. Black, wide and straight: the car stopped rattling. The tyres hissed again: the sound of smooth, swift motion. Air rushed through the half-open windows.

"Did you feel that?" Bobby was excited. "You can get some dangerous crosswinds here. They blow you off the road if you aren't careful."

The sun struck through the very top of the windscreen. Every deep scratch made the day before at the filling station was clear. On the gleaming bonnet minute scratches made circular patterns.

Linda said, "I knew it."

Beyond the white gleam of the bonnet, through the distortions of heatwaves, in the distance, black asphalt dissolving into light: a confusion of vehicles on one side of the road, an accident.

Linda said, "I thought it was too good to be true. It always happens when the road is as empty as this."

Approaching slowly, they saw a grey-and-magenta Volkswagen minibus parked level on the road; a blue Peugeot saloon parked on the verge; and, tilted to one side, half in the ditch, a shattered dark-green Peugeot estate-car, by its number-plate one of those used by Africans as long-distance taxis. There were other vehicles beyond this, but this was the only wreck: so new, in destruction so fragile and murderous.

As Bobby slowed down, an African in dark trousers and a white shirt came out from behind the minibus. Bobby stopped.

"Can we do anything to help?"

The African, squinting at the windscreen dazzle, looked uncertainly at Bobby and Linda and didn't reply.

Bobby edged forward past the fearful wreck. He saw a white Volkswagen; he stopped again. Like a hundred white Volks-wagens; like the Volkswagen of yesterday; but the man who came around from behind it was not white and short, but black, tall, solidly made. Not the blackness or the stature of Africa: there was about his hard features and warm complexion something that suggested other bloods, another continent, another language.

Linda, looking at the wreck for blood, a body, shoes, a blanket, responded at once to the authority of this man. She leaned out into the sun and called to him, "What's happened?"

He smiled at Linda and came close to the car.

"A fatal accident," he said. "Drive carefully."

He was not of the country. He spoke with the unmistakable accent of the American Negro.

The smile and the accent, and the unexpected compassion of the advice, gave his words authority. Bobby felt the little thrill of human fellowship. It was something more than the senti-mentality that overcame him whenever, innocent himself, and white, he met African officials or policemen doing a difficult duty. He was anxious to show that he obeyed, was responsive. He drove off carefully over the wavering black skid-marks that started and ended so abruptly on the black road. The sun was coming through the top of the scratched windscreen: he was aware of dazzle as a danger: he pulled down the visor.

The mirror showed activity around the estate-car and the minibus. There were more men than Bobby had noticed as he had passed. Then the road began to curve, and that view was lost.

Four or five army lorries, their axles high above the level road, were parked ahead. On the grass verge beside the lorries, in the shallow ditch, and in the shade of the stunted trees that grew in the field beyond, there were soldiers with rifles. Bobby drove slowly, to show that he had nothing to hide.

All the soldiers turned to look at the car. Below dark-green forage caps their black faces looked greased. The soldiers on the verge appeared to be frowning. Their eyes were narrow above their fat cheeks; foreheads that were so smooth during the entrancement of yesterday's run along the lake boulevard were now creased and puckered up between almost hairless eyebrows. Now they had guns in their hands, and no one else had. The soldiers beyond the ditch, in the shade of the trees, were smiling at the car.

Bobby lifted one hand from the steering-wheel in a half-wave. No one waved back. All the soldiers continued to look at the car, those who smiled, those who frowned.

Linda said, "That wasn't an accident."

Bobby was accelerating.

"Bobby, they've killed the king. That was the king."

The road was straight and black. The tyres hissed on the wet tar.

"That was the king. They've killed him."

"I DON'T KNOW," BOBBY said.

"Those soldiers knew what they were grinning about. Did you see them grinning? Savages. Fat black savages. I can't bear it when they grin like that."

"The king was black too."

"Bobby, don't ask me to talk about that now."

"I don't know what we're talking about. It probably was what that man said. An accident."

"That would be nice to believe. You know, I thought it was a joke. They said he would try to get away in a taxi in some sort of disguise."

"He must have picked it up around here somewhere. Between roadblocks."

"That's what everybody in the capital was saying he would do. I thought it was a joke. And that's just what he goes and does."

"Of course it was all bluff, all this talk about secession and an independent kingdom and so on. That was always Simon Lubero's private view, by the way. The king was just a London playboy. He impressed a lot of people over there. But I'm sorry to say he was a very foolish man."

"That's what everybody says. And I suppose that's why I didn't believe it. I thought it was too foolish to be true. All that Oxford accent and London talk. I thought it was an act."

"Simon was always level-headed about the whole thing. I happen to know that Simon very much wanted it to remain a purely police operation."

' And yet you would think that these people would have their secret ways, that they would always be able to hide in the bush and get away. Being African and a king. I thought the helicopter and those white men in it were so ridiculous."

"Yes," Bobby said, "the wogs got him." His bitterness surprised him, the discovery of anger, aimed at no one. He became calmer. "The wogs got him," he said again. "I hope the word gets back to London and I hope his smart friends find that funny too."

He was still driving fast, but he was no longer racing.

He said, "I should have telephoned Ogguna Wanga-Butere. He would have straightened out this curfew business. Not that I think there's going to be any trouble. We're making excellent time as it is."

"You know what they say about Africa," Linda said. "You drive these long distances and when you get to where you're going there's nothing to do. But I must say I'm beginning to feel it would be nice to see the old compound again."

The land opened out. The horizon dipped. Far away they could see the pale-blue hills, low, almost merging into the sky, and in the middle distance the isolated, curiously-shaped tors and cones, darker, greener, but still blurred in the haze, that marked this part of the Collectorate, the king's territory.

"Leopard Tor," Linda said.

"It's one of my favourite views."

"Like a John Ford western."

"How very film-society. To me it's just Africa. There's going to be an awful lot of foolish talk in the compound in the next few weeks, and a lot of comment in the foreign press. I suppose I wouldn't mind it so much if I felt that those people really cared."

"I don't know whether I care. That's the terrible thing. I don't know what I think. All I know is that I want to get back to the compound."

Later, the view not changing in spite of their speed, distances appearing to remain what they were, Linda said, "Why do you suppose they call it Leopard Tor?"

Bobby noted that her voice had altered and was growing mystical. He didn't reply.

She said, "I saw a dead leopard once."

Bobby concentrated on the road.

"In West Africa. A long red tongue hanging down from between the teeth. I wanted to touch it when they brought it in, to see if it was still warm. But you mustn't, because it's full of fleas. Then they began to skin it. Just below the skin it was like a ballet dancer in tights. You wouldn't believe the muscles. All that had to be cut up and thrown away, burnt on the fire. In the morning when I got up I thought, 'I'll go and look at the leopard.' I'd forgotten."

She spoke slowly. She had begun to listen to her own words.

Bobby said, "I don't believe they're going to skin the king."

"I can't bear it the way those soldiers grin. Did you see them grinning? You weren't here for the mutiny. Eighty marines flew in. Just eighty, and those same grinning soldiers threw away their guns and tore off those uniforms and ran off naked into the bush. They could run in those days. They weren't so fat. It was funny at the airport. Everybody from the compound was there. But the marines weren't waving back. Those young boys were just jumping out of the planes, guns at the ready, and running through the applauding crowd."

"I heard about that," Bobby said. "I don't think the Africans have forgotten either. They find it rather less funny. It's their big fear, you know, since the Belgians and the Congo. White men coming down from the sky."

"That's what Sammy Kisenyi was telling me."

"That's what many of them thought the king wanted."

"I feel like the colonel. I feel I should have gone out and done something to help the king. But then I know that wouldn't have made much sense either."

"That's just it. It's not your business or mine. They have to sort these things out themselves. And he nearly made it, you know. If he hadn't been spotted, in another ninety minutes or so he would have been up there, scuttling across the lake to the other side."

"Oh my God. You mean they're still waiting for him at the lake? They must have been waiting all last night. It's going to be awful in the Collectorate when the news breaks."

"I imagine they'll keep it quiet for a day or two."

"I feel I never want to stir out of the compound again."

"That would be quite a departure, for you."

"Of course," Linda said, responding to the provocation, "the soldiers may be rampaging around there at this minute."

The wide view was going. The land was becoming more broken; there were more trees; the road curved more often. They passed allotments, shops, huts: a village. But no one was to be seen.

"I hated this place from the first day I came here," Linda said.

"I felt I had no right to be among these people. It was too easy. They made it too easy. It wasn't at all what I wanted."

Bobby said, "You know why you came."

"They sent Jimmy Ruhengiri to meet us at the airport. For forty miles I had to make conversation with Jimmy. The conversation you make with the educated ones. Like playing chess with yourself: you make all the moves. And all I kept on seeing were those horrible little huts. I was screaming inside. I knew that nothing good was going to happen to me here. And that first day they put us up in a filthy room in the barracks they call a guesthouse. Martin didn't have enough points. We didn't know. Give Martin a points-system to live by, and you can be sure Martin will never have enough points for anything."

"You didn't do too badly," Bobby said.

"A girl in the next room was crying, and it was still only afternoon. That really frightened me. I don't think I ever wanted anything so much as I wanted to leave that day, to go back to the airport and take the next plane back to London."

"Why didn't you?"

"You go out driving with Sammy Kisenyi, making educated conversation, and you see a naked savage with a penis one foot long. You pretend you've seen nothing. You see two naked boys painted white running about the public highway, and you don't talk about it. Sammy Kisenyi reads a paper on broadcasting at the conference. He's lifted whole paragraphs from T. S. Eliot, of all people. You say nothing about it, you can't say anything about it. Outside you encourage and encourage. In the compound you talk and talk. Everybody just lies and lies and lies."

"You know why you came. You can't complain."

"It's their country. But it's your life. In the end you don't know what you feel about anything. All you know is that you want to be safe in the compound."

"You came for the freedom, though. You adjust very easily, remember?"

"No doubt we look at these things differently, Bobby."

"It doesn't matter now what you think, though."

8

"Every night in the compound you hear them raising the hue and cry, and you know they're beating someone to death outside. Every week there's this list of people who've been killed, and some of them don't even have names. You should either stay away, or you should go among them with the whip in your hand. Anything in between is ridiculous."

"Is that Martin? Or the colonel? I can't keep up with you, Linda. All those lovely weekends in the capital, with all those lovely open fires. Somehow I was expecting more. I was astonished at your taste, Linda. 'I adjust very easily.' Very nicely spoken, but it's nobody's fault if the people we find are just like ourselves. You've all been reading the same books. Of course, we read a lot, don't we? We mustn't let our minds grow rusty, among the savages."

"It isn't for you to talk like this, Bobby."

"I'm disqualified, am I? You should have told me. But I thought you wanted a houseboy to spread the news. I thought you wanted someone to excite by your screams in bed."

"That is one of Doris Marshall's absurd stories."

" 'Let's get Bobby to witness. He is one of Denis Marshall's.' " He was moving his head up and down. " 'Let's get Bobby. You can do what you like with Bobby.' 'That's a nice shirt you're wearing, Bobby.' Very funny. But you chose the wrong man."

"This is nonsense."

"Is it?" He took his right hand off the steering-wheel and tapped his head. "I notice everything. It's all there."

"I always thought you were a romantic, Bobby."

"You chose the wrong man."

"I wish it was the way you tell it. You can't have looked very carefully at the people in the compound."

"That's just it. It's nobody's fault if the people you find are just like yourself."

"Let's stop this, Bobby. I take back everything."

"You talk about savages and whips."

"I take that back."

"There are so many like you, Linda. We mustn't let our minds grow rusty. We are among savages and we need our cultural activities. We are among these very dirty savages and we must remind ourselves that we have this loveliness. Do we use our vaginal deodorant daily?"

"This is ridiculous."

"*Do we? Do we?* What brand do we use? Hot Girl, Cool Girl, Fresh Girl? Girl-Fresh? You're nothing. You're nothing but rotting cunt. There are millions like you, millions, and there will be millions more. 'I'm very adjustable.' 'I hope they've done nothing to the poor wives.' I don't know who you think you are. I don't know why you think it matters what you think about anything."

She leaned back in her seat and looked out of her window. A village again: dusty shacks, tropical backyard vegetation, a dirt side road: a vista of sun, dust and trees there; and then bush beside the highway again.

"There are millions like you. And millions like Martin. You are *nothing*."

"Please stop the car. I will get out here. I don't want to say anything more. Please stop the car."

He braked with a squeal on the hot road. The wind stopped rushing through the windows. The beat of the engine was like silence. Trees were throwing squat shadows across the ditches. The sky was hot and high.

Linda said, "You were right. It wasn't a good idea."

"You're a fool. You'll get into trouble."

"I'm very foolish."

"This is your idea, remember."

"I'll make other arrangements. I'll probably get a taxi or something."

As she turned to open the door he saw that the back of her shirt was wet. He was aware then that his own shirt was wet and felt cold. For a second, stepping out on the road, Linda appeared to be without a sense of direction. Her dark glasses masked her expression. She steadied herself. Bobby watched her start back towards the village they had just passed.

He called, "Your suitcase?"

She didn't turn. "You can take that."

He opened his door and stood up on the road. The sense of the moving road remained with him. He felt dizzy in the still hot air; he had again that sensation of the overcharged, exploding head.

"Linda!"

She continued to walk away with her brisk little steps, looking down, so alien on the high embankment of the empty road, so accidental-looking, the colours of her trousers and shirt suddenly so bright and noticeable that vivid colour seemed to come as well to the road and fields and sky, and the scene had something of the unreal quality of a colour photograph.

He got back in the car, slammed the door shut and drove off, rubbing his dry palms on the steering-wheel, studying the black road, feeling the heat thrown back from the bonnet, where the sun was reflected in a little ring of scratched glitter.

MINUTES LATER, AWARE all the time of the declining sun, the black shadows of trees, the empty fields, the empty car, the roar of the engine and the wind, he began to have the sense of nightmare. The colonel and the hotel, the soldier beside the wide riverbed, the white boys breaking out into the road like heraldic animals and running in slow, silent motion, Linda on the road: the pictures were clear, they had a sequence, but they were like things imagined.

He needed to be calmer. Acknowledging the need, he became calmer. The sense of nightmare was reduced to a memory of his own violence and a foreboding of danger. He was alone; he was inviting reprisal. But still he raced. There was danger at the end of the road, danger in his solitude. But still he allowed time to pass.

The car jumped, came down hard again on the road, and the steering-wheel momentarily kicked itself free of his hands. The road here had subsided. The thin asphalt crust, soft and melting in the afternoon sun, rose and fell. It was a stretch of road Bobby knew. He took his foot off the accelerator. Another bump, another slither, but he was in control. He stopped, and again was aware of the silence, the light, the heat.

He turned to go back. The road was as empty as before. On the wet tar he saw the tracks he had just made. In his panic, the road and the fields had been like things he was imagining. It astonished him, going back, to find he had seen it so clearly and remembered so much. His car had made perfect tracks, quite ordinary.

There was no sign of Linda on the highway. The little village that had been built all on one side of the highway, about the dirt road, looked shut up and evacuated. No one appeared when Bobby sounded his horn. The two or three shops, crooked wooden structures, were the colour of their bare, dusty yards. On tin advertisements nailed to the closed doors, the sheets of tin robbed by the sunlight of all colours except black and pale yellow, a laughing African woman in a turban-type headdress held up a jar of eczema ointment and a laughing African man smoked a cigarette.

Bobby turned into the dirt road. At once there was dust. At once all that the rear-view mirror showed was dust, dense and billowing, like the yellow smoke from a fierce fire. Bobby closed the windows; but as he drove along, obliterating what he had seen, bush, tall trees, an empty wooden hut, the dust in the car became thicker. He saw a large corrugated-iron shed standing in a junk-yard, old grease black and thick on dust; and next to this, behind two or three starved shrubs in hard earth, a white concrete bungalow on low pillars, squarely exposed to the afternoon sun.

Bobby stopped and rolled down his window. Dust billowed slowly around the car. When Bobby sounded his horn, a lanky Indian youth opened the front door of the bungalow. He looked at the car, and beckoned. Bobby hesitated. The boy stood where he was, between verandah and inner room, a puzzled intermediary between Bobby and someone inside.

Bobby went into the bungalow. The verandah, an afternoon

sun-trap, heat reflected from white walls and rising from the floorboards, was empty. In the suffocating little drawing-room, among paper flowers and paperbacks, chairs with chromium-plated metal frames and Hindu deities in copper-coloured plastic, Linda appeared to be having tea. With bared teeth she was biting the very tip of a pickled chili.

Bobby ignored the middle-aged Indian, Linda's host, and said, "We don't have too much time now."

Linda said, "I'm having a little tea."

"Well, I suppose there's no rush. I suppose I'll have a little tea too."

"Yes, yes," the middle-aged Indian said, and went out of the room.

Neither Bobby nor Linda nor the tall boy spoke. It was very hot. Linda was red; Bobby began to sweat. A young woman in a green sari brought a plate of pickles and an extra cup, and went out again.

"Nice place you have here," Bobby said, when the middle-aged man returned.

"Mrs McCartland," the man said, sitting down and rocking his legs from side to side. "She sold up in a hurry when she went South. House, furniture, books, business, everything."

Bobby said, "Nice books."

"You want a few?" His legs still, the man leaned towards the bookcase and pulled out a handful of paperbacks with his left hand. "Take."

Bobby shook his head. "Are you going South too?"

The man giggled and pushed the books back in place. "I am thinking of cloth business in the United States. Or Cairo. I am starting a juices-parlour in Cairo."

"What's that?"

"These Egyptians, you see, are drinking so much of the fresh fruit juices. As soon as I can get my money out, I will go. My brother is already there. Where are you going?"

"I live here," Bobby said. "I'm a government officer."

Slowly, the man's legs stopped rocking. He giggled.

Linda got up. "I think we should be starting."

Bobby smiled and sipped his tea.

"You knew Mr McCartland?" the man asked, after a time.

"I didn't know him." Bobby stood up.

"He died when he was very young," the man said, following Bobby and Linda out into the yard and the road, where the dust was still settling. "He was a great racer. He used to drive early in the mornings from here to the capital at a hundred miles an hour."

Bobby, walking slowly, looking up at the sky, not acknowledging the man's farewells, said, "That's what we'll have to do now to get to the Collectorate before the curfew."

They got into the car. The Indian went up to his verandah and watched them reverse in the garage yard. The dust began to billow again. When they drove away dust blotted out the road.

Linda said, "Do you believe that man drove to the capital at a hundred miles an hour?"

"Do you?"

"I wonder why he said that."

At the junction the shops were as closed and blank as before. The bleached Africans on the tin advertisements grinned; shadows had lengthened below the eaves.

They turned into the highway and rolled down their windows. The sun slanted through the scratched dusty windscreen. Everything in the car was coated with dust; on the dashboard every little grain of dust cast a minute shadow. On the soft tar, on the right-hand side of the road, Bobby saw one of the tracks he had made when he had driven back to the village. All his other tracks had been obliterated, by treads of a chunkier pattern. More than one heavy vehicle had passed, keeping more or less to the left, heading towards the Collectorate.

Bobby drove cautiously. He came again to the stretch of subsidence where the road, soft tar on an uneven surface, appeared to billow and melt. Here was where he had stopped: something still remained of the curving tracks where he had turned.

"Are we very late?" Linda said.

"We've only lost about half an hour. But I imagine you'll smile sweetly at them and they'll give us a cup of tea."

They both smiled, as though they had both won.

At first with private smiles, and then with fixed faces, they drove through the hot afternoon air, shadows beginning to fall on the road, slanting towards them from the right; and neither of them exclaimed when, abruptly, they saw Leopard Tor again, nearer now and larger, half in sun and half in shadow, its vertical wall less sheer, its sloping side, tufted with forest, more jagged.

Linda said, "Do you believe he's really going to Cairo?"

"He's lying," Bobby said. "Everybody lies."

She smiled.

Then she saw, what Bobby was gazing at, at the end of the road: the column of army lorries whose tyre-tracks they had been following.

9

HE HUNG BACK. He speeded up. He hung back again. Neither he nor Linda spoke. Leopard Tor, rising out of bush, was always to the right, its forested slope in shadow. The vegetation beside the highway had subtly altered. It was still scrub; no crops grew on it; but it was acquiring a rainy tropical lushness. They came nearer and nearer the lorries, a column of five, their slanting shadows falling just over the asphalt and jigging along the irregularities of the verge. Sometimes, through a break in the vegetation, Bobby and Linda could see the purely tropical land beyond the Tor, the territory of the king's people, a vast sunlit woodland, seemingly empty, with only scattered patches of a browner haze to show where, in that bush, the villages were.

The green-capped soldiers sitting with rifles at the back of the last lorry scowled at the car. The faces of the soldiers behind them were in shadow. Then Bobby saw the driver. His face and his cap, shakily reflected in profile in the wing-mirror of the cab, made a

featureless black outline against a background of dazzle. Sometimes, when the lorry bumped, or when he turned to look at the
mirror and Bobby, the face caught a yellow shine from the sun.

So for a time Bobby and Linda drove on, keeping at a fixed
distance from the last lorry. Behind the tailboard, with its heraldic
regimental emblem, the soldiers continued to scowl. Intermittently Bobby felt the gaze of the driver; every now and then
that face in the mirror shone.

Linda said, "If we go on at this rate we'll certainly be
late."

"It's not easy to overtake on this road," Bobby said. "It winds
so much."

They drove on. The soldiers continued to stare.

Linda said, "We're probably making them anxious."

Bobby didn't smile.

They came to a stretch of road that was straight and undeniably
clear.

Bobby sounded his horn and pulled out to overtake. The
soldiers became alert. Bobby, accelerating, looked up at them,
looked away, too quickly, and was dazzled by the sun. He began
to overtake, sounding his horn. The lorry moved to the right.
Spots streamed before Bobby's eyes; he raced; he was already
almost off the road. The lorry continued to move to the right.
Bobby was driving beside it. He felt his right wheels mount the
verge. The ditch came close. He braked and the car bucked and
bumped. The lorry pulled away. The soldiers' faces creased into
friendly smiles. The cab-mirror reflected the driver's laugh: suddenly he had a face. Then that reflection was lost. The car was
askew on the verge. The lorry moved further away, fell back into
line. The soldiers' faces became indistinct. A khaki-clad arm came
out from the driver's cab and flapped about awkwardly, hand
swinging from the wrist: it was a signal to overtake.

Linda said, "When you meet the army, play dead."

The back of Bobby's shirt was wet. His face began to burn.
He felt the heat of the engine, the bonnet, the windscreen. The
air was warm; the floor of the car was warm. Hot sweat broke out
8*

afresh all over his body. His eyes pricked; his trousers stuck to his shins.

He started the car and took it off the verge. Once more he followed the tracks of the lorries, chunky zipper-patterns on the soft asphalt. He drove slowly, never more than thirty-five miles an hour; and still from time to time they saw the lorries. The Tor grew larger; haze softened its shadowed forested slope. The afternoon light grew smoky.

And now the highway opened up, and for miles ahead was as straight as a Roman road, swinging from hill to hill. The army lorries, small in the distance, climbed, disappeared, and then were seen to climb again. They were entering the territory of the king's people; and the highway here followed the ancient forest road. For centuries, using only the products of the forest, earth, reeds, the king's people had built their roads as straight as this, over hills, across swamps. From far away Bobby could see the small white-washed stone building, a police post, that stood at the boundary of the king's territory. But the flag that flew there today wasn't the king's flag. It was the flag of the president's country.

Near the stone building the lorries turned off the road, and the road was empty again. But Bobby didn't drive any faster. There was no longer any point; it was past four, the hour of the curfew. Soon they could see the low, sprawling modern building, glass and coloured concrete, as bright as beads, that the Americans had built in the bush as a gift to the new country. It had been intended as a school, and symbolically it straddled the king's territory and the president's. It had been visited but never used; there had been neither pupils nor teachers; it had remained empty. It had a use today. The cleared space in front, partly bushed-over again, was full of lorries. And in the shade of the lorries there were groups of fat soldiers.

No barrier stood in the road here; no one waved them down. But Bobby stopped: the school, the lorries and the soldiers to his left, the stone building, over which the president's flag flew, across the road to his right. The soldiers didn't look at the car. No one came out of the stone building. Beyond the Tor was bright woodland, extending to the horizon through a deepening smoke haze.

"Do we wait for them here?" Linda said.

Bobby didn't reply.

"Perhaps there's no curfew," Linda said.

A soldier was looking at them. He was shorter than the soldiers he stood with, near the open tailboard of a lorry. He was drinking from a tin cup.

"Perhaps the colonel got it wrong," Linda said.

"*Did* he?" Bobby said.

The soldier moved away from the group by the tailboard, shook out his tin cup, and walked slowly towards the car. His head was shaved and bare. His stiff khaki trousers were creased below his paunch and down the round thighs that rubbed against one another. He sucked at the inside of his fat cheeks and bunched his lips and spat, carefully, leaning to one side to let the spittle drain out from his lips. He smiled at the car.

Then they saw the prisoners. They were sitting on the ground; some were prostrate; most were naked. It was their nakedness that had camouflaged them in the sun-and-shade about the shrubs, small trees and lorries. Bright eyes were alive in black flesh; but there was little movement among the prisoners. They were the slender, small-boned, very black people of the king's tribe, a clothed people, builders of roads. But such dignity as they had possessed in freedom had already gone; they were only forest people now, in the hands of their enemies. Some were roped up in the traditional forest way, neck to neck, in groups of three or four, as though for delivery to the slave-merchant. All showed the liver-coloured marks of blood and beatings. One or two looked dead.

The soldier smiled, wet hand holding the wet tin cup, and came near the car.

Bobby, preparing a smile, leaned across Linda and, with his left hand freeing the wet native shirt from his left armpit, asked, "Who your officer? Who your boss-man?"

Linda looked away from the soldier to the whitewashed stone

building and the flag, the Tor and the smoking woodland.

The soldier pressed his belly against the car door and the smell of his warm khaki mingled with the smell of the sweat from Bobby's open left armpit and his yellow back. The soldier looked at Bobby and Linda and looked into the car, and spoke softly in a complicated forest language.

"Who your boss-man?" Bobby asked again.

"Let's drive on, Bobby," Linda said. "They're not interested in us. Let's drive on."

Bobby pointed to the stone building. "Boss-man there?"

The soldier spoke again, this time to Linda, in his language.

She said irritably, "I don't understand," and looked straight ahead.

The soldier behaved as though he had been slapped. He gave a sheepish smile and took a step back from the car. He shook out his tin cup; he stopped smiling. He said softly, "*Don' un'erstan'. Don' un'erstan'.*" He looked down at the body of the car, the doors, the wheels, as though searching for something. Then he turned and began to walk back to his group.

Bobby opened his door and got out. It was cool; the sweated shirt was chill on his back; but the tar was soft below his feet. He could see the prisoners more clearly now. He could see the smoke from the woodland beyond the Tor. Not haze, not afternoon cooking-fires: in that bush, villages were on fire. The rebuffed soldier was talking to his comrades. Bobby tried not to see. His instinct was to get back in the car and drive without stopping to the compound. But he controlled himself. Quickly, right hand swinging, he crossed the bright road into the dusty yard and the shadow cast by the stone building, and went through the open door.

As soon as he entered he knew he had made a mistake. But it was too late to withdraw. In the cool dark room, with its desks and chairs pushed to the walls, with the new photograph of the president on the green noticeboard, among old notices about rates and taxes and wanted criminals and other printed and duplicated lists, there was no officer, no policeman. Three soldiers with shaved heads were sitting below the window on the concrete floor, their caps on their knees. They all stood up as Bobby entered.

"I'm a government officer," Bobby said.

"Sir!" one of the soldiers said, and they all stood to attention.

"Who your officer? Who your boss-man?"

They didn't reply and Bobby didn't know how, after his good start, to continue.

They saw his hesitation and they ceased to be nervous. They relaxed. Their faces became full of inquiry.

The soldier in the middle said, "No boss-man."

Bobby felt he had used the wrong word. He looked from the soldier in the middle to the soldier on the right, the fattest of the three, the one who had called him sir. "You give pass here?"

The fat soldier's cheeks rode up to his small liquid eyes. He waved his right hand slowly in front of his face, showing Bobby the palm.

"No pass," the soldier in the middle said.

Bobby looked at him. "Mr Wanga-Butere *my* boss-man." Smiling, he held his hands in front of him to indicate an enormous paunch, and he pretended to stagger under the weight. "Mr Busoga-Kesoro my *big* boss-man."

They didn't smile.

"Busoga-Kesoro," the fat soldier said, studying Bobby's face, and working his cheeks and lips as though gathering spittle. "Busoga-Kesoro."

"You no have curfew?" Bobby said.

"Car-few," the fat soldier said.

The soldier in the middle said, "Car-few."

"What time you have car-few? Four o'clock, five o'clock, six o'clock?"

"Five o'clock," the fat soldier said. "Six o'clock."

Bobby held out his wrist and pointed to his watch. "Four? Five? Six?"

"You give me?" the fat soldier said, and held Bobby's wrist.

Black skin on pink: they all looked.

The fat soldier moved his thumb over the dial of the watch.

His eyes were friendly, womanish. His cheeks and lips began to work again.

The soldier in the middle unbuttoned the pocket of his tunic and took out a crushed, half-empty packet of cigarettes. It was the brand which, in the advertisements, laughing Africans smoked.

Outside, lorries were revving up. There was chatter and shouting. Boots grated on asphalt; cab-doors slammed. Lorries whined away in low gear.

"I no give you," Bobby said. "I no have no more."

He had made a joke. They all laughed.

"No have no more," the fat soldier said, and let Bobby's wrist drop.

"I go," Bobby said.

He walked towards the door. He had a view of the sunlit road, the dusty yard with its diagonal line of shadow, the insect-spattered front of his car.

"Boy!"

He stopped; it was his error. He turned, to face the dark room.

It was the soldier in the middle who had spoken. He was holding out an unlit cigarette, very white, between his middle and index fingers.

"I give you cigarette, boy."

"I no smoke," Bobby said.

"I give you. Come, I give you."

And Bobby walked from the door and the brightness towards the soldiers, preferring that what was going to happen should happen here, in the dark room, rather than in the open, before the others.

The soldier's hand was outstretched still, open, palm down, the cigarette perpendicular between the middle and index fingers. Then the fingers widened, the cigarette fell, and in that same movement of finger-widening the palm came up at Bobby's face, only clawing, it seemed, but then landing hard on his chin. The other hand tore at the yellow native shirt.

"I report you," Bobby said, falling back. "I report you."

The other soldiers were behind him, to support him as he fell, to seize and twist his arms with practised hands; and it seemed then that the soldier in front of him was maddened not by his words but by the sound and sight of the torn shirt. He tore again and again at the shirt and the vest below the shirt, and with the right hand that had held the cigarette he clawed with clumsy rage at Bobby's face as though wishing to seize it by the nose, chin and cheeks alone.

"I report you," Bobby said.

His arms were twisted harder and he was thrown forward, and when he was on the concrete floor, feeling the boots thump him on the back, the neck, the jaw, he saw, with surprise, that the legs of two soldiers were quite still. It was the fat soldier, grunting as he squatted, tight in his khaki, who was beside him, seizing him by the hair, banging his head on the floor, rubbing his face hard on the floor, now this side, now the other. Bobby knew he was losing skin; but still he noticed that the other soldiers remained where they were.

He had thought at first that the soldier with the cigarette wished only to humiliate, denude, disfigure; and he had half understood, half felt sympathy. But they had gone too far; and now he felt that the fat soldier, who had asked for the watch, intended to kill. He thought: I must protect myself, I must play dead.

Sprawling on his front, he made himself heavy, his left arm jammed against the side of his head. The boots probed his ribs, his belly, probed and kicked. Bobby tried not to move; he didn't think he moved; the fine grit on the smooth plaster of the floor stuck to his wet skin. He didn't open his eyes, fearing to find that he might not be able to see. Then he felt the boot hard on his right wrist, and he could have cried then, at the clear pure pain, the knowledge of the fracture, so deliberate, the knowledge that what had been whole all his life had been broken. He shut out everything to concentrate on that wrist. He felt it grow numb; he felt the swelling come. And then he was on the road again, in a bright landscape, nervous at his own speed, his tyre-tracks and the wet, billowing road.

He awakened. He thought he would open his eyes. His whole
face burned. He could see. He could see that in the dark room
there were no more khaki legs. He waited to make sure. He felt
it was important to act at once, while he was lucid, while the
strength that had come back to him remained. He sat up, leaning
on his wrist. He had forgotten that injury; he remembered now.
He stood up, and he was steady. He didn't look at himself. Walking, he remembered to look on the floor. But he didn't see the
cigarette the soldier had dropped.

The light was yellower. Shadows had spread and were less
harsh. There was more dust and smoke. The sun caught the
windscreen of a lorry, a window of the school. Soldiers squatted
or sat around small twig fires, eating out of tin plates, drinking out
of tin cups, unhurried, deliberate, their eyes and voices bright
with the pleasure of food: forest people, kings of the forest, at the
end of another lucky day. Some way behind them, in the sun,
the bound black prisoners lay on the ground and didn't move.

A soldier saw Bobby and stared. The soldier's eyes glittered.
Without turning his head he spoke to the man beside him, and
the whole group looked. Bobby held his hands at his side and
stood in the doorway, allowing himself to be examined. He began
to walk to the car, which remained where he had left it, quite
exposed on the open road, the wheels slightly sunk in the
asphalt. The soldiers went back to their food.

Linda, still in her seat, leaned to hold the door open. No one
came to the car. The engine answered. Bobby rested his right
hand on the steering-wheel. No one stopped him from leaving.
The afternoon light made every scratch on the windscreen gold.
The almost perpendicular side of Leopard Tor was also gold; the
shadowed side was blurred, the forest on its lower slopes now like
part of the surrounding bush.

Four or five hundred yards away, over the brow of the hill,
they came to the roadblock. The soldier with the rifle, his face just
black below his cap, waved them down with the awkward flapping African gesture. But even before they stopped, the man in
the flowered shirt and dark trousers and his hair in the English

style, on the other side of the road, signalled to them to go on.

Bobby drove in and out of the white barriers and then slowly past the vehicles halted on the other side of the road, vehicles going out of the Collectorate: the Peugeot taxi-buses, the broken-down vans and African cars. The passengers were on the verge. Some were holding duplicated foolscap sheets, their passes; but others were already sitting down or lying on the grass, half naked, their clothes torn; the fully clothed soldiers moved among them. Some of the African women were in Edwardian costumes. So the first missionaries had appeared among the king's people; and so, ever since, but in African-style cottons, the women of the king's people had dressed on formal occasions or whenever they made a long journey.

The road continued straight, from hilltop to hilltop, a strip of asphalt in a wide swathe through the bush.

Linda said, "Let's stop for a little, Bobby."

He pulled up on the road, just like that.

She tried to dust his hair, to straighten the rags of the yellow shirt. There was little else she could do. He didn't allow her to touch his face.

She said, "Your watch is broken."

Bobby closed his heavy eyes and, in that darkness, thought, with sudden passing sorrow for her, for whom so much had also gone wrong: but these are the hands of a nurse.

He opened his eyes and saw the road. They drove on. The sky above was dark blue; the light was beginning to go. The tufted forest glowed where the king's villages were burning.

They were a people who lived, vulnerably now, in villages along their ancient straight roads. roads that had spread their power as forest conquerors, until the first explorers came. The villages were close together; the highway was normally full of pedestrians and cyclists. But the road now was empty; and the villages they passed were empty, dead, burnt-out. The villages that blazed were in the dirt tracks off the main road.

Linda said, "I wonder if they've burned down the compound."

But there was no other place to drive to.

The road dipped; they lost the view of the burning villages. The bush was tall and dark in this depression. They had entered forest, and the road, a straight black cutting, swung away between walls of forest, up and down, and then up to a high horizon. Bobby's wrist ached; he felt his eyes grow heavy. And then he was in a white storm. Like flakes of snow they came out of the forest, butterflies, white, on the asphalt, on the grass, on tree trunks, in the air, millions and millions of white butterflies, fluttering out of the forest. And the storm did not stop. They were crushed by the car wheels; they touched the bonnet and fluttered on the hot metal and died; they stuck to the windscreen.

Linda worked the washer; she turned on the wipers.

The road rose. The butterflies stopped as suddenly as they had begun. The forest ended. The sky above was the darkest blue. In the distance they saw the villages burning around the small town, showing in the quick dusk as a few broken lines of lights.

Bobby said, "I believe something's happened to my wrist."

"I wish I could drive."

He heard the panic in Linda's voice, and he didn't care. The road continued empty, the villages they passed gutted. Collapsed huts of mud and grass would have seemed part of the bush; corrugated iron made a ruin. Here and there women and children had returned to the ruins, the women plump in the manner of the women of the king's people, looking over-dressed in their Edwardian costumes. The car drove itself; and it didn't surprise Bobby, now only following the headlights of the car, that the women, shiny-faced with fatigue, should be where they were; or that in the little industrial estate just outside the town there should still be electricity and illuminated signboards; or that where once, behind its high double walls, the king's palace glowed dully there should be darkness.

The walls had been breached; there was destruction inside: lorries, soldiers, campfires. To that ancient site less than a hundred years before the first explorers had brought news of the world beyond the forest. Now the site had its first true ruin, a palace built mostly in the 1920s, the first palace built there of materials less perishable than reeds and grass.

Between the palace and the colonial town was an open, indeterminate area: caravanserai, rubbish dump, pastureland, market place, shanty town. Few lights burned there. Wholesale warehouses, traffic lights: road signs became complicated. Army lorries and jeeps stood at some intersections. Sometimes the headlights picked out the green cap and shining face of a dazzled soldier. But no awkward hand waved Bobby down. In the main street, where half a dozen three- or four-storeyed concrete buildings rose above the old pioneer wooden structures of the original Indian-English settlement, some Indian furniture shops had been looted. But most of the shops were boarded up and whole.

After the main street the town was open again: a park, looking across to the scattered lights of the main residential area; a roundabout, with soldiers; then, straight ahead, going out of the town again, into the darkness again, towards the glowing sky, another nondescript African area, houses and huts and roadside standpipes, motor-repair yards with decrepit lorries, shops and stalls and backyard vegetable plots, stretching all the way to the compound. Usually this road was busy, and at this time of evening dangerous with drunks or Africans from the deep bush who hadn't yet learned to assess the speed of motor vehicles. Now it was clear. But the road was rough, potholed after the rains, and bumpy with asphalt that had melted and run together and grown hard. At every bump Bobby grew weaker.

Trees screened the compound from the road. At the end of the short drive two dim globes burned above the pillars of the iron gates. The gates were closed; the red-and-white wooden barrier was down. Bobby stopped. A torchlight flashed inches away from his face, and just outside the dazzle he saw lorries and soldiers.

The torchlight played about the windscreen, smeared with the yellow-white mess of mangled butterflies, and rested on the compound pass stuck on the inside.

"*Boswa et bévéni. M'sé, mem.*"

It was one of the compound watchmen, offering a laughing welcome in the patois which was his distinction and his pride. He was neither of the king's people nor the president's. He came from another country; in the Collectorate he was neutral, a spectator, and as safe as the compound he watched over.

The compound was safe. The soldiers were there to protect it. The wooden barrier flew up, and the watchman, in his old-fashioned red-and-blue uniform, ran to open the gate, as though anxious to display his zeal, and the authority of the people he served, to the watching soldiers. He pushed half the gate inwards and held it open; he saluted as the car passed in; and then he ran with the gate to close it again.

The big compound road-map was illuminated. The neatly labelled streets, artificially winding through the compound's land-scaped grounds, were well lit. Fluorescent light fell on hedges and gardens. The open windows of bungalows and flats showed bark-cloths and straw-work on walls, African paintings, bookshelves. The little club house was crowded.

Linda said, "How's your wrist?"

Bobby didn't answer. Linda's voice was lighter, brisker; he could tell her panic had gone. The compound was her setting; she had news.

INTERMITTENTLY DURING THE night Bobby awoke from the drive and the confused dangers of the road to the comfort of bandages. As it grew lighter he began to wait for Luke, his houseboy. He was awakened by radios from the boys' quarters. Then he was awakened by the sound of Luke's brisk bare feet in the next room. There was guilt in that briskness; and when Luke tiptoed into the bedroom, his shrunken khaki trousers catching in the crotch and high above his small ankles, Bobby could tell, from the delicacy of his steps and from Luke's crumpled white shirt, that Luke had been drinking and had slept in his clothes.

Luke drew the curtains and said in his heavy, drunken voice, "Blue Dress out in garden this morning." This was one of their private jokes, about a compound wife, an American and a newcomer, who for several weeks had appeared to wear the same blue dress.

Then Luke turned and saw Bobby. He stood where he was and pulled in his lips hard. Luke was of the king's people and came from one of the nearby villages; he knew the ways of the president's army. His red eyes stared; his nostrils widened and his long, thin face quivered. He sniffed; his pulled-in lips flapped open. With a snort, and with swift little stamps of his right foot, he began to laugh.

Afterwards, still briskly, but now without his delicacy, moving as though he was alone and unobserved, he gathered up Bobby's travelling clothes.

Bobby thought: I will have to leave. But the compound was safe; the soldiers guarded the gate. Bobby thought: I will have to sack Luke.

The Circus at Luxor

The Circus at Luxor

I WAS GOING TO Egypt, this time by air, and I broke my journey at Milan. I did so for business reasons. But it was Christmas week, not a time for business, and I had to stay in Milan over the holidays. The weather was bad, the hotel empty and desolate.

Returning through the rain to the hotel one evening, after a restaurant dinner, I saw two Chinese men in dark-blue suits come out of the hotel dining-room. Fellow Asiatics, the three of us, I thought, wanderers in industrial Europe. But they didn't glance at me. They had companions: three more Chinese came out of the dining-room, two young men in suits, a fresh-complexioned young woman in a flowered tunic and slacks. Then five more Chinese came out, healthy young men and women; then about a dozen. Then I couldn't count. Chinese poured out of the dining-room and swirled about the spacious carpeted lobby before moving in a slow, softly chattering mass up the steps.

There must have been about a hundred Chinese. It was minutes before the lobby emptied. The waiters, serving-napkins in hand, stood in the door of the dining-room and watched, like people able at last to acknowledge an astonishment. Two more Chinese came out of the dining-room; they were the last. They were both short, elderly men, wrinkled and stringy, with glasses. One of them held a fat wallet in his small hand, but awkwardly, as though the responsibility made him nervous. The waiters straightened up. Not attempting style, puzzling over the Italian notes, the old Chinese with the wallet tipped, thanked and shook hands with each waiter. Then both the Chinese bowed and got into the lift. And the hotel lobby was desolate again.

"They are the circus," the dark-suited desk-clerk said. He was as awed as the waiters. "*Vengono dalla Cina rossa.* They come from Red China."

I LEFT MILAN IN snow. In Cairo, in the derelict cul-de-sac behind my hotel, children in dingy jibbahs, feeble from their day-long Ramadan fasting, played football in the white, warm dust. In cafés, shabbier than I remembered, Greek and Lebanese business-men in suits read the local French and English newspapers and talked with sullen excitement about the deals that might be made in Rhodesian tobacco, now that it was outlawed. The Museum was still haunted by Egyptian guides possessing only native knowledge. And on the other bank of the Nile there was a new Hilton hotel.

But Egypt still had her revolution. Street signs were now in Arabic alone; people in tobacco kiosks reacted sharply, as to an insult, when they were asked for *Egyptian* cigarettes; and in the railway station, when I went to get the train south, there was a reminder of the wars that had come with the revolution. Sun-burnt soldiers, back from duty in Sinai, crouched and sprawled on the floor of the waiting-room. These men with shrunken faces were the guardians of the land and the revolution; but to Egyp-tians they were only common soldiers, peasants, objects of a disregard that was older and more rooted than the revolution.

All day the peasant land rolled past the windows of the train: the muddy river, the green fields, the desert, the black mud, the *shadouf,* the choked and crumbling flat-roofed towns the colour of dust: the Egypt of the school geography book. The sun set in a smoky sky; the land felt old. It was dark when I left the train at Luxor. Later that evening I went to the temple of Karnak. It was a good way of seeing it for the first time, in the darkness, separate from the distress of Egypt: those extravagant columns, ancient in ancient times, the work of men of this Nile Valley.

THERE WAS NO coin in Egypt that year, only paper money. All foreign currencies went far; and Luxor, in recent imperial days a winter resort of some style, was accommodating itself to simpler tourists. At the Old Winter Palace Hotel, where fat Negro servants in long white gowns stood about in the corridors, they told me they were giving me the room they used to give the Aga Khan. It was an enormous room, overfurnished in a pleasing old-fashioned way. It had a balcony and a view of the Nile and low desert hills on the other bank.

In those hills were the tombs. Not all were of kings and not all were solemn. The ancient artist, recording the life of a lesser personage, sometimes recorded with a freer hand the pleasures of that life: the pleasures of the river, full of fish and birds, the pleasures of food and drink. The land had been studied, everything in it categorized, exalted into design. It was the special vision of men who knew no other land and saw what they had as rich and complete. The muddy Nile was only water: in the paintings, a blue-green chevron: recognizable, but remote, a river in fairyland.

It could be hot in the tombs. The guide, who was also sometimes the watchman, crouched and chattered in Arabic, earning his paper piastres, pointing out every symbol of the goddess Hathor, rubbing a grimy finger on the paintings he was meant to protect. Outside, after the darkness and the bright visions of the past, there was only rubbled white sand; the sunlight stunned; and sometimes there were beggar boys in jibbahs.

To me these boys, springing up expectantly out of rock and sand when men approached, were like a type of sand animal. But my driver knew some of them by name; when he shooed them away it was with a languid gesture which also contained a wave. He was a young man, the driver, of the desert himself, and once no doubt he had been a boy in a jibbah. But he had grown up differently. He wore trousers and shirt and was vain of his good looks. He was reliable and correct, without the frenzy of the desert guide. Somehow in the desert he had learned boredom. His thoughts were of Cairo and a real job. He was bored with the antiquities, the tourists and the tourist routine.

I was spending the whole of that day in the desert, and now it was time for lunch. I had a Winter Palace lunch-box, and I had

seen somewhere in the desert the new government rest-house
where tourists could sit at tables and eat their sandwiches and buy
coffee. I thought the driver was taking me there. But we went by
unfamiliar ways to a little oasis with palm trees and a large, dried-
up timber hut. There were no cars, no minibuses, no tourists, only
anxious Egyptian serving-people in rough clothes. I didn't want
to stay. The driver seemed about to argue, but then he was only
bored. He drove to the new rest-house, set me down and said he
would come back for me later.

The rest-house was crowded. Sunglassed tourists, exploring
their cardboard lunch-boxes, chattered in various European lan-
guages. I sat on the terrace at a table with two young Germans.
A brisk middle-aged Egyptian in Arab dress moved among the
tables and served coffee. He had a camel-whip at his waist, and I
saw, but only slowly, that for some way around the rest-house the
hummocked sand was alive with little desert children. The desert
was clean, the air was clean; these children were very dirty.

The rest-house was out of bounds to them. When they came
close, tempted by the offer of a sandwich or an apple, the man
with the camel-whip gave a camel-frightening shout. Sometimes
he ran out among them, beating the sand with his whip, and they
skittered away, thin little sand-smoothed legs frantic below swinging jibbahs. There was no rebuke for the tourists who had offered
the food; this was an Egyptian game with Egyptian rules.

It was hardly a disturbance. The young Germans at my table
paid no attention. The English students inside the rest-house,
behind glass, were talking competitively about Howard Carter
and Lord Carnarvon. But the middle-aged Italian group on the
terrace, as they understood the rules of the game, became playful.
They threw apples and made the children run far. Experimentally
they broke up sandwiches and threw the pieces out onto the sand;
and they got the children to come up quite close. Soon it was all
action around the Italians; and the man with the camel-whip, like
a man understanding what was required of him, energetically
patrolled that end of the terrace, shouting, beating the sand,
earning his paper piastres.

A tall Italian in a cerise jersey stood up and took out his camera. He laid out food just below the terrace and the children came running. But this time, as though it had to be real for the camera, the camel-whip fell not on sand but on their backs, with louder, quicker camel-shouts. And still, among the tourists in the rest-house and among the Egyptian drivers standing about their cars and minibuses, there was no disturbance. Only the man with the whip and the children scrabbling in the sand were frantic. The Italians were cool. The man in the cerise jersey was opening another packet of sandwiches. A shorter, older man in a white suit had stood up and was adjusting his camera. More food was thrown out; the camel-whip continued to fall; the shouts of the man with the whip turned to resonant grunts.

Still the Germans at my table didn't notice; the students inside were still talking. I saw that my hand was trembling. I put down the sandwich I was eating on the metal table; it was my last decision. Lucidity, and anxiety, came to me only when I was almost on the man with the camel-whip. I was shouting. I took the whip away, threw it on the sand. He was astonished, relieved. I said, "I will report this to Cairo." He was frightened; he began to plead in Arabic. The children were puzzled; they ran off a little way and stood up to watch. The two Italians, fingering cameras, looked quite calm behind their sunglasses. The women in the party leaned back in their chairs to consider me.

I felt exposed, futile, and wanted only to be back at my table. When I got back I took up my sandwich. It had happened quickly; there had been no disturbance. The Germans stared at me. But I was indifferent to them now as I was indifferent to the Italian in the cerise jersey. The Italian women had stood up, the group was leaving; and he was ostentatiously shaking out lunch-boxes and sandwich wrappers onto the sand.

The children remained where they were. The man from whom I had taken the whip came to give me coffee and to plead again in Arabic and English. The coffee was free; it was his gift to me. But even while he was talking the children had begun to come closer. Soon they would be back, raking the sand for what they had seen the Italian throw out.

I didn't want to see that. The driver was waiting, leaning against the car door, his bare arms crossed. He had seen all that had happened. From him, an emancipated young man of the desert in belted trousers and sports shirt, with his thoughts of Cairo, I was expecting some gesture, some sign of approval. He smiled at me with the corners of his wide mouth, with his narrow eyes. He crushed his cigarette in the sand and slowly breathed out smoke through his lips; he sighed. But that was his way of smoking. I couldn't tell what he thought. He was as correct as before, he looked as bored.

Everywhere I went that afternoon I saw the pea-green Volkswagen minibus of the Italian group. Everywhere I saw the cerise jersey. I learned to recognize the plump, squiffy, short-stepped walk that went with it, the dark glasses, the receding hairline, the little stiff swing of the arms. At the ferry I thought I had managed to escape; but the minibus arrived, the Italians got out. I thought we would separate on the Luxor bank. But they too were staying at the Winter Palace. The cerise jersey bobbed confidently through bowing Egyptian servants in the lobby, the bar, the grand dining-room with fresh flowers and intricately folded napkins. In Egypt that year there was only paper money.

I stayed for a day or two on the Luxor bank. Dutifully, I saw Karnak by moonlight. When I went back to the desert I was anxious to avoid the rest-house. The driver understood. Without any show of triumph he took me when the time came to the timber hut among the palm trees. They were doing more business that day. There were about four or five parked minibuses. Inside, the hut was dark, cool and uncluttered. A number of tables had been joined together; and at this central dining-board there were about forty or fifty Chinese, men and women, chattering softly. They were part of the circus I had seen in Milan.

The two elderly Chinese sat together at one end of the long table, next to a small, finely made lady who looked just a little too old to be an acrobat. I had missed her in the crowd in Milan.

Again, when the time came to pay, the man with the fat wallet used his hands awkwardly. The lady spoke to the Egyptian waiter. He called the other waiters and they all formed a line. For each waiter the lady had a handshake and gifts, money, something in an envelope, a medal. The ragged waiters stood stiffly, with serious averted faces, like soldiers being decorated. Then all the Chinese rose and, chattering, laughing softly, shuffled out of the echoing hut with their relaxed, slightly splayed gait. They didn't look at me; they appeared scarcely to notice the hut. They were as cool and well-dressed in the desert, the men in suits, the girls in slacks, as they had been in the rain of Milan. So self-contained, so handsome and healthy, so silently content with one another: it was hard to think of them as sightseers.

The waiter, his face still tense with pleasure, showed the medal on his dirty striped jibbah. It had been turned out from a mould that had lost its sharpness; but the ill-defined face was no doubt Chinese and no doubt that of the leader. In the envelope were pretty coloured postcards of Chinese peonies.

Peonies, China! So many empires had come here. Not far from where we were was the colossus on whose shin the Emperor Hadrian had caused to be carved verses in praise of himself, to commemorate his visit. On the other bank, not far from the Winter Palace, was a stone with a rougher Roman inscription marking the southern limit of the Empire, defining an area of retreat. Now another, more remote empire was announcing itself. A medal, a postcard; and all that was asked in return was anger and a sense of injustice.

PERHAPS THAT HAD been the only pure time, at the beginning, when the ancient artist, knowing no other land, had learned to look at his own and had seen it as complete. But it was hard, travelling back to Cairo, looking with my stranger's eye at the fields and the people who worked in them, the dusty towns, the agitated peasant crowds at railway stations, it was hard to believe that there had been such innocence. Perhaps that vision of the land, in which the Nile was only water, a blue-green chevron, had always been a fabrication, a cause for yearning, something for the tomb.

The air-conditioning in the coach didn't work well; but that might have been because the two Negro attendants, still with the habits of the village, preferred to sit before the open doors to chat. Sand and dust blew in all day; it was hot until the sun set and everything went black against the red sky. In the dimly lit waiting-room of Cairo station there were more sprawled soldiers from Sinai, peasants in bulky woollen uniforms going back on leave to their villages. Seventeen months later these men, or men like them, were to know total defeat in the desert; and news photographs taken from helicopters flying down low were to show them lost, trying to walk back home, casting long shadows on the sand.

August 1969 – October 1970